PERLA

PERLA

Carolina De Robertis

First published in the United Kingdom in 2012 by
HAUS PUBLISHING LTD
70 Cadogan Place, London SW1X 9AH
www.hauspublishing.com

This edition published by arrangement with Alfred A. Knopf, an imprint of
The Knopf Doubleday Group, a division of Random House, Inc.

ISBN 978-1-908323-21-7

Typeset in Garamond by MacGuru Ltd
info@macguru.org.uk

Printed and bound by CPI Group (UK) Ltd, Croydon, CR0 4YY

A CIP catalogue for this book is available from the British Library

Para ti, Rafael

The aim of the Process is the profound transformation of consciousness.

– GENERAL JORGE RAFAEL VIDELA
General Commander of the Argentine Army, 1976–1981

Not drowned entirely, though. Rather carried down alive to wondrous depths where strange shapes of the unwarped primal world glided to and fro before his passive eyes; and the miser-merman, Wisdom, revealed his hoarded heaps…He saw God's foot upon the treadle of the loom, and spoke it; and therefore his shipmates called him mad.

– HERMAN MELVILLE,
Moby-Dick

ONE

1

Arrival

Some things are impossible for the mind to hold alone. So listen if you can, with your whole being. The story pushes and demands to be told, here, now, with you so close and the past even closer, breathing at the napes of our necks.

He arrived on the second of March, 2001, a few minutes after midnight. I was alone. I heard a low sound from the living room, a kind of scrape, like fingernails on unyielding floor – then silence. At first I couldn't move; I wondered whether I had left a window open, but no, I had not. I picked up the knife from the counter, still flecked with squash, and walked slowly down the hall toward the living room with the knife leading the way, thinking that if it came to fighting I'd be ready, I'd stab down to the hilt. I turned the corner and there he lay, curled up on his side, drenching the rug.

He was naked. Seaweed stuck to his wet skin, which was the colour of ashes. He smelled like fish and copper and rotting apples. Nothing had moved: the sliding glass door to the backyard was closed and intact, the curtains were unruffled, and there was no damp trail where he might have walked or crawled. I could not feel my limbs, I was all wire and heat, the room crackled with danger.

'Get out,' I said.

He didn't move.

'Get the hell out,' I said, louder this time.

He lifted his head with tremendous effort and opened his eyes. They were wide eyes that seemed to have no bottom. They stared at me, the eyes of a baby, the eyes of a boa. In that moment something in my core came apart like a ship losing its mooring, anchor dismantled, the terror of dark waters on all sides, and I found that I could not turn away.

I raised the knife and pointed it at him.

The man shuddered and his head collapsed against the floor. My instinct was to rush to his side, help him up, offer him a hot drink or an ambulance. But was he pretending, hoping I'd come closer so he could overpower me? *Don't do it. Don't go near him.* I took a step backward and waited. The man had given up on lifting his head again, and was watching me from the corners of his eyes. A minute passed. He did not blink or lunge or look away.

Finally, I said, 'What do you want?'

His jaws began to work, slowly, arduously. The mouth opened and water poured out, thick and brown like the water of the river, seeping into the rug. The murky smell in the room intensified. I took another step back and pressed against the wall. It felt cool and hard and I wished it would whisper *Sshhh, don't worry, some things are solid still,* but it was only a wall and had nothing to say.

His lips worked around empty air. I waited and watched him strain to form a word. Finally he spoke, unintelligibly and too loudly, like a deaf person who has not learned to sculpt his sounds. 'Co-iii-aahh.'

I shook my head.

He made the sound again, more slowly. 'Coo. Iiiii. Aaaahh.'

I tried to piece it together. 'Coya?' I asked, thinking, a name? a place I've never heard of?

'Coo. Miiiii. Aaah.'

I nodded blankly.

'Coo. Miiiii. Dah.'

And then I understood. '*Co-mi-da*. Food. Food?'

He nodded. Drops of water fell from his face, too copious to be sweat; they seeped from his pores, a human sponge just lifted from the river – though even sponges would stop dripping at some point, and this man's wetness had not. Without turning my gaze away from him, I pressed the knife against my arm, to see whether I was dreaming. The blade broke skin and drew blood and I felt the pain but did not wake out of this reality into another one. If my father had been here he surely would not have seen this ghoulish man, or if he had, he would have stabbed him already, without a word, then poured a glass of scotch and watched Mamá clean up the carpet. I met the stranger's gaze and felt my heart pulse like a siren in my chest. I should attack him, I thought. I should chase him out. But I couldn't bring myself to do either. Later, I would look back on this moment as the one when my real life began: the moment in which, without knowing why, to my own shock and against all reason, I lowered my weapon and went to forage for food.

The kitchen was just as I'd left it, only the pot had boiled over on the stove, water hissing as it leaped out onto the burner. I had been cooking squash for Lolo, the turtle, who stood by the refrigerator, neck craned from his shell, unperturbed. My cigarette had gone out on the counter. I was shocked to see it, as it did not feel like the same night on which, just a few minutes earlier, I had stood there smoking and chopping squash, thinking to myself, as though repetition would make me believe it, it's good to be alone, the house to myself, and isn't it wonderful, I can do anything I want, eat toast for dinner, whirl naked in the kitchen if I choose, leave dirty dishes on the sofa, sit with my legs spread wide, cry without explaining myself to anyone.

I turned off the fire under the pot of squash, and began to rummage through the refrigerator. Mamá had left the house well stocked. I gathered an array of foods on a tray: Gouda, bread, last night's roast chicken and potatoes, white wine, a glass of water, a few bonbons in a gold box – and headed back down the hall. I still had the knife with me, nestled between the dishes. My parents protested, from nowhere, from the air at my back, and I had no answer for them. I felt the heavy cape of their disapproval, their dismay at my breach of common sense. *Perla, what are you doing?* I imagined them calling as I kept on down the hall and into the living room.

He had not strayed from his position, folded into himself like a foetus. He did not shiver. The burgundy rug was almost black with water. He was motionless except for one bare foot that tapped silently against the floor. He stared at the wall and his eyes did not blink. In the morning I would wake up and he would be gone and the carpet would be dry, dry, because none of this ever happened.

I put the tray down on the floor beside him. He stared as if it held objects from a strange and sunken kingdom. He made no move to rise and eat, and, I realised, he probably couldn't, since he'd barely had the strength to move his mouth. He was as vulnerable as a dazed infant, and might be waiting for me to feed him, bite by bite. The notion repulsed me – my hand at his mouth, his damp skin brushing against mine – and so I waited. He made a sound, unformed and plaintive, all vowel and longing. Another minute passed.

Finally, I asked, 'Would you like some chicken?'

He shook his head, almost imperceptibly.

'Cheese?'

He shook his head again.

'Chocolate?'

Again.

'Water?'

He nodded, and his eyes widened. Pleading.

There was no avoiding it. He could not serve himself. I lifted the glass from the tray, toward his lips, and he raised his head a few centimetres from the floor. Now that I was closer, I saw a bluish tinge to his lips, and a sheen of moisture on his face. I tipped the glass, carefully, and he chewed as though he were eating the water, as though it were as solid as bread. I was careful not to touch him with my fingers, although even then my repulsion warred with a prick of curiosity: what on earth would his skin feel like?

He finished eating and sank his head back to the floor.

'Who are you?' I said, but he had closed his eyes.

I didn't know what to do with myself, so I sat on the floor for a while, next to the stranger. I thought of trying to move him somewhere, to the backyard, to the street. But he seemed too heavy, it would be worse if the motion woke him up, and in any case what if the neighbours saw? Easier to just do nothing, go to bed and in the morning he'd be gone the way he came. Not a rational solution, but one to get me through the night.

I felt so tired. It had been ten days since my fight with Gabriel, since I'd left him on that Uruguayan beach with empty hands and emptier eyes and no promise of ever seeing him again. Since then, unpalatable visions had not let me sleep. But in the morning I would always rise and polish the surface of myself, a gleaming, confident young woman, an excellent student and good daughter starting her fourth year at the university, moving smoothly through the world, and even though inside the chaos scraped and railed I would push it into the crevices of the day so it could not be detected.

The only person who could be counted on to see through my masks was Gabriel. When we first met, four years ago, I thought it was because he was seven years older, and therefore more sophisticated. But surely there were twenty-five-year-old men who were barely men and didn't know how to see the black hole in a poised eighteen-year-old girl. I had managed to deceive professors, friends, my parents and their friends, everyone except Gabriel. Early on, when I said I had to go study for a psychology exam, he had said, *All that Freud, and yet you can't see your own demons.* Then he kissed me, laughing, which enraged me. My own desire to kiss back enraged me more. Don't talk to me about demons, I said, until you've wrestled down your own. He looked at me as if I'd just spoken the secret of seduction. I did no studying that night; not of Freud – only of the slopes of his body, the urge in his hands, his mouth against my skin, his sex hard against me through his jeans. That was our first year together, the least complicated of our years, when I was simply Perla and not the people I was linked to, before we talked about his work or my family let alone the explosive combination of the two, before our images of each other started cracking, fault lines spreading, as happens to mirrors hit by tiny stones. It was enough, then, to kiss and laugh and argue, to smoke and drink and undulate against each other until the heat we generated hauled the sun out of its sleep.

I thought of this as I left the stranger on the floor and went back to the kitchen, where I put the boiled squash in a bowl on the floor for Lolo, who was hiding somewhere but would surely come in the night, when the house was asleep. I walked up the stairs toward bed, feeling both exhausted and viscerally awake. I longed to turn back time and re-enter those early nights with Gabriel, re-enter Gabriel himself, the scent of him, his vigorous voice, the gaze that made me feel transparent. Wrapped in his presence I would look for the woman I had been with him, or believed that I could be. *And who is that woman, Perla?* A braver woman, a woman from underground, carrying secrets like subdued snakes in both hands. Inklings of that woman had flared at me during nights with Gabriel; I could imagine burning through my own reality to become the snake-woman, hair on fire, ready to rise. But these were only absurd imaginings, and anyway ten days ago I'd shut that door, and shut the door on Gabriel. He was gone from me now and it was my own doing. I had to do it, there was no other choice, I thought, night after night, running the words through my mind, *no other choice, no other choice,* an incantation whose power grew with repetition. I had thought he might call me, but he did not. He had been angrier than I'd thought. If he doesn't call in seven days, I thought, it's absolutely over – and when seven days had passed with no Gabriel I thought my heart would come apart but instead of shedding a single tear I went to a bar near the university, found a shy classmate called Osvaldo, and let him take me home. It was shockingly easy, all it took was a split second longer gaze than usual and five minutes later he'd bought me a drink, thirty minutes later we left the bar for the raucous night. On the walk to his apartment he acted like a miner who had stumbled on a vein of gold. He was a kind person, but when he reached into my body he found my body only. He never sensed the inner shape of me that even I could barely face but that Gabriel had always seemed to reach for, to touch, to want to understand. There was pleasure in the way Osvaldo touched me, the way he wrapped my legs around his neck like rope, the way his sex quickened its pace from sheer enthusiasm, but the pleasure seemed to belong to someone else, a girl who had taken my body for the night and whom I scarcely recognised. Afterward, I lay naked beneath him in the dim light and thought, Now, Perla, you've got what you want, freedom from exposure, a self so well hidden it cannot be found. I should have felt relief or at least some scrap of triumph, but I only felt terribly alone.

And I was alone, for three more nights, until this stranger broke in without shattering a single pane.

He wakes up in the morning from a sleep that heaves like tides. There is sunlight in the room, more intense when poured through air than through the water. He was in the water before, was he not? From the wet blur of his memory comes the feel of light through water, its slow rhythm, the dispersion of beams through a dense realm. There is so much he can't remember, but he does remember this: he lost his body, once, though he's not quite sure how. Somehow he disappeared, then died, then floated in the water for a very long time. The sea and the river were his homes. Until finally, last night, he rose into the air, buoyant, invisible, and the darkness rubbed against his naked mind, he had no form, he had no bulk, he was translucent as the air, which was black and sweet and weightless, and he felt that he could rise up to the sun, but in the night there was no sun, nor was there any moon. And in any case he wasn't drawn into the heavens, he was drawn toward the earth, toward the shore, where little lights winked and gleamed and boasted. The city. His city. Buenos Aires. He was starved for something there but he didn't know what. He knew only hunger and specks of light.

He glided toward the city, and as he did, his form began to change. He slowly took the shape of a man. At the edge of the city there were houses full of light and darkness. He was pulled toward them. He was pulled toward one.

And then suddenly he was here, in this room, where light moves so fast, it shoots right into him. He is not accustomed to it. He is not accustomed to anything – not this large room; this wet and limber body he's encased in; not this morning sun that shouts its presence, ricochets from the walls and the paintings hanging from the walls, the ship and hills and disfigured clocks inside those paintings, this sun that makes the room cry out. The sofa seems to swell, the bookshelf looks over him, the rug glows at the edges and the song is broken, chromatic, invisible. Fast light cuts into all of him and he can't shout, he hears the room and hears the light and he can smell it, also, he lets in the scent of light, the lemoncrush and greensweat of morning.

She enters the room, the woman from last night, she is wearing something red and she is marvellous, a marvel. There is something about her that chafes at him. Something important, though he doesn't know what it is. Knowing comes to him haphazardly, sharp and sudden, his mind is a bowl full of splinters that he cannot sift through, cannot gather, cannot see, all he can do is wait for them to cut him so he'll know that they are there. She comes closer. She looks at him with thinly veiled disgust.

You're still here, she says.

He stares at her.

You seem stronger.

He is silent.

I have to go out.

Colours, he thinks, there are colours in her face he's never seen.

Why are you here?

He shakes his head.

You don't know?

Her lips are as red as the clothes she's wearing. Her hair is long and dark, a heavy curtain around her shoulders. Once there was another woman with dark hair around her shoulders, he remembers now, a memory cuts into his mind, her name was Gloria and the day the black boots came for him her name rang out inside his mind, Gloria, Gloria.

The woman rises. I have to go. I'll be back in the evening.

She is gone.

He stares at the window, where the sun ebbs in, along with the gentle sound of a car passing. The shard is cutting deeper. The black boots and Gloria's name grow vibrant. He remembers.

On the train into downtown Buenos Aires, I almost missed my stop and had to barge through a knot of men in suits to make it through the sliding doors before they closed. I rushed up the stairs in a thick mass of people, all moving in the same direction on separate legs, not speaking or even looking at each other, focused only on speed and destination. Usually I took these stairs without noticing the bodies all around me, my mind absorbed by a friend's romantic problems or an upcoming exam, but today I keenly felt their presence, their momentum and their folded psyches as they emptied out of the station into the broad light of the day.

The street met us all with blaring horns and impatient cars. The tall buildings loomed over us, as always, casting their implacable shadows. Today they stood taller than ever. The strangers around me seemed to walk to the inaudible clicks and clacks of a hidden potent timepiece, the invisible machine that powers Buenos Aires, and though I usually fell in step without a thought, today I could not walk like them. My legs were loose, unleashed. I had lost the gait of reason within myself. You cannot walk with perfect reason when a dripping man who may not even be a man has appeared in your house. Purses and satchels swung in irritation as their owners overtook me. It's not my fault, I thought, it's the water: it leaked into my consciousness and soaked it, bloated it, ruined the regular mechanics. I wondered whether I had gone insane. If so, I thought, then this is what it feels like; I would never have guessed the world would still appear so sharp and vivid, the streets the same, the clouds the same, nothing different except your mind has come unhinged, its cogs whirling loose and wild and hazardous.

As I walked up the noisy boulevard toward the university I thought of all the years that I had dutifully walked through the world with careful sanity, as though all were well, as though my family were well, as though nothing rotted beneath the surface, until I broke away from expectations by enrolling in the department of psychology. That was the first time I ever went against my father's wishes on anything significant. He had always planned for me to become a medical doctor, a paragon career for his paragon daughter, the only path he would accept for me, chosen by the time I was born. When I first told him my decision, he would not speak to me for days, and even in my first year at the university, the campaign continued: You still have time, Perla, you could switch to medicine, it would take you longer but at least you won't be making this mistake.

'But it's not a mistake, Papá. It's what I want.'

He shook his head. 'You're too young to know what you want.'

'Everybody decides at my age.'

'I'm not talking about everybody.'

His hands were broad and large and calloused, resting on the table as he leaned in to persuade me, and his voice was stern but his eyes were pleading, almost tender, only the best for my princess, and I wanted to take his hands and cup them in front of me so I could pour in what I was learning. Look look, here are the secrets of the mind, the deep-sea treasures I am diving for, lost keys that can unlock what has long remained shut down in the dark. How I longed for my father's reach. How I hated myself for doing so.

I arrived in class fifteen minutes late. My professor raised an eyebrow – Perla, the eyebrow said, this is not like you – and kept talking. I took out my notebook and tried to turn my attention to the evolution of Freudian dream theory. The field's understanding has deepened and expanded over the years; we are all responding to the constant cues of our subconscious, only the insane see dripping ghouls in their home. I looked up, startled, but of course no one had heard my thought. I made notes dutifully, but even as I wrote the page seemed distant and even hazy, as though seen through a windshield blanketed with rain. Inside, I was riding a torrent, to who knows where, back to my living room, to the madness of seaweed in my living room, and to the figure of a naked man or not-man lying on the floor at this very moment, moaning or muttering or just dripping in absolute silence. God, what was he? A ghost? A monster? Just a sad pale man? Would he still be there when I got home? What an absurd predicament. Gabriel, I thought, if only I could call you; you of all people would know what to do or at least would invent some way to respond, or barring that might at the very least put your arm around me as I face the living room tonight, how I long to see you, but surely, after the way we parted, you would never want to hear from me again. The professor glanced over at me – she'd made some point she thought would spark me, and I, Perla, excellent student, nodded thoughtfully. I'd missed what had been said. I was a liar, nodding Yes, Yes, like a dutiful machine.

My friend Marisol looked at me from across the room, and smiled hello. Her eyes added, *Where have you been?* I answered with a halfhearted smile back, and hoped she wouldn't approach me after class. If she did, I'd make a quick getaway, or, if she caught me, I'd tell her I had an appointment. We usually went out for coffee every few days, but I'd been avoiding her this week, ever since my return from Uruguay. We had spoken only once on the phone.

'Well?' she'd said. 'How did it go?'

'Fine,' I'd said, and once it was out of my mouth it was too late to take back the lie.

'You didn't get caught?'

I had told my parents I was taking a trip with Marisol and her family. 'No, that all went smoothly. Thanks for covering for me.'

'And his family?'

'Whose family?'

'Perla. Come on. Gabriel's family. How was meeting them?'

'Sorry, Marisol, but this isn't a good time. Can we talk later?'

'Sure, sure. Just call me when you have time.'

But I never had the time. Or I did have the time, but lacked something else essential to making the call, and such an ordinary call at that, to catch up with a friend. It wouldn't even have to be particularly involved; Marisol wasn't the best of listeners, and would soon turn the conversation to her latest fight with her mother. But I didn't have it in me. And now, even less so – with the whoknowswhat in my living room, I felt incapable of feigning chatter.

What would she say if she knew? And what would the rest of my classmates say? I imagined my professor presenting the case study, my story told: a young woman believes she saw a wet ghost just like you see me here, that she gave him water from a glass and he chewed it. Now remember, your patient is convinced of her reality, attached to its veracity even though it plagues her. What treatment would you say she requires? The hands shoot up.

When I woke up that morning I'd lain in bed, staring at the ceiling, the impervious ceiling, asking it for a normal day. A normal living room. A normal fist of silence in my mind. Not like these raucous thoughts, these eddies, this whirlpool of wondering what the hell had poured into my house.

The day the black boots came for him was a pretty day, with bright blue slices of sky between the buildings. He remembers, now, the café he went to on his way home. It was halfway between the office and his apartment. It was beautiful and ordinary, with ivory walls, bitter coffee, little cookies. People walked sharply outside the window. It was just another cup of coffee to him then, and just another window. He was tired. He had stayed up too late fighting with Gloria, about a stupid thing, the apartment, something about the apartment, whether or not they should move and what they should do with the apartment if they did, though he couldn't remember what had raised the question about moving, where they would go and why, all he knew was that her mouth was pursed in profile, she turned and showed her shoulder blades, they didn't touch in sleep that final night, what an idiot, not to have touched her. He dreaded going home, the chance that she was still angry, the dance-step of apologies, and so he stopped for coffee. The coffee came with little almond cookies, not the butter ones today, what a shame. He remembers. He tastes the coffee and the almond cookie, tinged with his petty disappointment. Then home. He turned the key and pushed the door open and there was Gloria, bound to a chair, blindfolded, still as a doll. The first fist sent him to the floor and he stayed there, there were many of them, dozens, a dozen boots around him, in his ribs, kicking, speaking, the boots were speaking, they wanted to know things but he couldn't speak. Blood filled his mouth. A hand caught his hair, lifted him from the ground, then came a fist and he was down again, sinking in a vortex of men. He understood that they had come for him, it was his turn, he would be gone, Gloria was right about people being taken and he wished that he'd believed her, held fiercely to this wish as though believing her could have staved off this moment, there was red in his eyes, wet copper in his mouth, two teeth floating across his tongue like hidden shipwrecks, and Gloria was pleading please don't hurt him, shut up Gloria, a slap and then a cry, that's right darling, don't say a thing, sit still until it's over and then maybe they won't take you, please shut up. She didn't shut up and they weren't done and he was on the floor and pulled up and back down again, they wanted to know where Carraceli was but he had never known a Carraceli, it was no

17

use, the hood came over his head, the room went quiet, by now it was the middle of the night, he was rolled into a carpet, he was carried down the stairs of his apartment building past neighbours' doors that did not open, everybody seemed to know to keep their doors closed on such nights, and then he was in the footwell of a car that drove and drove and drove and drove and that – he now remembers – is how he disappeared.

2

A Secret Dimension

I arrived home with brown bags full of food. I was ready for anything – ready to find an empty living room and accept that I had hallucinated and was clinically insane, and also ready to see him there still, in which case perhaps the world was crazy and not me. I imagined this, the world on the couch, the whole of it lying prone and anguished, a globe deflating in the grip of confession, and my professor scribbling on a tablet, *Suffers from delusions, psychosis. Acute.*

He was still there. I smelled him as soon as I opened the door, a gust of metallic fish and rotting apples. He still looked wet, as if he'd just emerged from water. He sat on the floor, staring at the painting on the wall, Tía Mónica's blue rendition of a ship on tumultuous seas. The monochrome approach was inspired by Picasso's blue period; that's what Papá always said about it. Intermittently, Mamá would make a case for them to take it down, or at least hang it in the upstairs hallway, the last thing I want in my own living room is to be reminded of your sister, but none of the appeals ever worked. On most decorating points my father caved to my mother, but there was no moving this vestige of Tía Mónica.

'I brought more food,' I said.

He didn't move.

'I had no idea what you wanted.'

He turned his head toward me, slowly.

'Are you hungry now?'

He didn't answer and I felt like a fool, standing in my living room with two bags of groceries I had painstakingly chosen – lingering in the aisle, thinking, Pasta? surely he'd like pasta? – for a guest I had never invited and whose humanity was in question and whom I had no reason at all to long to feed and who now would not even deign to speak. 'You must be hungry.'

'Rain.'

'What?'

'It's going to rain.'

'Oh.' I looked out the window, at the heavy sky beyond the trees. It had been a hot summer day, humid as always, and rain had not occurred to me. 'Maybe.' I put the grocery bags down on the table. 'You can talk.'

He nodded. 'I am remembering.'

'What do you remember?'

He said nothing.

'What are you?'

Through the wall, I heard Belinda, the neighbour child, shrieking with pleasure in the yard. Another child laughed; there was a friend over. I wanted to hurl a loaf of bread at this stranger who would barely talk to me.

'I'm going to make us dinner. You want dinner?'

'Water.'

'What?'

'Water.'

'That's not dinner,' I said, and stopped myself before adding *not for real people, anyway.*

His eyes probed and entered me, his eyes were looking into my mind, they were all sight, they were all dark, they had no bottom. 'Water. Please.'

He eats the water, chews it, it has substance, it's the only thing with substance in this world. It sparkles in his throat as it goes down. It flows into this unfamiliar flesh, not like the living flesh he had before he disappeared, but something else; he doesn't understand what; he can't answer her questions, still doesn't know it all, the who and what of his presence, after so much absence he must defend his presence, that's how it is, how the world is, a dry dry world, he wants water to pour into him, over and over, fill him up, like it did in the cradled years, the deep-in-river years, when everything was water and he not only ate water but the water – sparkling, ravenous – ate him.

I ate my bread, torn from the loaf, unbuttered. I felt both restless and paralysed, yearning for motion yet unable to do anything ordinary such as open a book, cook dinner, call friends and meet them for drinks. I needed a drink. I couldn't imagine what I would tell my friends. How's your week going? Oh really? As for me, there's a pale wet man who smells like a dirty beach sitting in my living room. No, I don't know how long he's staying. No, he looks too weak to steal the stereo. Don't worry. Let's buy another round.

I poured myself a scotch from my father's good bottle. I would have offered some to the man but he wanted only his plain water, which he consumed with such intensity it should have been a private act. He finished and looked up at me.

'Thank you.' His voice was clearer now, just a little blurred.

I nodded. The window was open. Outside, I heard a dog bark, a man silencing the dog. It didn't rain.

'I was in the water.'

It was difficult to hold his gaze. 'In the water?'

'Yes.'

'Which water?'

'All of it.'

I finished my scotch and filled my glass again. 'And before that?'

'I disappeared.'

I reached for my cigarettes and matches. The small flame moved down the match toward my fingers. I let it scorch me, and it seemed incredible that my fingers didn't shake. 'Are you alive?'

He cocked his head to the side and stared at me; it was maddening, terrible, corrosive, the way he didn't blink. 'I don't think so.'

I smoked the cigarette, watching the smoke curl on itself in the air between us. 'I don't think so either.'

I poured my third glass of scotch and tore another piece of bread from the loaf, but didn't eat it. I pulled out the soft, white centre and pressed it into a ball. Disappeared, I thought. I should have felt bemused, disturbed, at the very least surprised, but all I felt was the low burn of scotch inside my throat.

'Why did you come here?'

He stared at the white ball in my fingers. Bread with all the air crushed out of it. 'I don't know.'

We spent the next few hours in silence. He stared at Tía Mónica's painting, the ship and sea evoked with the same hue and brush. This painting seemed to engage him far more than the print on the other wall, Dalí's *Persistence of Memory*, with its melted clocks draped over a barren branch, an angled surface, a sleeping creature of inscrutable origins. I had not caught him looking at the Dalí even once, whereas Mónica's painting seemed to have the effect of a gripping story, as though a part of him could leap over the frame and into its blue world. When I was a child, I had done the same: watched the painting in naked fascination, certain the ship was in motion and would lunge toward me at any moment, as if to save me from perilous shores. The brushstrokes were thick and dynamic, blending ship with sea, creating the illusion that they interpenetrated. A ship melting into the ocean waves, or being born from them: my child-mind could never decide which was more true and always longed to ask the woman who had made the painting. *Does the ship form the water or the water form the ship?* But I could never ask her this, of course, because she was gone, to an unknown place, a woman even more enigmatic than her art. I drank and smoked and pretended not to watch the man who watched the painting. The street lifted its low voice into the room. The air swirled. I put my head down on the table, and slept.

Perla, Perlita, my mother said, don't believe the lies about the disappeared. You're going to hear things in school and I'll tell you now that they're not true, Perlita, these people are hysterical, they don't understand a lot of things. Don't say anything to them about it. Just stay quiet and remember they're confused.

I nodded then, and my tight braids brushed against my dress. Mamá smiled at me, helped me into my coat, and gave me a hug. As always, I wanted the embrace to last longer so I could dissolve into my mother's soft blouse and bright perfume, but the touch was perfunctory, a means to an end, delivered in the rush of a busy morning. Mamá loved me very much, but she had many things to think about, and very nice clothes that should not wrinkle so early in the day.

I was six years old. The democracy was about to turn one. And yes, there were people now who clearly did not like Navy men like Papá. Romina Martínez's uncles had been gone for seven years, or so she'd told me in the coatroom at school. There are many people like that, she'd whispered. Many people who never came home in the Bad Years. Her grandmother still marched in the plaza downtown every Thursday, wearing a white scarf over her head, so that her uncles would return. But, Romina said, taking off her green galoshes, Mamá said that's crazy, they won't come back, because they're dead.

I said nothing to this because I was a goodgirl. But later, weeks later, one night after homework, I asked my own mamá about it: Where are Romina's uncles? Will they come back?

Mamá sighed. She was holding a scotch, and she swayed it back and forth, so that the ice cubes chimed against the glass. 'Who knows?'

'Where are they?'

'They probably went off to live lazy lives in Paris.'

I felt sorry for Romina then, with her hand-me-down galoshes and her grandmother wandering the plaza and uncles too lazy to come home. She did not have a mamá like mine, the kind that had her nails done every week and wore imported French scarves that draped across her collar like bright plumes. Mamá had beauty all around her, Papá was a strong man who arrived home in the evenings with his uniform still pressed, and I was a lucky girl to have parents like these.

But Romina was not the only one who spoke about these things. We're a democracy now, said the puffy-haired lady on the television news; the dictatorship is behind us. I had never heard the word *dictatorship* – *dictadura* – before. I tried to understand what it could mean. It had the word *dura* inside of it, meaning *hard,* so perhaps there had been something hard about that time, which might explain why Romina called them the Bad Years, but did not explain why Papá seemed not to like that they were over. Maybe it wasn't a bad kind of hard. Like walls. Everybody knew it was good that walls were hard, because that way the rain couldn't come in. But you wouldn't want your pillows to be hard, or your father's hand, or many other things.

Whenever the puffy-haired lady came on television, I watched intently so I could better understand this word, *dictatorship.* From her, I learned that in those years a thing had happened called El Proceso, the Process, and some people said it was a good thing, while others said it hurt a lot of people, especially some people who were called *desaparecidos.* The disappeared. At that point, I waited for the puffyhaired lady to name Romina's uncles, maybe even show Romina and her family on the screen, but she did not. Instead, she was busy talking about a man called General Jorge Videla, who had commanded the country (I could see this clearly, the commanding: Argentina at the table like a schoolgirl, Videla the headmistress, passing the bread, telling Argentina to keep its elbows off the table and chew with its mouth closed), and now people were mad at him and other generals because of the disappeared, and so there were going to be trials. On the first day of the trials, my parents watched the news after dinner without saying a word. I watched them more than I watched the footage of stern military men and shouting people on the street. On the second night, they watched for five minutes, until my father got up quickly and turned it off.

'We're not watching that shit.'

'Language,' said Mamá.

Mamá and Papá bought another television for their bedroom. I didn't see the news anymore. But still, I learned at school that the former commanders went to prison. And as the years passed, I learned that the disappeared had not reappeared. The word *disappeared* kept ricocheting, through rooms, down streets, in grocery stores, in plazas, in newspapers, in whispers and in wails and all tones in between. A new number of *desaparecidos* was calculated, denied, defended. Thirty thousand. That number was a lie from foreign groups. That number was a truth that had occurred. The number was of people that the government had taken. No. It was people who simply had gone somewhere else. No. There were mass graves. There were exaggerations. They were dead. There must be survivors. El Proceso was a national shame. El Proceso had been necessary. The disappeared had been innocent. The disappeared had endangered the security of the nation.

So many words, so many versions, always pushing back and forth. I wanted to believe everybody, wanted to find the space where everyone – my father, the journalists, strangers in the store – had a little piece of the truth. When I was eleven, I read Borges in school, and it occurred to me that everything was possible. Because, in Borges's stories, there were men who dreamed grown men into being, and points in space that contained the universe, and gardens that forked the paths of time itself. If all of this could happen, then there must be a way to understand the vanished people. Maybe El Proceso had tapped into an unknown seventh dimension. A crack had opened between our plane and another secret realm. And thirty thousand people had fallen through, by a slip of the foot, a slip of the tongue, a slip of reality. In which case, the disappeared were still somewhere. Still alive. But not with us.

I wrote a story for Spanish class in which the thirty thousand clustered, waiting, wakeful, trapped in a secret dimension. I was twelve when I wrote it; the democracy was five years old. Videla had been released from prison, pardoned by President Menem. In the story, the thirty thousand crowded their new homes and survived by taking in memories instead of air, craving recollection the way the rest of humanity craves breath. Their mouths grew large from telling their own stories. They kept looking for the rift in their reality, the crack they'd slipped through, a way to go back home, or at least tell those they'd left behind what happened so they wouldn't have to worry. But the slipping-place was gone. I wrote this story for myself, in the depth of the night, spilling over beyond the demands of the assignment, which was a story of three pages while my own version continued on for thirteen, and every page surprised me, made me wonder where it came from, where the words and memory-breaths and tangled translucent avenues and ethereal lost people with distorted mouths had come from, what this force that pushed my pen across the page could be. When I finished, I didn't dare to read it over. Instead I put it under my pillow and slept the three remaining hours of the night.

The story won a school contest, and a briefer version was published in the newspaper. My teacher had me stand up at her desk while the whole class clapped, and though they did so with wooden duty and even envy, the sound still showered through me and reached inner chambers I had not known were there.

When I came home that night, at ten o'clock from studying

at a friend's house, my father was waiting for me in the living room. He was drunk.

'Come here.'

I didn't want to go there but I did.

'Sit down.'

I sat.

He held up the clipping of my story. 'What is this?'

'A story.'

'Who wrote it?'

I grasped my fingers in my lap. 'I did.'

'Oh yeah? And who are you?'

Papá looked old, gray around the edges. I thought that he might shout or hit me, but he didn't. His tone was a slap already. He stared at the wall and then at me and with his eyes upon me I wanted to shred that story and swallow it, piece by piece, pull the whole thing back into my body and make it disappear.

'Perla. There are a lot of things that you don't understand.'

I nodded.

'We're your parents. Your mamá and I.'

I felt Lolo amble up to me. He leaned his cool shell against my ankle, and this calmed me a little. I nodded again.

'Do you want to lose us?'

I shook my head.

'You want to be an orphan?'

'No.'

'Then why the hell would you write a thing like this?'

Mamá was in the doorway now. 'Héctor,' she said, 'that's enough. Stop it.' She walked over, hard shoes echoing, and put her hand on Papá's shoulder, her long red nails against his white shirt like exotic insects. I leaned forward, into the sweet edge of her perfume.

Papá looked at me with an open face, a face more open than I'd ever seen on him, afraid, exposed, a man lost in the jungle. At that moment, I felt as though I understood nothing, not a single thing about the world, except one: I would not write. I moved forward and put my hand on his knee to comfort him, or to calm him, or to keep myself steady.

'Perla,' he said, 'you're killing me.'

'I'm sorry,' I said.

'All right then,' said Mamá. 'Let's all go to bed.'

♣

His eyes are closed but he isn't sleeping. He recalls the time when he had no eyes. They hooded him, a simple way to take eyes from a man. He wore the hood day and night, and day and night did not exist, there was only dark, the dark was everywhere, all around him, in the air while he swung from the ceiling, in the cold water thrown over his sleep, in the steel mesh of the electric table. The men said You are nothing, We are God, and pissed and spat on him, his countrymen, all in a day's work. Sometimes they said it shouting, and other times mechanically, duty done, mission accomplished; in his other life when he had eyes he might have asked them for their names, or for some shred of who they were, perhaps he'd known them, their feet may have once kicked a soccer ball his way in some park in the city, it was possible, there had been many games in the park, but this was not soccer and he was not a ball and their feet had their own marching orders.

He missed his eyes at first. He longed for light and thought that light might save him. He wanted to see his welts, his bruises, he was worried about his balls. The way they hung it

seemed they'd swollen to the size of grapefruits from the twisting and the twisting, from the electric shocks, they throbbed
and throbbed, there was a time when Gloria had cradled them
in her fingers, in her mouth, squeezing playfully, a daring
squeeze, how could they have imagined what could be done
to balls? how much more daring things could get? where was
she now? his wife *safe, safe, safe* drinking coffee with her girlfriends, typing letters for her boss, taking off her earrings in
the bedroom, taking off her blouse, leaving on her wedding
ring, wondering where he was. His mind returned to her over
and over, finding her in bed, her body warm, hair redolent,
opening arms and legs to him, *shhhhh you're back, don't worry,*
he'd shrink to baby-size and be enfolded, crawl between her
legs into her body where the baby was growing, *shhhhh there's
room for both of you,* he stayed inside her, warm, lush, halfway
between worlds, all three of them resting in one nest of flesh –
until cold water and spit made him return.

Days passed. Weeks. He couldn't tell. He learned that there
are things worse than the dark. Light in the wrong places, like
his ass, the hole of him, filled up with a metal rod that lit with
current. The questions kept coming and coming, over and
over, he no longer knew what he answered, he no longer knew
what they wanted, what his body could survive. He longed for
dark, retreated there, a microscopic coil of a man.

The men said You don't exist.

They said it loud and also said it low and there was no day,
no night, no slope of time between light and darkness.

You don't exist. You're nothing.

Little did they know those words could be a refuge. What
does not exist can feel no pain. Pain still approached with
jaws wide open, but it found nothing to clamp onto. Nothing

mattered. He slipped away. Even his name was gone from him, erased from the past, from all the mouths that ever made the shape of it to call him from the street for dinner, to call on him in class, to sing him to sleep, to punctuate a question – did you steal that? are you cold? do you still love me? How many oranges? where do you think you're going? Where there are no questions there's no life. Where there is no name there is no calling. Better not to be called, not to feel yourself again, the skin and cold nightwater and the boots, the three other men in the small tube of a cell, whom he smelled nearby though they were strictly forbidden to speak. They too had no names. They only had numbers, called out by guards when they arrived to take them to the interrogation room down the hall.

The men in that room. They existed. They were hot unyielding they were everywhere. He hated them. He needed them. Sometimes he loved them – he despised himself for it but couldn't help it, they could grant reprieves, could halt the beating and say *Look what I did for you,* could fill his mouth with a sweet pastry when he was starved, the same hand brought the pastry and the electric jolts, stroked his forehead dry with a cloth and pushed levers, and he was so debased that when the pastry came and the voice said *Say thank you, sir,* he would not only repeat the words but mean them. I want to live and so I want your love. Men who could grant life and thresh it to oblivion. The guards were myriad, they gave him *mate* sometimes and sometimes a crust of bread, a bowl of gruel, a small moment to lift the hood off and eat. Sometimes they laughed, the laughter of a bored man or of a boy watching ants drown in the water he'd just poured over them.

In the end it was light that broke him, light worse than the dark. Light revealing colours that never should be seen. He was tied to the table, as usual, facedown, beaten first, then shocked, poked, twisted, as usual. A hand touched his face, caressed it, two fingers soft along his cheek, then drawing up his hood. His head was pulled back by the hair. His eyes were stung by the light, it had been days or months, he blinked several times and the voice said *Do you know what this is?* And so he blinked again and strained to focus. There was another hand in front of him, holding a rag that dripped with blood; he had no answer and anyway there was no time, the voice went on – *It's your wife's panties, that's what* – and then the hood came back down and the dark, the dark, the dark clasped him and swallowed his whole mind.

I woke up, not in bed. I was at the table. What had I dreamed? Of swimming through dark waters, full of broken fish. And I was cold. And then? Already I couldn't quite remember.

The man was still on the living room floor. His eyes were closed, so I took a long look at him. There was a drenched translucence to his skin, an unnatural paleness, that did not belong to the living. His limbs were as limp as tentacles. His lips were blue and swollen, and his genitals drooped. I had never offered him clothes, I realised, and he had not asked for them; somehow, the notion of clothing seemed extraneous and even strange. He did not seem cold, after all, and appeared to have no way of becoming dry. As for modesty, he seemed to have none, and I had no desire to draw attention to his nakedness by making the suggestion. In any case, I did not feel the embarrassment I would have expected to feel in response to a naked stranger; I might as well be embarrassed at the nakedness of a fish. He had a few bits of seaweed stuck in his hair. I thought of the seaweed on the beach in Uruguay, that last night with Gabriel, how it glistened obscenely in the moon-light. How I ran away and left him there, alone on the beach, calling after me. I thought of his face right before I turned from him, washed in moonlight, the lost look of a man who's exited the train at the wrong stop. I didn't want to think about that moment, couldn't bear to think about it, but this man's presence was pushing at the dam I had erected to keep it out of my thoughts. This man's presence was wet and heavy and seemed to have this effect, he threatened to collapse the dam so anything could pour into my mind, memories, urges, melted question marks. I was afraid of what would happen if he stayed here, who I would continue to become.

It was quiet in the room; there were no cars on the street, all the neighbours were home behind closed doors. The tall lamp in the corner illumined a wide circle in the room, hemmed by silent shadows. The light was low, but gleamed gently in the wet drops on the man's skin. I wondered whether he would ever dry, or whether he'd always appear this way, damp and clammy, as if freshly risen from the river. He was uninvited moisture. He had leaked into this house. I had every reason to find his presence an affront, to be enraged at his invasion, or at least to eject him in calm tones. Certainly he made me feel combustible, unsafe in my own skin. But though I didn't know why, though the feeling shocked me, I did not want him to leave. It occurred to me then that there might be something the two of us had to do together, something ineffable, some-thing I could not possibly do alone.

Perla, I thought, you're delirious with the night.

Outside, it began, very softly, to rain.

3

Waters and Sorrows

Morning came. I didn't go to class. I left a message on my professor's voice mail, something I'd never done before but it was so unlike me to miss school for any reason that I felt the need to explain. I'm running a high fever, I said, a strange summer virus. It wouldn't be responsible to expose the rest of the class, and anyway, with my head in this state I won't be able to apply myself. I said it all thinking I was weaving a big lie, but as I hung up it occurred to me that everything except the fever could be true.

The wet man slept on his patch of floor, his body curled into a loose ball. The rug around him was stained with water. I watched him breathe for a few minutes, taking in air, expelling it, his mouth slack. I wondered how old he was. In the morning sun his hair was still black with hints of green, his ash-white face unwrinkled – he could be my own age, twenty-two, or perhaps a couple of years older, twenty five at most. But then again, he had been somewhere that could have changed his skin, darkened his hair, shifted his constitution in ways I couldn't grasp. I was trying to fathom him, the bare essentials of his being; trying to open my thinking, my world, to contain what he claimed to be: one of the disappeared. One of the people who left for work and never arrived, or arrived at work and never came home, or went home and never emerged. People who left holes more gaping than the ordinary dead, because they can't be grieved and buried, forcing their loved ones to carry their perpetual absence as though the absence itself were alive. Like Romina, with her missing uncles, and her involvement with the Madres de Plaza de Mayo, with whom she marched in sight of the Presidential Palace, a white kerchief around her face in protest. In the single year that we were close friends, I had always imagined the uncles' absence as a dominating current in her house, sweeping the walls along with sunlight, murmuring under dinner conversations, lining the copious shelves of books. Of course that was all before we turned fourteen and Romina cut our ties in a single brutal gesture of disgust – or rage? or grief? or – after which there was no more speaking let alone dreaming between us, only glares at me in the hall that spoke with such ferocious naked force that I came to spend my high school years studiously avoiding Romina's face. I imagined finding Romina now – an apparition in stern glasses, hovering in the hall – and saying Look, look, one of them is here, I don't know how he got here but it's true, he drips and stares like a human trout but he says he's one of them, halfdead, undead, disentangled from the threads of nonexistence, he has not aged, could he be your uncle?

The apparition of Romina scowled and said, That's impossible.

I know it seems impossible, but he's here.

Not that, bitch. It's impossible that my uncle would come to your house.

I stood, to dispel the vision, unsteady on my feet. I didn't want to stay home, nor did I feel equipped to leave. I washed my face, but didn't shower. Two cups of coffee for breakfast. For Lolo, boiled squash, which he picked at for a moment and then abandoned. I'd been boiling his food faithfully ever since I was old enough to be let near the stove. He hadn't been able to eat lettuce in thirty-nine years, since before I was born, when he was my father's turtle, and so mean, it is said, that my grandfather kicked him and broke his mouth. His mouth was still crooked from the injury. Occasionally he disappeared for days, and the squash I boiled for him would go untouched. I would worry about his hunger and demise until I saw him again, out in the open, alert, unperturbed, crooked jaw shut tight around the secret of where he'd been. He was capable of immense stillness as well as a surprising gallop up and down the hall when the mood struck him. That bastard is strong, mean and strong, my father would always say, and shake his head in vexed admiration. Now, as I watched Lolo amble out, I wished I could crawl into his leathery head and dig up memories like buried stones. Because he was there when my father was a child, long before he became my father, when he was just a little boy called Héctor watching his own father kick a turtle in the face and break his jaw. A forceful boot, the rapid shatter of a mouth. Lolo had brought it on himself, or so the story went. What had he done? Walked too slowly? Too fast? Been too much underfoot? Perhaps he'd bitten his attacker first, though I'd never seen him bite anyone and could not imagine him doing so without provocation. And surely there were some provocations in the house that formed the boy who became Héctor, a house four kilometres away that smelled of medicines and disinfected floors, in which a childhood had unfurled that I had little knowledge of, barely a fistful.

Once, my mother had told me, when I was small and crying in my room because Papá was angry and I'd been bad and had to be punished, *Your father's good to you, you know, he never hits you like his father did with him.* I was spoiled, the one who was not hit, escaping the fate of Héctor, and of Lolo. When we visited my grandfather, I saw a man who everyone said was ill but who seemed to possess a terrible charm, wearing his Navy colonel's jacket just to sit at his own kitchen table, capable of mesmerising a child, launching his special game that sent me hiding in the house without any seek, no one to come after me, no one to find me and pull me by the arm into the light. Yet still I breathed with quick exhilaration in the dark, counting to sixty as instructed, and then emerged a changed girl, always a changed girl, to find my grandfather talking to the grown-ups and to wait patiently (eyes on his feet, trying to discern which one had wounded Lolo years ago) until he looked at me and smiled, saying, *Well?* And I'd say, *Well,* not knowing what else to say. *Did you hide in the dark?* I nodded. Dark places were always the best, the only true ones, for hiding. *How was it?* I never knew how to answer, what the right response was for the game, but no matter what I said, he always sent me out again. *This time count to eighty, if you can.*

The wet man awoke as I lit up my third smoke.

'Good morning.'

His body had not moved. His eyes wide open.

'Did you sleep well?'

'I don't know.'

I tapped ash into the saucer on the table and tried to smile. 'I'm staying home with you today.'

He glanced at the window without moving his head. He looked back at me. Eyes from the depths. Octopus eyes.

I got up, went to the kitchen, and returned with a glass and pitcher. 'Hungry?'

He nodded, as if to say, I am voracious, I could devour the sea.

As I held the glass to the mouth of my guest, I felt terribly sad, and the sadness gaped inside me, faceless, formless, bottomless, ready to draw everything down into it, books, skies, cigarettes, the very texture of the day. It was not an unfamiliar sensation, but one that always came without warning. I struggled to keep it concealed, as I usually do, but this time the effort was futile: he stared at me with eyes so clear they could have read the emotions of a stone.

Sometimes, to hide your sadness, you have to cut yourself in two. That way you can bury half of yourself, the unspeakable half, and leave the rest to face the world. I can tell you the first time I did this. I was fourteen years old, standing in a bathroom stall holding the last note I would ever receive from my friend Romina, a note consisting of a single question in furious capital letters.

We had been in class together for years, but did not grow close until we were thirteen, when Romina began to have her *experience*. That was her own word for it, *experience*, spoken in a hallowed tone that gave it an aura of great mystery.

'An *experience*,' I repeated blankly, the first time I heard of it.

'Come over tonight, I'll show you,' Romina said.

I nodded. I wondered whether the *experience* had something to do with breasts. If so, Romina's change was no great secret: on the contrary, it was sudden and astonishing, and had rapidly transformed a perennially mousy girl into an axis of hushed attention. Boys and also girls had started glancing sidelong at the blouse of her school uniform, under which those early and voluminous globes hummed – surely they hummed! – and pushed out curves that incited whispers and giggles and stares. They were fecund; they were bolder than their bearer; they sang themselves into the rounded air. I was fascinated by them too; I wanted (though I would never say this) to touch them, to explore their bulk and shape, the buoyant slope of them, their quiet yet absolutely incontrovertible presence. My own breasts had grown only a little so far, and could not possibly equal this capacity to command the centre of a room. At night, in bed, I stroked my own breasts and wondered at their fresh swells, the soft-then-firming nipples, and, as I did, I wondered what Romina's breasts would do under my fingers, how they would curve, how the supple skin would respond. The only thing more unbelievable than Romina's breasts was her own reaction to them. She barely seemed to notice all the new attention. She had always been the kind of girl who stared out of the window and chewed her pencil to shreds and looked perfectly comfortable lunching alone, and her new reknown left that unchanged.

As it turned out, Romina's *experience* had nothing to do with breasts, not talking about them and most certainly not touching them; it was nothing more and nothing less than the philosophical and aesthetic expansion of her world. She had begun exploring her parents' bookshelves. That was all. I tried to hide my disappointment. That afternoon, she walked me back and forth in front of them, pointing out the spines of Kierkegaard, Sartre, Storni, Parra, Baudelaire, Nietzsche, Vallejo, pulling out the volumes and spilling them open in her hands as if they had wills of their own. She had been sleeping with them under her pillow. She had been waking in the middle of the night and opening them to arbitrary pages, imbibing words, and then reciting them in her head as she drifted back to sleep. She had been rolling words around her mouth, consuming them like food, even instead of food. She had been thinking – and this, I realised, was a very concrete and important action in Romina's world: her father, after all, was a philosopher, which meant that he had forged a life out of thinking, and that the university even paid him to do it, a notion that amazed me, far as it was from anything I had seen in my own family. Imagine! A man who is paid to think! What happens in such a mind (and such a household)? As Romina spoke, the sun gradually faded from the living room, casting huskier light along the books, and I touched the spines, with their embossed titles and names, wondering what it would be like to draw so passionately from a mere printed page, or, for that matter, draw so passionately from anything at all. By the time night had fallen, my disappointment had given way to curiosity: there was something hallowed and ecstatic about Romina's relationship with the books that I had never seen before. I wanted to feel what she felt.

That night, I stayed for dinner, and Romina introduced me as That Girl Who Wrote the Story About the Disappeared, with a glow in her voice that surprised me and made me blush. It had been a year since the story had been published, and she had never said anything to me about it. The parents exclaimed, *A wonderful story, we loved it, how brave of you,* and a hot shame ran through me at accepting praise for this story that had brought so much trouble at home, that I had willed myself to renounce, because surely it was a bad story, wasn't it, and I had been bad for writing it? Wasn't it an embarrassment? Hadn't it been woven out of lies? Romina's parents did not seem to think so; the father grinned, the mother served me more potatoes, delicious potatoes, perfectly salted, crisp around the edges. At this table, I realised, it was not my story that was embarrassing but something else, other parts of my life, the things my parents said. Even things they had done. It was a confusing thought, surrounded by cacophonous thorns. I pushed it down and said nothing so I could stay at this table and eat potatoes without breaking the spell.

We began to spend hours together after school, after home-work was done, exploring books, ideas, poems, life's great questions. We pillaged her parents' bookcase, pulling volumes down, reading, and sharing our findings with each other. We built small fortresses around ourselves, with volumes as the bricks. We read chaotically, opening books at random, reading a page aloud, watching each other for wordless excitement or disinterest. If it lit us up, we continued. If it did not, we discarded it without a thought, like greedy children with an enormous box of truffles, abandoning one flavour for another after a single bite. I often had no idea what the words meant, but I didn't say so, and if Romina didn't understand them, she didn't say so either. Tasting the words was enough. We approached them freely, without the pressure of analysis or even understanding, for the pure pleasure they incited. The words began to spin inside me, to sing to me of wakefulness and wanting and mystery and pain, to thread through my days and accompany me to class, to bed, to meals with my mother and father who I thought could not possibly understand what I was discovering, who read newspapers and popular novels but never lines of words like these, lines that could whip you from the inside.

This is how I discovered Rimbaud, one rainy evening. The

first time I opened *Illuminations,* I read, *In an attic where at the age of twelve I was locked up, I knew the world and illustrated the human comedy.* My hands shook. I felt cut open. It was not a line I could read to Romina. I turned the pages back toward the beginning.

Waters and sorrows, rise up and bring back the Floods.

This line hooked into me and would not let me go, the way a song from the radio repeats in the mind, a chant to which my feet beat on the pavement, left foot, *Waters,* right foot, *sorrows,* left, *rise up,* right, *bring back,* on and on as I walked wherever I was going. Perla, where are you going? To the moon, I thought, to the city, to myself. I had no idea what the line meant, but it shook me. There's that feeling that comes when you read something and the lines speak directly to you, and to you only, even though the person who wrote them died long before you were born, or, even if alive, has no idea you exist. The words seep right into your mind. They pour into your secret hollows and take their shape, a perfect fit, like water. And you are slightly less alone in the universe, because you have been witnessed, because you have been filled, because someone once found words for things within you that you couldn't yourself name – something gesturing not only toward what you are, but what you could become. In that sense, books raise you, in a way your parents can't. They emancipate you.

For my fourteenth birthday, Romina gave me a copy of *Illuminations,* complete with a handwritten dedication. *To Perla, So your truth will always burn bright. Abrazos, R.* I slept with the volume under my pillow. In the mornings, before rising, I would open the book to any page and read a line. My hands opened the book, the book opened the day. The line I read accompanied me, furled in my mind, a mantra beyond meaning.

Needless to say, the other girls found this new friendship strange, even laughable. But I didn't care. I had never had a friend who ignited me like Romina. I no longer pitied her as I had years before, when she first told me about her uncles, but rather saw her as fearless and free, and I wanted to be more like that, even if it meant that the other girls stopped calling my house, gave me berth. In some ways, I was in fact free then, perhaps more so than at any other time in my life – though there were limits. Every Thursday, Romina went to the Plaza de Mayo, where she marched in a long, slow circle with her grandmother and many other women in white kerchiefs carrying placards with enormous black-and-white photographs of men and women who had vanished long ago, and messages also: WE DEMAND JUSTICE, WE WANT THEM BACK WITH LIFE. It was a part of her world that made me sting with discomfort. I could not reconcile this aspect of her life with the rest of her. Mamá, after all, insisted that the accusations about *desaparecidos* were untrue; if these women in the plaza were caught up in a big mistake, unable to accept the wanderlust of their sons (and wouldn't it be good if it had always been that, if Romina's uncles had just gone roaming the world like Rimbaud! if they arrived back one day with too-long hair and exotic tales to tell!) – then wouldn't Romina with all her sophistication see through her family's delusions?

Unless they were not delusions. Unless the people in the plaza were the ones with the truth, and I was the one who breathed in lies. This strange thought hovered inside me, a live grenade. I did not know what to believe. I wondered whether Romina was as sure of her beliefs as she seemed. I wondered what went through her mind as she marched the plaza, what it meant to her, what she privately thought about her family's weekly ritual. Whether she participated for herself, or just to placate her abuela, and, above all, whether she also harboured doubts.

But these were not questions I would ever ask aloud. The topic was hazardous, to be avoided at all costs. She asked me to come with her to these demonstrations – *We can go to my house afterward,* she said – but I always found an excuse, spoken in a carefully casual voice. I had told her that my father worked in the port, a vague description that was not exactly a lie, was it, considering that the port had to do with water and the Navy did as well? It was just a slight blur of reality. No. I could not fool myself. It was a lie. I had to do it, I told myself, to protect our intimacy, our hours together, the radiant bond I could not bear to lose.

I finally had Romina over to my house, and that was my great mistake. We were at the dining table, doing homework, textbooks spread around us. My parents were both out.

'Are there more books in your father's study?'

'Some.'

'I want to see them.'

'You can't.'

I said it too quickly, and Romina put her pencil down and looked up. 'Why not?'

'We're not supposed to go in there.'

She looked surprised, then hesitant. She returned to her work. I thought the danger was gone, but then, an hour later, she went to the bathroom and twenty minutes passed and she still had not returned. I found her in the study. She stood completely still, in front of a bookcase, her profile to the door. Her hands were at her sides, frozen with fingers far apart like startled starfish. I thought of my father coming home at that moment, the invasion discovered, sharp words in front of my friend. We had to leave the room. I searched for the words.

Romina said, 'What is this?'

Her voice was tight, almost foreign. I followed her gaze to the bookshelf, where a photograph stood in a silver frame, of my father in full uniform, standing in a row of officers in front of ESMA, the Escuela de Mecánica de la Armada, with stately door and soaring ivory pillars that, to me, had always evoked the unshakable laws of an ancient world. Romina was staring at it, concentrating furiously, as though working through a complex algebraic equation. *Speak,* I thought. *I need to speak.* I opened my mouth, but it was empty.

'He's one of them, isn't he,' Romina said. 'Your father.'

The silence spread through the room, long tentacles that wrapped around my throat and slid into my belly. I felt seasick. Romina turned and stared at me, and she looked like a girl lost in dark waters, a girl who had just stumbled on evil in those waters, for the first time, in its wild form. A girl looking evil in the face. *My face? Mine?* No, it could not be, this was terribly wrong, we had fallen through the world's ice into a mistaken place. I took a step toward her in an attempt to shift the story but her face wrenched into a brutal wail that would not come.

'Don't touch me,' she said, and began to cry without sound. Her body shook violently, straining to sob, straining not to sob, at war with itself.

'Romina,' I said.

She hurried past me, to the dining room, where I heard her packing up her textbooks. I knew I should go in there, say something, persuade her to stay, to understand. But I myself did not understand what had happened, what had spread through the study, the nausea at the pit of me, the look on her face. I could not move. I stared at my father's desk, which was long and wide and freshly polished, the cherry-dark wood as smooth and gleaming as a mirror. A leather bound cup of pens stood reflected on the desk, and I knew they all had ink in them; my father was scrupulous about discarding pens as soon as they ran out. I stared at the pens' reflections. I counted them. There were seven. I counted them again. I was still counting when I heard rapid footsteps, the front door opening, the loud slam shut.

The next day, in class, Romina would not look at me, her back a rod of steely reproach. The naked horror had been replaced by something else, something shuttered and cold. I pretended not to care, although my hand shook as I copied Latin lessons from the blackboard. The fear of losing my friend consumed me. Romina's voice, surprisingly throaty, reading aloud from a book in the diminishing light. Romina's face, eyes closed in pleasure, absorbing the sound of a paragraph or poem. Her breasts. Romina bent over her homework, her hair a fine brown wall around her, her pencil turning to shreds between her teeth. Romina in the study, wrestling down sobs. I wanted nothing more in the world than to rebuild our friendship. It seemed a looming task, but in those first days it did not yet seem impossible. The more I thought about it, the more the situation seemed like nothing more and nothing less than a misunderstanding – though, granted, one of epic proportions, historic proportions, a tragic disconnect between two poles of reality as much as between two schoolgirls. It seemed to me that the rift between us was larger than us, larger than either of our understandings – wasn't it? surely that's how it was? – since to understand it fully would mean seeing things from all sides, and neither of us had done such a thing. For all I knew, no one in all of Argentina had truly seen all sides. Maybe no one had ever stood in the gales between men like Papá and men like Romina's uncles and somehow absorbed all of it, the whole scope of the story, every inch of shadow and light. Maybe no one had ever loved a person on both sides of that chasm. It seemed impossible, too far for a heart to stretch. I was trying to do it, and felt dismantled by the effort – and yet in those first days I still longed to occupy that space and swallow everything, mend everything. I still believed in such mendings, with all the fervour and deaf hope of adolescence. Romina, I wanted to say, it's not what you think, I'm not what you think, I don't know what we are but I want to discover it with all the roving intellectual boldness we found together. We can rewrite this story; come with me, come back, I'll explain. I'll try to explain.

But I never found my chance.

A week after the incident, I found a note tucked into my science textbook, on torn paper, in Romina's unmistakable capital letters:

ARE YOU A MURDERER TOO?

My hand shook, holding the paper. I couldn't breathe. I looked around the classroom: the other students were raucously packing their bags, talking about lunch, and Romina was nowhere to be seen. I had read the note undetected. I stuffed it quickly into my pocket and hurried to the bathroom, where I locked myself into a stall and stood with my eyes closed and my face against the door. The stall smelled of urine and cigarettes and the cheap perfume someone had sprayed to disguise the smell of smoke. The note seemed to burn through my pocket, scalding me – I would surely take off my trousers that night and find red puckered skin. I closed my eyes and saw my father, face full of love, at my bedside at night as he stroked my hair and sang a lullaby off-key. I heard his laugh, watching television, the sound of him round and generous and dropping slowly in pitch, *ha-ha-ha,* as if somersaulting down steep stairs. I heard the long push of his breath as he filled an inflatable pool for me, in the summer, the *pffhhh, pffffhhh* of his dedication to my joy. I saw him eating breakfast, about to leave for work, in proud clean uniform, the golden buttons shining on his cuffs. He was not a – no. Could not be. I was enraged. I was ashamed. I felt like breaking everything in sight, only there was nothing in my sight except the blistered paint on the stall door.

The stall door stayed closed in front of me, dispassionate, unyielding worn.

I stood and stood while time stretched and moaned and pressed around me, until the bell rang to signal the end of lunch. I had forgotten to eat, I was late for class, I was not hungry. I took the note back out, unfolded it, and read it again. It had not changed. I read it and read it and read it. Then I tore it into many little pieces and flushed it down the toilet, a futile act that could not keep me from reading those words incessantly in the coming months, in the dark of night, where they blazed and hovered over my bed.

After this, the crimes of my father – the crimes of the nation, also, crimes to which I had not given words – settled on me, rode my back, draped my shoulders, stuck to me and refused to wipe away. They were not delusions. I could no longer believe they were delusions. Things had happened in this nation, they were true, and Romina's family had played one role while my family had played another, a role that could not easily be cleansed, and that clung to the underside of my skin like a dense sheet of lead that made it difficult to rise from bed in the mornings. I couldn't clearly see what my father had done – the images only came in fractured pieces, his gleaming cuffs against a desk, his face gazing through iron bars – nor did I want to see any more clearly. But I had accepted that the disappeared had truly disappeared, and this was enough for condemnation. I was guilty by inheritance. There was no trial, no choice, only the *here you go this belongs to you* of guilt, which increased with every bite of bread from the dinner table, every absent smile from Papá as he looked up briefly from the morning paper, every brisk kiss I accepted from Mamá as I left for school, every night I burrowed into fresh linens that had been washed by a woman who was paid with pesos that my father earned the way he'd earned them. With every turn and motion and common daily act, the stain occupied more space beneath my skin. It was inescapable. I could no more free myself of it than I could free myself of my own face.

I said nothing to my parents, and they did not seem to suspect that I had changed, that the secret at our family's heart had become exposed.

At that time, of course, I was sure that it had.

My old friends accepted me back, though gradually and not without a few barbs, which I met with amiable shrugs. I did not explain and they did not ask for explanation. They were popular girls who did not care about French poets or Thursday marches or *experiences* that led down hazardous roads. Instead they were obsessed with eye shadow and hairstyles gleaned from fashion magazines and losing weight they didn't have and movies from Hollywood in which things went terribly wrong but always ended well for everyone except, of course, the villain. I buried the parts of myself that seemed radioactive. My friends made it easy to pretend, so convincingly that on good days I lulled myself into believing my own act, and became a girl who was not haunted by the echoes of a question on a torn sheet of paper. She was an easier girl to be. So I became her.

From then on, there were two Perlas: one on the surface who had good grades and good friends and smiled a lot and for whom everything was going fine, and a secret Perla under the surface where sins and shame and questions lay buried alive, like land mines.

4

The Chorus in the Depths

The morning flares open, slowly, filling the air, piercing his mind. They are quiet together. He watches her smoke cigarettes, flip through magazines, flip through television channels. She doesn't laugh when recorded laughter issues from the screen. He listens to the sound of her in the kitchen, clattering around, cooking nothing. The turtle crawls up to him on squat, scaly legs. It cranes its neck out of its shell. Its jaw smacks open, then closed, with a low clack. There were jaws in the water, many jaws of differing shapes and hardness, the toothy eel-jaw, the sluggish trout-jaw, the whole-body opening of jellyfish. Water has so many mouths. They ate his body while the rest of him drifted on, penetrated, porous, unperturbed. Now there is no water for him to drift through and he doesn't want to be eaten, he doesn't want to go away. He bares his teeth at the turtle. The turtle opens his jaws and lets his narrow tongue hang out. Neither of them blinks. The turtle is the first to close his mouth.

He sits up on the floor. His spine creaks. There is sensation in him, power of touch, he can feel his body beneath his fingers. The flesh is real, though soggy. He can feel pain. He feels the pain of sunlight in his head.

51

There is a world beyond this house. He hears the groan of a car outside, the lilt of voices. They are close to the city, his city, but they are not inside it; the quiet is too great; the streets do not roil and purr as they did where he once lived. There, he had felt the city under every sound like the sharp drone of a bee in flight. He was never alone in the city, a place where solitude was always tinged with strangers' voices, the low blare of a radio, the smell of someone else's steak on the grill, the brush of a rough shoulder on the street. He recalls these now in a tumble of sensations. The city: how it accompanied him unceasingly, the way the devout claim to be accompanied by God. On visits to the country – rolling pampas, breezy beaches, the vast ice of Patagonia – he enjoyed the beauty of each place but always felt relieved to return home, to be folded once again in the great fabric of a living place imbued by the breath and noise of millions. He remembers this with a sting of longing for his city, for Buenos Aires. For a moment, he is tempted to stretch his mind wide the way it stretched inside the sea, so he can go and feel it, the incessant pulse and sprawl, legions of feet. But no, he will not. This is not the sea and it is painful and difficult to stretch here. In any case, there is no need: this room is a world within a world. He turns his attention to his surroundings, seeking the inner soul of the place. On the bookshelf, books stand shut, their secrets tightly pressed inward. These are not books that open often, nor do they want to. On the contrary, they seem to say to their own words, you are captives, we won't let you out, you cannot fight us. The spines are tidy and betray no signs of the battle within. In front of the books sits a porcelain swan, its head bent in defeat or from carrying a terrible burden for too long. It throbs with unsaid thoughts. One shelf above the swan, there are two photographs, a bride and groom in one, a little girl in the other. He notices them for the first time. The little girl wears her hair in pigtails, she is sitting on a sofa, the sofa in this room. Her smile is too big for her face, her face is perfect, beaming and spilling what her features cannot hold. The wedding couple are young and handsome, both smiling with their mouths closed, the woman's chin in a high slant of pride or defiance, the man's eyes searching the camera for clues to an unsolved puzzle. Now the camera is gone but the man's eyes keep searching, roving the living room for signs of what he sought. On the other wall, over the ominous sofa, the painting of the sea, the sea, slashed in thick blue paint not made of water but he knows it is the sea, with something riding it the colour of the water, a ship, plunged in water, made of water, a ship risen from the wet arms of the sea itself, and he can swim-pour-flood into those brushstrokes and ride the swelling curves of blue, dreaming the waves of his lost home.

She comes back from the kitchen with a plate of empanadas. On the way, she watches the turtle amble past her with an expression that he recognises as tenderness. She loves the turtle, he thinks, and his mind is stabbed by the word *loves*. She sits down at the table, and eats without looking up. Her hair is pulled back in a rubber band. Gloria used to pull her hair back when she was serious about something: scouring the stove, taking a test, winning a fight. Gloria always won their fights. She was able to turn his words around and hand them back to him, hard, polished, proof of her triumph. She was going to be the greatest lawyer in the nation, that's what he always told her, throwing his arms up in defeat. He had such faith in her. Thanks to her fighting prowess they wouldn't always live in a small apartment with gray water leaking through the roof from the third floor. Good things would happen. They were sure to.

They both said this. They were happy. The gray water didn't matter, anyway. But they didn't know that; they didn't know, back then, how little the leaks mattered, how happy they really were. Didn't know how good it was to have all of their toes. To drink too much red wine. To feed their animal joys, naked, slippery with sweat. To take doorknobs, showers, speech for granted, and complain bitterly about getting up early in the morning, as if it were some monumental sacrifice. What brats we are, he thinks, when we are happy.

The woman at the table glances over at him, though when their eyes meet she stares down at her empty plate. Her body is young and beautiful, it is so whole, uncut, unbruised, unburned. She has the luxury of sinking in a vague sadness. She has never been raped with rods that deliver electric shocks. The skin has never been peeled from the bottom of her feet. She has never hung from a ceiling hook, basted in shit. She has never been shown panties, bloody, torn, in the hand of a man whose voice is intensely familiar but whose face is unknown. She has never even had the smallest bullet wound. And all of this is good: he is nourished by her wholeness. A wholeness that he knows she cannot see.

They are linked, he and the girl. But how? By a rope of light, a truth that flickers for an instant before fleeing into the morass of his mind.

The phone rang and I didn't want to talk in front of the dripping man, so I ran from the living room to my father's study.

'Hello?'

'Perlita.'

'Hi, Papá.'

'It rang so long, I thought you weren't home.'

'I'm home.'

'Yes. Well, we're just calling to make sure everything's all right.'

The room was dim, the curtains were drawn, and I hadn't turned on the light when I came in. I leaned against his desk. 'Everything's fine.'

'You're fine?'

'Yes.'

'And the house?'

'What would be wrong with it?'

'Perla, I'm just asking.'

'But what could happen? I don't see why you need to ask.'

'Because it's my house.'

'Only yours?'

'What's the matter with you?'

I was wondering the same thing myself. I hadn't meant to pick a fight, hadn't meant to expose him to my private chaos. 'How's Punta del Este?'

'Beautiful. We're having a great time.' He sighed, the heavy sigh of a man beseiged by a child. 'Look, just be careful. Here's your mother.'

I waited. There were distant murmurs before she came.

'Perla?'

'Hi, Mamá.'

'What's happening over there? Is everything all right?'

'Everything is fine. Papá's just being paranoid.'

'He worries, that's all.' She said it soothingly, almost in a purr, and I could see him at the other end of the room, pouring them drinks. 'So you don't need anything?'

'No.'

'Good. We miss you. I wish you'd come.'

But Mamá, then who would stay home to water the ghost? 'I couldn't miss the start of classes.'

'Right. Well, maybe next time.'

'Maybe.'

'Call if you need anything, okay?'

'Okay.'

'Take care of yourself, Perlita.'

I hung up. The sun hovered at the window, reticent to fill the room. I thought of my parents in Punta del Este, enjoying the sun and the food, forgetting their troubles. That's what my mother always said about it: Punta del Este is where we go to forget our troubles. There was a time when I was very small, long before Romina, when I had no idea what she could be referring to, what troubles my Mamá and Papá might face. All I knew was that when we took the ferry to Uruguay, troubles remained miraculously bound to the shores of Argentina, unable to cross the waters, waiting for our return. Whatever we might be escaping from, I'd feel relieved to be doing so, our family taking refuge in a high-rise apartment that overlooked the Atlantic Ocean.

For me, the best of Punta del Este was not the boutiques, the brazen yachts in the harbour, the waves crowded with people, or the bustling restaurants to which Mamá wore her most elegant summer dresses every night. It was that hour when twilight began to run its lightest fingertips over the beach, whispering of the impending dark, *I know, you don't believe it, or don't want to believe it, but it's coming.* At that hour, my father would usually suggest we go for a walk. I'd always say yes, and my mother occasionally did, but more often she'd say, No, you two go on. I always preferred it when we two went on. We'd walk along the damp sand near the water, not talking,

I rooting for seashells and then jogging to keep up. Around us, other families would splash and play or start to fold their towels and umbrellas. Not every group had children in it, but the ones that did usually had several, and you could see them running through the foam together or bickering over plastic spades. Not everybody built their sand castles alone, like I did. We were a small family, just the three of us, no brothers or sisters, no aunts or uncles living nearby, but at that age I never thought to see us as incomplete. It was just the way we were. A constellation of three stars, and I the faint one, like the pinprick at the tip of Orion's sword. What shape we might have made among the heavens, who can say.

On our walks, I thought about how it would be if we kept walking, beyond the little peninsula of Punta del Este, along the edge of Uruguay, all the way to the country's end. A perfect place to start from, since the town sat right at the formal border between the Río de la Plata and the Atlantic Ocean, like a guard watching their bodies mix. If we walked with the water on our left, we would trace the shore of the wide river and eventually wind our way back to Argentina. With the water on our right, it would not be river but ocean, and we'd end up in Brazil. I always asked to walk with the water on our right. Of course, to reach another country the walk would have to be extremely long. It would take days, or maybe months, which was almost the same thing as forever. I liked the idea of perpetuating the walk forever, or at least until the last of my father's sadness had been shaken out by our steps. You are my light, he'd sometimes say when I ran up to him with a particularly beautiful seashell. I had to time this at the right moment, so it wasn't a bother to him, but a welcome interruption of his mood. When I succeeded, he would hold my palm in his as he admired the shell, paused on the beach, commenting on its pattern, its colour, its size. Look at that swirl along the edge, how lovely. And such a nice pink, so deep, like raspberries. Like wine. You are my light, you know that? As if without me he'd be stumbling in the dark. And so the star of me would shine that much brighter. My bare toes would revel in the sand between them. The sun was going to set soon, but it didn't matter; I was light for my father, and the world was well.

Except that now, in his study, I felt so far from him. The very word *father* raw and open in my mind, like a wound.

Searching his mind for the strange flicker that he'd lost he thought of God and how he lost Him. When he first disappeared he had a God, and when the dark swallowed his mind he reeled and broke and soared out to find Him, pray to Him, God as final refuge. Save us from this hell, forgive my sins, forgive my crime of not protecting Gloria, send your angels please like flying armies to save her and the child she carries. Gloria is alive, she has to be, the red rag might have been a trick, after all, just a cloth with which they'd mopped the floor. You've protected her, haven't You? Give us this day our daily bread and keep her safe? Because, in the name of the father and the son and the holy spirit, if I could only fly to her I'd give my life to mend her body, offer myself to her like a needle for the sewing, mend the nest where baby was, no, is, still has to be. But I cannot fly, please go for me. And hallowed be Thy name. He had not prayed so much in years. He was a bad Catholic, too fond of soccer and slow sex on Sundays, but surely God remembered him, the child he'd been, the altar boy with his frock perfectly white, gazing piously at the candles, the bloodsoaked cross, the yeasty body of Christ breaking apart in the hands of priests. He had loved the cold air in the vaulted church, the ceilings he would never ever be tall enough to touch, not even jumping, not even standing on the shoulders of ten men, and the stonecold air tautened his skin and made it tingle with the subtle gust of what must surely be God's breath. And even though, when he grew up, he never bothered to pray, he had still felt God's peculiar presence, in the colours of the dawn after a long night in the bars, the sway of wheat stalks in the country wind, the opening inside him as he opened a good book, the touch and sigh of Gloria, the memory of prayers pouring from his mother's lips, by turns rapid and languid, mumbled in church pews, droned at home with the urgency of swarming bees, *Pater noster qui es in caelis,* at times in Latin, at times in Spanish, at times in the Italian she had gathered in slivers at her own mother's heels, infused with magic power in every language, though who knew whether that power came from God or from the robust whip of his mother's tongue. Everything his mother set her mind to either came to pass or spawned infinite warfare in which she unfurled all her weapons, word and will and fistful of rosary beads brandished alike and he could not would not think about what she might be doing now that he was gone from the normal world; what his absence was now doing to her; he could not bear to reach for his mother and so instead he reached for God, resurrecting the old prayers, *Pater noster qui es in caelis* our father who art in heaven save her, my Gloria, raise her from this place, I'll go to mass each week for the rest of my life, I swear it, show me a sign. And then it came. He was on the machine. The explosions were in his mouth and on his genitals. And then they stopped, the hood raised up, he saw the composed face of a priest.

Confess, my child.

Father.

You must cooperate.

Father, please, tell them to stop, they're going to kill me.

My son, how can they stop when you won't help them?

I have nothing else to tell. I don't know anything.

Confess, my son. Confess.

Please, I have a wife, don't let them kill her.

Death is in the hands of God.

Then tell God not to kill her.

The priest smiled sadly. God knows this is all for the good of the country.

The hood went down, the machine began again and *the Lord is with you* everything seared with light and *o ye of little faith* his skin burst open in gashes of pain and *thy will be done* he screamed and screamed but not to God, God wouldn't hear him, He was gone, He was on the side of the captors and their will was now His will: or else, far worse, the captors had stolen God out of his heaven and torn him slowly apart on their machines, and if it was so, then God was truly lost, God Himself was a *desaparecido*.

She smokes a cigarette. It grows dark. He hears a dog bark, then silence, then a passing car. He hauls his attention back into the room; he is not on that machine; he is deeply relieved to be here instead of there. The more memories come, the more his mind feels cut open, wounded, and the more he looks to this house to hold him, even though this place is not entirely safe – he knows this, he can feel it, this house has its own spectres. But he has a chance here, a chance at – what? At accomplishing what he came for, a purpose he still doesn't know, but whose presence he senses, afloat on the air, vague and as yet unseen. There is a purpose. He needs to be here, in this particular house, with the turtle and the windows and the woman. That much of his knowing he's pieced together, that many shards in place. He sits on his haunches, forward on the floor, like a dog. The rug on the floor is moist as a sponge from all his drippings. Leaning into it is like leaning into underwater mud, or into coral. There is a dangerous voluptuousness to coral, a cradling quality that lulls and surrounds you at the same time. The sofa glowers at him for soiling the rug, look what you've done, you are not welcome, intruder! drencher of rugs! Its pillows flare like a beast about to pounce, he is almost afraid, it is large and could easily crush him, but it has not moved since she walked in and sat on it, pinning it down, reinforcing its function, dominating it without a word. She has showered and her hair is different, glistening, heavy with wetness. It shines in the lamplight, and the lamplight fills his consciousness (it does not lacerate him like the sun, it does not shoot as quickly, these are duller blades of light that cut in slowly), his consciousness is clear and open, and everything is this now, this moment, watching the young woman smoke a cigarette. He can't stop staring at her. He feels the heavy presence of her mind.

What are you thinking about? he asks.

Nothing.

What kind of nothing?

Same as usual.

I want to know more. He is surprised by the force in his own voice. For the first time he hears longing in his voice.

You're talkative all of a sudden.

I'm waking up, he says, and even as he says it the waking unfurls further, there is more room inside him.

———

61

I see.

Little by little.

The turtle crawls in from the kitchen. He goes to her. He rests his shell against her naked ankle.

How is it? Being awake?

It makes my head hurt.

The memories?

No, memories don't hurt. I just see them. What's painful is the sun.

I don't understand.

The turtle yawns his mouth open and closes it, snap. The eyes don't blink. He wants to shake the turtle, without knowing why.

It doesn't matter, he says.

At least you can talk now.

Yes.

Were you gone a long time?

Yes. I think so. More or less.

You were kidnapped?

Yes.

And you died?

Yes.

She lights another cigarette and taps the arm of the sofa with her lighter, as if bored, as if killing time with little questions. Do you remember what happened in between?

Almost.

And it doesn't hurt to remember?

Not like sunlight. Not like thirst.

You want more water?

Please.

She leaves for the kitchen and comes back with a large blue jug.

Thank you, he says.

Take your time.

He takes his time. Water pliant between his jaws, coruscating, brilliant in his throat. Water sturdy and enduring, the liquid flesh of the world. He eats and eats and she is watching, silent in her faint haze of smoke, and when he's done and wiping the last streaks from his chin, she says, What else do you remember?

Why?

I want to know.

Why?

I want to understand.

Understand what?

Why you're here.

The light, the light, small flecks of it are catching in her hair. It hurtles in through the window and lands everywhere, walls, shelves, picture frame, but there is something in the way light mingles with her hair that hurts him. He says, Why wouldn't I be here?

You're dead ...

He nods, waits.

... and we didn't know each other. Didn't you have anyone you loved?

Of course I did.

I'm sorry. I didn't mean it that way.

I had many people. A wife.

Sorry.

They took her.

Her cigarette has burned down, but she's still holding it. They are silent for a while. The turtle has closed his eyes. The woman looks out of the window, at the deep blue sky. Buoyant voices rise from the street. She gets up and goes to the kitchen, and as he waits for her, he returns to the painting. He roams the painted waves, tastes their expansive salt, and takes comfort in the curves that dissolve barriers between sea and ship, path and voyager, object and world. As though brushstrokes could unify reality. She returns with a glass in one hand and a bottle of gold-brown liquor in the other. By the time she sits down, she has emptied one glass. She doesn't look at him, and the distance is vast between them, she has shrunk away from him into some invisible shell and he can't stand it, her distance, the hard line of her jaw, he wants to get close, he would curl against her naked ankle if he didn't think she'd pull away in horror.

He says, Are you happy?

What?

In your life.

I don't know. She finishes her second glass and pours another. You're talked about, you know.

Me?

All of you. The disappeared.

What do people say?

Depends. Mostly, how bad things were.

You weren't born yet?

I was born during.

Ah.

It is not her naked ankle that he wants to press against: it is the Who of her, the inside sound, the secret aural texture of her being. He wants to hear the chorus in the depths of her, where the past and all the unseen futures gather to sing.

Tell me what you were like at fourteen.

She pulls back in shock. Why that age?

Why not that age?

She stares at him in silence. He isn't sure why he picked that number, fourteen. He could have started elsewhere, anywhere. Finally she says, I was studious. Great at Latin. I wanted to be a poet.

What else were you like?

I wore my hair long.

In a ponytail?

Sometimes. She swirled her drink.

The boys must have liked you.

Not the ones I wanted.

What else?

I don't know. I was sad.

Why?

My parents were sad.

Is that why?

No. It was me. I don't know why. I was afraid.

Of what?

Everything.

Did you cry a lot?

Never.

Did you write poems?

Rarely.

Did you have friends?

Yes. No. I lost a friend that year, the year I was fourteen. Then I made new friends.

How did you lose her?

We fought.

Over what?

Why should I tell you?

She is becoming resistant, he can feel a shield rising around her, but his hunger to know will not let him stop. He leans forward, onto his elbows, into the moisture of the rug. What happened after that?

Then I turned fifteen, sixteen.

Were you still sad?

Yes.

Then what?

I started at the university.

How was it?

Why do you want to know?

I do. I just do.

I don't see why.

I want to know all of you. Every instant since you were born.

Now she looks him right in the eyes and the room goes bright, too bright, and something in her stare slices him open, the ease is gone and the disgust is back and there is something else, too, something new that fills him with confusion.

That would take forever.

I have time, he says.

She gets up so quickly that the bottle falls to its side. Liquor spills onto the table. She stares at it, then goes to the stairs and rises out of view. He hears steps down a hall above him.

I don't have time, she shouts, and just before the door slams: I'm not dead.

I hid in my room. I thought the stranger might try to drag himself upstairs and knock on my bedroom door with his damp knuckles, but he didn't come. I reached for a magazine and attempted to distract myself with its pages, to care or at least pretend I cared about the fashion spreads and photos of celebrities with their ostentatious teeth, as if it were a normal night and the silence in the living room were normal also, why wouldn't it be silent when my parents were gone and I was alone? Only I couldn't fool myself, I was not alone, he was downstairs in the living room. I couldn't stand the lack of sound. Silence prickling with the stings of incursion. I'm not crazy, I said to myself, and tried to believe it. Sometimes, when I was very small and cried too much, my father would say *Don't be crazy* and I would quickly become quiet, brush away the tears and try to forget the lost doll or scraped knee or the punishment freshly meted out. There was always that fear of going mad, of falling off the edge of the family. Such a paralysing fear. Girls who fall off the edge of their family have nothing left to stand on in this world. Or so it seemed, and not a fibre of my being dared test the theory. Not even now. That man, that *thing,* his presence downstairs threatened my sanity and my house and the very tenets I'd grown up on and now my thoughts were curling in on themselves, twisting into dangerous shapes; I had to get rid of them. I wished the man would vanish. If only I could make him leave: but how? Pack up your things was a futile thing to say, as there was nothing to pack. I could simply say Get out, and see whether he could devise a way to exit – I pictured him scanning the room, at a loss for where the doors were and how to use them; trying to heave his body forward and failing; dragging himself to the sidewalk with slouching steps, neighbours staring at him through their curtains. Maybe he wouldn't go of his own volition. Maybe he would hover in the living room, refusing with one of those ghostly stares of his and then I'd have to grab him by the arm and drag him out, all the way out, more neighbours at more curtains that would blatantly pull open to watch me haul a soggy naked man to the curb. And then there he would be, out on the street, wet, abandoned, naked, trying to find his way through the suburbs, the train station, the cafés, the ruthless cars. I saw him razed by a fast taxi, or fallen in an elegant front yard (he seemed so weak, he could collapse, I'd never even seen him walk), or arrested for his inexplicable demeanor. Worst of all, I saw him staying at the front door of this house, ringing, knocking, ringing, waiting for me to open, filling the threshold and driveway and street with the smell of rotting fish, and me inside, trapped in my own home. Trapped, I thought, I'm trapped already. I wanted to scream.

Perla, I thought, if you stay here like this much longer you're going to come unglued, and in fact you're already on your way.

So I changed my clothes and came out of my bedroom, went down the stairs, and grabbed my purse without looking at the strange wet man who looked up as if snapping from a dream and said, 'Where are you going?'

I slammed the door behind me as an answer.

I didn't know where I was going. It didn't matter, it couldn't matter. I headed toward the city. I emerged from the train a little past midnight and the streets were swollen with people. I was out in the world again, out in Buenos Aires, where everyone lives above water and where restaurants are full of little candles and clinking knives, where people stroll or sit without ever leaning forward on damp haunches, where look look people were smiling as if the past were just a flattened thing beneath their feet, easily sidestepped, or at least possible to ignore long enough to go out for a drink. True, not everyone was smiling, but that's the street, that's the city. Ever since I was a child, walking through Buenos Aires in my thick winter coat with Mamá's hand firmly on mine, I had heard a strange voice in the city. It was subtle and unpredictable, as thin as a fairy's wing, and all it would say was *psshhh, psshhh, you* – and then I would turn and look around the sidewalk, across the street, but no one would have opened their mouth or tried to meet my eye. The strangers around me would look bored or busy or distracted, gazes averted, and I would wonder whether my father was right, whether I was, in fact, a little crazy – or whether I was hearing the voice of the city itself, a disembodied sound that sprang from the mesh of all other sounds, from the cars and constant footsteps, the private lives through open windows, the creak of ornate doors, the glad moan of sunlight, the hum of humidity, the twisted whispers of crumbling walls, all combining into something neither human nor inhuman, neither real nor imagined. My mother would keep leading me as though nothing had happened, maintaining a brisk pace, focused on our destination rather than our surroundings. And I would wonder what would happen if I broke from Mamá's hand and followed the voice, pursued it around the corner and down the block, into alleys and out of them and around more turns until I knew I was alone in the great maze of the city, sublimely lost, wandering on cobbles and asphalt toward something for which I had no words. I never did it, I was always too afraid, Mamá's gloved hand a steady anchor – but still I wondered. Could a voice like that lead me to a place where I'd belong? Even now, as a grown woman, part of me listened for the fluid voice of the city. I did not hear it. I walked. The streets smelled of bread and gasoline, gutters and coffee, stone and age and sadness. The summer air was humid and it didn't look like rain.

I walked into a bar, a regular spot, and scanned the tables from the doorway. My friends weren't there. A couple of men near the back looked up and tried to meet my eye. I didn't look at them and didn't sit down. I knew the bartender, who grinned at me and raised his hand in greeting – Perla, he said, smiling – but I turned and left and walked on. I would have liked to see my friends, but it was probably for the best that I failed to find them; I was always the confidante, the mature one, the shoulder to lean on when drunk or in pain, and my friends had grown so accustomed to my composure that any other face became invisible. You can lean on Perla. Talk to Perla, she'll understand. I looked generous to people, with so much room for tending to their problems, but people rarely saw the power it gave me, the shield from scrutiny, Perla Who Has the Answers, Perla Who Can Help You, Perla Without Problems of Her Own. How I liked to see myself through the eyes of a grateful friend. How strong I seemed, floating above the earth with all its human tangles. Not at all like a girl who feels out of place in her own home. And they appreciated me, called me kind for it, Leticia with her constant love troubles, Marisol with her hard-drinking mother, Anita with the faltering grades and the childhood rapes that continued to haunt her dreams. They needed me, and I needed to feel needed – a perfect symbiotic fit. These were the friendships I had chosen, the ties I'd formed, with girls who wanted to be listened to, grateful for a friend who demanded no attention in return. But tonight I would not be able to sustain the act; the façade would surely break and burden my relationships with more weight than they had been designed to bear. I was lost tonight, the cage lay broken, even my mother's rules lay shattered on the ground, *always neaten your clothes before you leave the house, always think before you speak, always make sure your hair is in place,* so thoroughly drilled into me, so familiar and now so savagely abandoned, my mouth was capable of anything, my hair was surely a disaster. I could roam the city, just as I was. I had never wandered the city much as a girl; our family forays were always focused, purposeful, and in any case my parents mostly kept me in our neighbourhood. They were protective. They enfolded me in great protective wings. They did everything for me, they said so, and it was true. Perla, we do everything for you. There was so much shouting in my mind, about my father, about my mother, doubts and questions I had spent these recent days struggling against with all my desperate strength. And now, with the ghost's arrival, I could not escape the questions, and yet I still couldn't bear to put them into words, even in silence, even inside. I was walking and walking the lambent streets and had nowhere to go. I could have swallowed all the buildings in this city, could have swallowed anything, the sky, a corpse, a lie, a truth, the sea. I was starved for something that had no name. Buenos Aires was so beautiful, full of noise, full of night. I couldn't go home yet. I needed to hear the voice of another human being, someone who didn't smell of river or of death and who could hear the whole of me no matter what I said. Of such people there was only one. I hesitated for a moment, imagining him hanging up on me, but then I stopped at a public telephone and dialled. He answered after two rings.

'It's me,' I said.

Gabriel was silent. For a moment I thought we'd lost the connection.

'Are you there?'

'I'm here.'

'I just wanted to hear your voice.' Now that I'd said the words, they sounded stupid. And naked. Why had I picked up the phone?

Gabriel said nothing.

'Am I disturbing you?'

'No. No.' He sounded uncertain. 'I'm just surprised.'

'I know. I mean, I can imagine. Look, if this is a bad time – '

'It's not. It's really not.'

'Okay,' I said.

There was a pause. 'I was starting to think you'd never call.'

'You didn't want me to?'

'That's not what I said.'

'Okay,' I said again, like an idiot.

'Are you all right?'

'I'm fine.'

'You sound strange.'

'I am strange.'

I said it without thinking, and he laughed, hesitantly, but enough to ease the tension. 'Tell me about it.'

I smiled into the phone receiver.

'Why did you call?'

I didn't answer. The words sounded harsh. Until ten days ago, I'd never needed a reason to call him. I would simply turn to him, for company, comfort, or pleasure; to hear how he was, to be with him. But now there was a wall between us that had to be taken down. If it even could be taken down, because, having heard his voice, it seemed possible that it was now too late. And of course I should have known, should have shielded myself and gathered my tools, but instead, in my disoriented state, I'd reached for the phone out of longing, impulsive, unprepared.

After a long silence, he said, 'You're so quiet.'

'So are you.'

'But you're the one who called me.'

'I know, I know.'

'And so? Why did you call?'

Because a phantom of the disappeared is in my living room, and he won't go away, and the things he's tearing open only you would understand. 'It's complicated.'

'What isn't?'

'Nothing. You're right. Everything is complicated.'

'But still,' he said, exasperated, 'some things are simple, Perla. It's simple to say, *because I miss you.* Or to say, *I'm sorry.*'

The hurt and anger in his voice were palpable. What a huge mistake, I thought, to make this call. 'You know – ' I said, then stopped.

'"You know" what?'

'Never mind.'

'Perla?'

'It doesn't matter.'

'How can you say that?'

'That's not what I mean. I didn't mean us. *We* do matter.'

'Is there still a *we*?'

How easily he could cut me, even when that wasn't his intention. 'You think there isn't?'

'I don't know what to think. If there were a *we,* you would have called.'

'You didn't call either.'

'But you,' he said, 'are the one who ran away.'

I could have said *because you made me,* but we would only have descended further into a hole that seemed to have no bottom and for which I had no words, no verbal tethers that could pull us back to the surface. 'Listen, Gabo, this isn't a good time. I'm at a pay phone.' I closed my eyes. My forehead ached. 'And for other reasons too.'

'Such as?'

'I can't tell you.'

His voice softened. 'Are you really sure you're all right?'

'Yes. No. I will be. I have some things to deal with, and then I'll call again.'

'And how long will that take?'

'I have no idea.'

'But you won't tell me what's going on.'

'No. That's not possible.' There was no language for it, after all, no place to begin. 'But please don't give up on me.'

He was silent.

'Gabriel?'

'I don't know what to say to that.'

'Just say, "Of course I won't give up on you."'

'Perlita. Listen to yourself.'

'I'd rather not.'

He laughed. I wanted to live inside the gauzy folds of his laugh. They could lilt up on the wind and I would float there, suspended, surrounded, at home.

Before his laughter could abate and deposit us back on hard earth, I quickly hung up the phone.

I took the subway to Puerto Madero and walked along the promenade, flanked by glossy restaurants and clubs to my right, and the water to my left. Through the doorways came the scent of freshly grilled *churrascos,* the thrum of techno music, bursts of people dressed for the night. It always amazed me that the old, abandoned docks of Buenos Aires had been changed into such a fashionable destination for tourists and well-heeled locals, with its long brick warehouses refurbished to hold upscale businesses and lofts. You never know what a city can become. I was the only person by myself, and I felt out of place, unkempt, though in fact I probably blended in just fine, judging from the way I was ignored. There was no reason for someone looking at me to suspect that anything was wrong, any oddness at home, any drenched interlopers to contend with, any nightmares rearing up and demanding to be seen, and this was good; this was how it worked, wasn't it? You don't walk in the truth, you walk in the reality you want to inhabit, you walk in the reality you can stand. This is how realities are made.

The sky spread above me, black and cloudless, robbed by the city of its stars. I was separated from the water by a metal rail, which a couple leaned against to kiss, while an older, well-groomed couple glanced at them with a mix of amusement and envy. Behind the rail, the water glimmered darkly, holding the bellies of yachts and a weak reflection of the Hilton Hotel on the other side. Just a ribbon of water, really, though I knew it came from the river, which, I suddenly realised, was why I'd come here: to see some piece of the Río de la Plata, which was not a river really but an estuary, a big wide-open mouth that swallowed the sea, gulped it in toward the land. Such wide water that the other side, the shore of Uruguay, was too far to see. The river made a long seam with the horizon, stitching the world closed in a great sphere of water and sky, a vast ethereal cloth hemmed around Argentina. As a child, I had imagined that the city did not end at the shore but rather continued underwater, down in the depths, in the great low cradle between two countries. I would stare at the water and picture streets, castles, and houses flooded with brackish water, fish lacing through windows, waving coral, the high distorted songs of mermaids, sailors drowned in long-forgotten vortices of time. I tried to imagine the secret laws of such a place. I imagined hieroglyphs that painted shimmering tales in the water and vanished with the shifting of the tide.

It had been so easy, as a little girl, to believe in such a city.

As a grown woman, of course, I knew better than to believe in an underwater world, except that now, on this night, with no compass to tell me who I was, I had no idea what I could believe. And so I had wanted to come here, to the old port, that was now the ultramodern port, to lay eyes on a strip of water.

Its surface shone with electric light, and revealed nothing.

I slowed to light a cigarette and leaned against the rail to smoke it. Dark, quiet water licked the bodies of the yachts. Nearby, a group of young women shrieked with laughter and spoke to each other in a rapid foreign tongue. I thought of Gabriel, his delectable laugh, and how he must have felt when I cut off the call without giving him a chance to say good-bye. He must have said *Hello? hello?* into the receiver, dismayed, affronted, then stared at it and perhaps decided in that moment that he was tired of this, tired of me, ready to find a woman who was less of a headache and fit better into his life. Sadness engulfed me at the thought.

I looked out over the water in search of reprieve. Light from electric streetlamps fell and broke against it, glimmering shrapnel, caught in the ripped cloth of the river.

That night in Uruguay, when I last saw Gabriel, sand had filled the gaps between my toes, wet and dark. I couldn't see it but after he spoke I looked down anyway, at the dark water tearing open at my ankles, thinking, there are grains of sand down there, millions of them, burying my toes, burying themselves, as if they knew that some things can never be exposed. As if hiding were a matter of survival.

I walked on. I reached the construction zone for the Women's Bridge, which was well under way. A sleek white walkway with a great fin rising at an angle, spearing the heavens, or so it seemed through the scaffolding. A bridge like nothing you've ever seen, one columnist had said. I stopped at its edge and stared at the bridge, thinking of things that were like nothing I had ever seen. I stood for a long time. Water beckoned from below. I gazed down and imagined myself plunging, swimming, in search of unthinkable places that could not and yet seemed to exist.

5

Failed Geraniums

I have to tell you more about Gabriel, and about who I was when I met him. I can't fully paint my world without those strokes – and I need you to take in the whole picture, which is made of words instead of colours because it's the best way I know to give you this story, here, tonight, six years after the stranger came, sitting at this window, torn by pain and ecstasy in alternating waves. As though the world itself were surging through my body and my body had to stretch to give it space. That's how it feels. But I can't stop. There is no place to stop this story, which, in being voiced, has taken on a life of its own, as stories inevitably do. Now I myself am whirling in its orbit, suspended in it, unable to do anything but ride. It's the only way I can think to do the telling: careening around the centre, circling and circling, in a spiraling path, whirling gradually closer to the source. Though you may not understand, though it may sound strange, this is the best way in. Linear routes seem faster, but they lack dimensions, they lack flesh, they are dead – and this is not a dead story, it's a living story, it breathes and palpitates. Keep following me. This is the best way I know to show you who I really am – and it's urgent for me to do so, here, now, while there is time.

From the start, it was dangerous to pursue Gabriel, like walking calmly into a burning house. I knew this, of course, and some part of me sought him out for just that reason: to be scorched, to catch fire, to search for myself in the flames of danger.

I met him at a party in his honour, invited by a friend of a friend. He was celebrating his new job as assistant editor at *Voz,* an amazing feat, my friend explained, for a twenty-five-year-old man. Her eyes lit with admiration as she told me about it. I had never read *Voz,* but I knew what my father thought of it: that pack of lies, not good enough to wipe my ass with. He said that but he feared it. He only bothered, after all, to insult the things he feared. And there were few things that he feared more than reporters. Which, naturally, made me extremely curious to meet Gabriel.

I was eighteen years old, in my first year at the university, studying the axis of repression, the dance of consciousness, the hidden havoc of the id. I dreamed of becoming the sort of psychologist who could reach into people's minds, touch the unspeakable, and guide them to it and beyond it, for don't we need to pass through the unspeakable to be truly free?

Even if it meant facing, for example, what lay within my father. The ugliness there.

But not only that, my father was not only that. He was also the man who, long ago, prowled to the kitchen at 3 a.m. only to find his daughter barefoot on the tile floor, a small insomniac in a pink flowered nightgown. *You can't sleep, can you, Perla, you are your father's daughter,* he would say, smiling, and search the cupboards for chocolate we would break into little jagged squares, our midnight prize for being the wild ones, the two who could not wrestle themselves down to sleep, just because the lights went out, just because the clock said it was time. We were not like Mamá, the Queen of Sleep, who could lie down when the extended ritual of cotton balls and makeup removal was complete, and doze as soon as she closed her eyes, and who could not understand why her husband and daughter tossed and turned, rose and roamed the night. Only we shared this fate, Papá and Perla, and when we were together in the kitchen in the hours before dawn, what could have been a defect came to seem like a boon, a source of stolen pleasure and shared pride.

On those nights the chocolate was sultry-sweet on my tongue. My father would look relieved and glad as if my presence had eased whatever plagued him. He would stroke my hair and look at me as though we shared a profound understanding, beyond language, beyond time, and he'd say something like *God was good to send you to me,* or just *Eat, eat.* And I felt happy, so happy with the chocolate and his touch.

But then came the revelations of his profession. So much in one man, I could not grasp it. I could not comprehend how it all resided in one skin, and yet this seemed essential to grasping who I was. I longed to understand him, not to exonerate him, but to extricate myself, and perhaps to save him, or at least to be able to see clearly and without fear. Surely somewhere in the annals of psychoanalysis lay the secret to seeing without fear. He became my phantom patient, on whose analysis I depended for survival.

And so, at the university, I dug through the theories and case studies the professors presented to us as maps to the subconscious, in search of the workings of my father's mind. I exhausted my textbooks, and not only my textbooks but the other tomes assigned to more advanced classes that did not yet belong to me – curled up on the floor of the university book-shop for hours, or forsaking homework to linger in the library stacks – but nowhere could I find a profile that described a person like my father, a person who had done the kinds of things that he had done. Freud had never analyzed a man like him, or if he had, his pen had refused to tell of it. (What a time Freud would have had with Héctor Correa! He would either have run away or salivated at the thought of sessions.) There were references to men like him in sociological texts, but only with the word *evil* attached, a word that, for all its moral strength, flattened the picture of a man rather than plumbing the depths of his consciousness. I read and read but still could not unravel the thick dark knots that I encountered; they were too tangled, I got lost over and over in the mire of my own mind. I was searching for answers to questions I had not fully dared to form. I had never lain on an analyst's couch – my parents would not have permitted such a thing, and I did not have money of my own to do so without being discovered – and in any case, though our professors considered it essential to our development, I didn't want to. The notion terrified me. When I imagined it, I saw myself talking and talking on the couch, only to meet with silence and turn to see my analyst staring at me with Romina's face, that night in the study, the horror and urge to run. I would not take that risk. Better that I pursue the slippery things I was pursuing by myself, surrepti-tiously, ravenously, each theory and case study a nest of clues. Books were already a familiar refuge, after all, and they still took me in without the slightest judgment. They don't close to you the way a person can. You might feel as though you don't belong anywhere, least of all in your own home, you might feel bound to a person whose actions you abhor yet unable to divorce yourself, struggling to individuate in their shadow – all these feelings you wouldn't dare articulate to another person, no matter how highly trained – but you can bring your whole untempered self to books. You can ask them anything, and though you may need to search for the resonant lines, though the answer may come at a slant, they will always speak to you, they will always let you in. And so I entered and entered. Back then, in my first year of university, I trusted books more than people. If I was lonely, if I wished for something deeper with living breathing human beings, I didn't know it – until the night I met Gabriel.

As I got ready for his party, I thought of *Voz* and brave young journalists and frightened fathers and broken rules and printed sentences that could shake the page that held them. I applied more makeup than usual, heavier eyeliner and shadow. The skirt was short already. I didn't know exactly what I planned to do, or, if I did, I told myself that I didn't know it. Just preparing, I said to myself, for whatever is offered by the night. I looked at myself closely in the mirror and the reflection didn't look like me. Another woman stared out of the mirror, with bright eyes and a generous mouth, red-lipped, round with confidence. Such a daring mouth, to whom did it belong? I wanted to let that mouth loose, an animal off its leash, to see what sounds might tumble from it when it opened. Surprise me, I thought to the woman in the mirror, and she laughed at me with her eyes. There was the thrill of rebellion, that night (he was a fearless journalist! the very kind they'd warned about!) but also something more. What begins as rebellion can quickly become something else, something with flesh of its own.

He had no idea I was eighteen. He was not the kind of man to seek out a girl so young. And he never did seek me out in the first place: I, Perla, a goodgirl and a virgin, was the one to make the advance. I found him in the kitchen, polite, confident, and almost haughty, the sleeves of his black linen shirt rolled to the elbows. He was the kind of man made beautiful by the generous conviction of his gestures. I watched him while pretending not to. The party came to him in steady waves. Three different girls approached him at the counter, asking him questions, smoothing their hair. Finally he glanced over. All I did was look at him, across the room, biding my time, holding him in a gaze that spoke and spoke and did not flinch or cool. As if I'd done such things before, as if I knew exactly how to calibrate the temperature of lust, as if I were some kind of vixen rather than an inexperienced girl exploring her own strength. As if I held the secrets of Eros in my power, instead of Eros having its sharp hold on me. And it did have its hold, it scratched fire across my skin, the terrible sweet wound of it, what had I begun? We stared at each other until another guest approached him and broke the spell. I slunk to the living room; I was not breathing; my own boldness seemed a cause for both triumph and alarm. I found my friends and joined their conversation, steadying my breath. If I was flushed, no one seemed to notice.

Half an hour later, he approached me in the hall. The heat immediately returned.

'Are you having a good time?'

I nodded.

'I don't think I've met you before.'

'Perla.'

'Gabriel.'

'I know.'

He smiled, with a coy shyness. 'Can I get you another drink?'

I looked at his hands. They were slender, surprisingly long, the hands of a woman, the hands of a languorous pianist. I wanted them to bring me things – a drink, a feather, broken glass, shards of unfamiliar songs.

He brought me a beer and stayed beside me. He was easy to talk to. We didn't talk about politics that night: we talked about his sisters, Bob Marley, Nietzsche, my dream of travelling the world.

'Where would you go?' he asked.

'Morocco. Laos. Indonesia.'

He looked surprised. 'Not Europe?'

'No.'

'Why not?'

'It's too close.'

'Not r – '

'I don't mean geographically.'

He looked intrigued. 'Then what do you mean?'

'Buenos Aires, the Paris of South America, and all that. I want to go to a place to which *argentinos* have never thought to compare themselves. Where no one knows a thing about Argentina.'

'People don't know about Argentina in Laos?'

'I don't know. I hope not.'

'I see. And what would you do there?'

'Look. Listen. Smell.' *And lose myself,* I thought, but this part I did not say.

'You could do that in Buenos Aires.'

'I already know Buenos Aires.'

'Are you sure?'

I started to say yes, then couldn't.

'How,' he said, waving toward the balcony door, 'can you ever fully know a city like this one?'

I looked toward the balcony, where a cluster of people

smoked and laughed, while, beyond them, the city's heart beat with electric light, and the great gray wall of an apartment building rose across the street, hoarding the secrets of centuries. In that moment the night's pulse seemed to come roaring in through the windows, the delirious blend of a million human hearts. The city, incorrigible and sprawling and awake. For all its long and freighted history, for all its cracked façades and streaks of sorrow, on this night the city seemed young, renewed by the vigour of its people. I could have leaped from the balcony to the streets and wandered them until the sun came up, only I did not want to leave the party.

'Let's dance,' I said.

It had been a long time since I'd danced with a boy or a man. In high school I'd begun to dance alone at parties and those around me had learned to keep their distance, that's Perla, she's a bit strange, there she goes moving like she's the last person left on the planet, or, from less kind sources, like the bitch thinks music plays only for her. My friends saw me dancing with Gabriel and made faces of mock alarm, *What, you?* I laughed. I moved to the rhythm of my laugh. Gabriel looked at me strangely, *Who is this girl, where is the joke,* and I came closer so his cologne could fill my nose and coat my tongue when I opened my mouth to smile and though I longed to touch him I did not, we danced with our desire, we danced desire into being, we danced to the Rolling Stones, to U2, even to a tango when someone cued up those old songs and then his hand landed on my waist with all the sureness of a bird making a nest for itself; our bodies touched, shouts and laughter filled the room as a young generation revived the old steps their grandparents had taught them. When the song ended, we lingered close for an instant, not wanting to draw apart, and I felt his body listening for what mine wanted to say. I pulled away quickly.

'Are you all right?' he said.

'Let's go outside and get some air.'

We stayed on the balcony for hours. My friends left the party, and, eventually, so did his. At five in the morning only a small cluster remained, drinking beers in the living room, leaving us the balcony as our kingdom. And I did feel like royalty, strangely exalted, poised up on my perch over the city, watching people walk the streets of San Telmo, leaving bars or friends' apartments with their arms around each other. Perched up there I felt for the first time that I could own the city, and it could own me back.

'I love your apartment,' I said. 'It's the best in Buenos Aires.'

He laughed. 'How do you know?'

'I know things,' I said, with mock imperiousness.

'Ah! So do I.'

'Oh really? Like what?'

That's when he kissed me. He tasted of cigarettes and eucalyptus and beer. I had only kissed high school boys before, never a grown man, and everything about his kiss took me by surprise: its skill; its supple confidence; the measured pleasure his tongue took in my mouth, the hints it gave of skills and pleasures yet to come; and my own response to the kiss, the places that opened widely to receive it, not only my lips but my thighs (and this alarmed me, I rushed to close them but his hand was there and so they stayed half-parted, listening to his light touch) and hidden places in my being where I'd long stashed parts of myself that could not be allowed into the light. I'd never guessed a kiss could do that. I should have stopped but I could not, we kissed for a long time and I could have kept on longer. I didn't want it to end. I could have toppled over the rail and continued as we crashed together down the streets of Buenos Aires, limbs entangled, joined at the mouth, tumbling blindly through alleys and boulevards, knocking down kiosks and café tables on our way to the sea.

He took me out to dinner the following week. We sat in a warm Italian restaurant, the kind with dim lights and dark red walls and black-and-white photographs of other eras crowding every corner. I felt far from the suburbs, transported to a Buenos Aires that, though only a train ride away from where I had grown up, still felt somewhat foreign. I had determined that I would not talk about my family yet, and had devised various strategies for avoiding the topic, but as it turned out, it was shockingly easy. Though, I thought as the meal progressed, perhaps I should not be so shocked: he was a man, after all, accustomed to filling the air with his voice and being listened to, all the way from the reading of menus to the last spoonfuls of dessert. With just a few prompting questions from me, he told me about his father, who was from Mar del Plata, and his mother, who was Uruguayan, and how they had met on vacation in Piriápolis, a little town on the Uruguayan coast. His father was in medical school at the time, though he had hidden this fact from the girl he was pursuing to make sure that, if she returned his attentions, it would be for the right reasons, as he did not want to marry a social climber who would try to keep him from his dream of ministering to the poor. When he finally told her, at the end of an idyllic seaside week, he expected her to light up with delight, All this in a man and he'll be a doctor!, but she looked at him without expression for a long time and then said, So you're a medical student.

He nodded.

And a liar.

No, he said quickly, of course not, I don't lie.

And that story, she said, about dropping out of school?

He stopped cold, or so it was always told to Gabriel throughout his childhood, by both tellers; they agreed on the fact that he stopped cold in that moment and had no idea what to say. It was a test, he finally confessed.

She said, And you failed.

He thought of protesting this, pointing out that he had not been the one being tested, but then he gave up and nodded. I'm sorry, he said, I'll never lie to you again.

And therein, they told their son years later, lay the secret to their long and happy marriage.

They moved to Buenos Aires, where Gabriel's father worked for a clinic that served the slums at the edges of the city. When the dictatorship took over, Gabriel was five years old, and his sisters were four and one; fearing for their safety in a political atmosphere where anyone working for the most vulnerable elements of society was in danger of being labelled a subversive, they fled, and since they obviously could not return to Uruguay because of its own dictatorship, they went to Mexico City, where Gabriel grew up in a cluster of exiles from the Southern Cone who carved out homes for themselves in that cacophonous, phenomenal, disorienting city. How he loved it, with its palatial colonial buildings layered uneasily over and beside Aztec ruins that whispered – no, not whispered, he corrected himself: the ruins *sang* – of ancient days and powers we *rioplatenses* down south have long forgotten in our stubborn amnesia over what this land has been, the life it had before Europe crashed in and transformed it with paving stones and spilled blood. Here, he said, we talk about the pretty paving stones but not the blood. We act as though the founding of Buenos Aires were the beginning of time rather than an interruption of what Time had long been doing. We think four hundred and something years is old, but please, that's just a young snotnose of a city when you've experienced México D.F. You should really try these cannelloni, here, have some, they're spectacular. Mm, see? In any case, I loved it there, but my mother couldn't stand the pollution, the whorls of noise, and above all she could never get used to the edge of violence that accompanies you there as constantly as your own shadow. She pined for the tranquillity of Uruguay, where even the capital has the bucolic calm of a village. And so, after the Uruguayan dictatorship ended, we moved to Montevideo. I was fifteen then. My father would have preferred Buenos Aires, but my mother won that fight. No, she said, I can't stand that many Argentineans at once. Despite her intermarriage, she never shook off the Uruguayan belief that Argentineans all too often suffer from excessive arrogance, and, to put it bluntly, are sons of bitches. She would sometimes throw up her hands in the house and say, My husband, my children, they're all *argentinos,* I'm surrounded! So, I finished high school in Montevideo, and by my first year at the university I was writing for newspapers. Small, insignificant pieces at first. Then I started writing about political issues, the imprint left by both dictatorships, and I wrote an article about Uruguayan nationals who'd disappeared in Argentina. You know, I'm sure you've heard about it, they came here seeking refuge from their government, but then the junta took over here and – paf! – Operation Condor, lists of names, and the regimes are doing each other's dirty work. A disgrace. But anyway, after I wrote that piece, I became obsessed with the *desaparecidos* in general, and I felt that I had to come back here, to Buenos Aires, to dive further into those stories. Now I feel like I can't leave, he said, taking a bite of almond torte. I love Montevideo too, my family's there, I visit, but this is home.

'What makes Buenos Aires home?' I said.

'I don't know. The streets. I never get tired of these streets, their noise, their colours, even their sadness. Even the cracks in run-down buildings seem beautiful to me.'

I drank the last drops of wine from my glass. The bottle stood empty. I felt warm, sated.

Gabriel looked as though he'd just woken. 'But wait. We haven't talked about you.'

'We don't have to.'

'This is terrible. I've talked the whole night.'

'I like to listen.'

'You're very good at it.'

'You sound alarmed.'

'Perhaps I am. I don't usually tell my whole life story on a first date like this.'

'No?'

'No.'

I smiled.

'I'm a journalist, for God's sake. I'm supposed to get people talking.'

'And I'm an aspiring psychologist,' I said. 'I'm supposed to do the same.'

'Looks like you won.'

'I liked hearing your stories.' I meant this. I could have listened for hours more.

'Well, you owe me some next time.'

He invited me back to his apartment that night, and I

declined, though I did kiss him long and slow at the subway gate before descending to catch my train. On the next date, at the same trattoria, he was ready with his questions.

'I don't want to talk about my family,' I said.

'Why not?'

I waved my hand, hoping that the gesture seemed both confident and casual. 'Your family doesn't define who you are.'

'It doesn't?'

'No.'

'But it's where you come from. Where you begin.'

'Not where I begin.'

He looked slightly amused. 'Where do you begin, then, Perla?'

Without thinking, I said, 'With Rimbaud.'

He laughed. 'What? The poet?'

'The poet.' I spent the next hour weaving a creation story for myself, miraculously devoid of parents. I described my experience at Romina's bookshelves, opening volume after volume as if opening the gates to textual cities. In those cities, among those words and meanings, I said, the true trajectory of my life began. Everything I said was true, though of course I left out details of my friendship with Romina – her discovery in the study, her uncles, the note I read and reread in the bathroom stall. Instead, I focused on the appetite with which we'd open book after book, picking out delectable lines to roll against the tongue of the mind, the wonder of those hours, the way the words and visions and ideas sparked from those pages and dug into my flesh like splinters of a fire started on the page by a writer long dead. It made me fall in love with the mind, I said. It made me see how everything – ideas, poems, buildings, even wars – ultimately began in the mind. First comes a thought, then words to carry it, and only then does a thing take shape in a concrete way. In the beginning there truly was the Word. Eventually I became a student of the mind, the place where words begin, so that one day I could accompany people's journeys into the dizzying labyrinths within them, and help them navigate, help them change. It felt good to tell the story without the context of my mother this, my father that. My own story, unhampered, as if my parents did not exist. I had never described my life that way to anyone. I felt entranced by my own telling, and wondered how much of it was fiction and how much a new way of looking at the truth.

'So Freud has the keys to the labyrinth?' Gabriel asked.

'Some of them.'

'Do you believe everything he said?'

'Even Freud didn't believe everything he said. He contradicted himself, he made mistakes. But he was the first to unlock certain rooms of the psyche.'

'Such as?'

'Unconscious desires.'

'Mm hm. Unconscious desires.' He looked at me with a subtle smile. He was so confident with his lust, I found it both maddening and impressive. 'Do you have any of those?'

'If I did, I wouldn't know it, would I?'

That night, I did go back to his apartment, and he turned on Coltrane's *A Love Supreme* and poured us wine and we kissed in the middle of the living room, on our feet, swaying, a kiss that started with languor and rapidly intensified as though it had a will of its own. We were on our knees, kissing, we were on the floor, his hands on my breasts and in my hair and everywhere else all at once or so it seemed, and my hands too, we were there a long time, we didn't take our clothes off but we pressed so forcefully it seemed the fabric might burn away from our bodies. Finally, I said, reluctantly, 'I should go.'

'Do you have to?'

'I have to.'

He brushed my hair back, very gently. 'I've never met a girl like you.'

'Oh, shut up.'

'It's true.'

'You're good at this, Gabriel. But I'm still not going to have sex with you.'

He made a face of wounded innocence. 'Sex? Who said anything about sex?'

I laughed.

He pouted. 'I feel so used.'

'Poor thing.'

He grinned. 'I have something for you,' he said, and left the room. He returned with a file folder, and opened it to show me a small stack of clippings. 'If you'd like to borrow them. To read some of my work.'

The article on top was called 'Gentlemen of the Sea: The Role of the Navy in Disappearances.' The room went cold. I did not want to read his work. But I smiled and took the folder from him. 'Of course I do.'

I started reading on the subway ride home. The article was smart and eloquent. Outrage emanated from every sentence, hard as a spear, flung at men who had participated in atrocities and now held immunity under the law when obviously they had no right to roam free in the world *with their daughters* – no, it didn't say that. The train was nearly empty. I leaned back in my seat and closed my eyes. I had been so stupid. I had thought that we could find some kind of common ground, or if not find it, then create it for ourselves, out of nothing, out of sheer desire for each other. As if common ground could exist between our worlds.

The train hummed on. I felt Romina's phantom presence in the empty seat behind me, lit with triumph. *Perla, Perla. Who do you think you are?*

Go away.

He'll never love you.

Go away.

You have to stop.

I know. I know.

I broke off the next date, but Gabriel called and called and the thought of his smell when I last saw him, deep sweat under sharp cologne, decimated my resolve. I finally agreed to visit his apartment on a Sunday afternoon.

'What happened?' he said, as soon as I came in.

I stood uncertainly in the centre of his living room. 'I just wasn't sure.'

'About me?'

'About this.'

'Why?'

I looked around the room as though the answer could be culled from it. Afternoon light poured in from the balcony, gilding the books strewn on the floor, the dirty coffee mugs, debris from a long night of research. 'How old do you think I am?'

'Twenty-two?'

'Eighteen.'

'God. Oh God. Are you joking?'

I just looked at him.

'Why didn't you tell me?'

'You didn't ask.'

'You're too young for me.'

'Don't be so sure.' I didn't know where my words were coming from, there was a woman speaking whom I barely knew, a Perla who could not be trusted to keep to any script.

'What are you saying?'

'That you don't know me.'

He stared at me, and I met him without flinching. 'You're right, Perla. I have no idea who you really are.'

'I didn't mean it as – '

'No, it's a good thing. You're complex. I never feel like you say things just to impress me.'

'Why the hell would I say things just to impress you?'

He laughed. 'You see what I mean?'

'So can I stay?'

'Do you want to?'

I should have left right then, taken the revelation of my age as an exit door, ensured the safety of my world. 'What do you think?'

I stayed, that afternoon. After that, we continued to see each other and I stopped resisting it. Those were delectable times. Our nights were long and full of beer and heat and urges that were probed but not satisfied; we cleaved to each other, we seemed to fit the convoluted curves of each other's inner lives. This surprised me: I'd imagined him to be the kind of man who moved from girl to girl with distracted ease. You don't know me, then, he said. *Oh, come on,* I answered, *you've never been that way? with all those ex-girlfriends?* This made him laugh and run his tongue along my ear, so that when he said *You do something different to me, Perla,* I could barely hear the words through streaks of pleasure.

And on some level, I understood. He was not a man who could be penned in. He succumbed to bouts of writing during which the phone went unanswered, the dishes unwashed, schedules rearranged for the sake of the story, and in those bouts a woman could lose her footing by demanding too much. Other girlfriends in the past had badgered him – What are you writing? Can I read it? Can't I sit beside you while you work? What are you thinking now? – but I had no desire to enter that sphere of his life; I understood the need for private spaces, the need for inner chaos to spin its whorls, because I needed the same thing.

In any case, it was safer this way for both of us. I preferred his journalism stashed outside of our relationship, part of him yet separate, like a shadow. I did not make too many demands on his time. I did not insist that he come home to meet my family. We stayed in the present moment. When you are with me, give me your lithe hands and green eyes and use your wit to make me laugh, don't talk to me about the article you published, the letters that streamed in, I don't care, I only want to speak of what the sun is doing to our skin, what my skin does to yours and what yours does to mine, what our bodies generate and how our minds catapult together to new realms.

Believe it or not, I kept my father's identity from him for a year.

Finally, one day, as we were getting ready to leave his apartment for a party, he told me about a meeting friends of his had organised. They were part of an exciting group called HIJOS, like the Madres de Plaza de Mayo, only by and for children of the disappeared who were now young adults. They were wonderful, they had the coolest tactics, they named perpetrators on the radio and listed not only their crimes against humanity, but their phone numbers and home addresses, and called protests at those addresses, an amazing method, *eserache,* what an innovation. There was going to be a rally next week outside a general's house, why didn't we go together?

I felt hollowed out from the inside. I imagined a crowd of young people, Gabriel among them, shouting on a lawn that, in my mind's eye, happened to resemble my own. 'I'll never go to anything like that with you. Don't ask me again.'

He looked shocked, but his comb kept moving through his hair. There was a party to get to, after all. 'But why?'

I had dodged these subjects before, with elliptical remarks and timely silence. But it had become exhausting. 'Gabo. Listen. My father is in the Navy.'

The comb stopped moving. He held it in midair. He stared at me, and though I'd imagined this moment many times, I still was not prepared for the look on his face. 'Was he in the Navy … when … ?'

I couldn't bring myself to speak, so I just nodded.

He was silent. He stepped away from me, sat down on the bed, and covered his face with his hands. I didn't move. The city blared in through the window, cars and murmurs and the heavy groan of an overloaded bus.

'Perla,' he finally said, 'why didn't you tell me?'

'Why do you think?'

'He must have taken part in it, you know.'

'Don't lecture me.'

'But how can you talk to the man?'

'You don't know him.'

'Do you?'

'You don't know what I know and what I don't know.'

'Fine. No need to shout.'

'I'm not shouting.'

'It was just a question.'

'Are we going to the party or what?'

'Can't we talk about this?'

'What for?'

He opened his mouth as if to say something, then closed it. I hadn't meant to speak with such hardness, and I thought I might see him lose his temper for the first time. But he only sighed. 'Fine, let's go, we'll talk about it later.'

We went to the party and afterward we came back to his apartment and stood in the light of one dim lamp, staring at each other like two jaguars in the jungle, quiet, drunk. He looked at me as though he'd never seen me before, as though I had just broken into his home. I wanted to run but could not tell whether the impulse was to run away or run toward him. I longed to say but did not say so many things, *I am not my father* and *When will I ever be free of this* and *Mea culpa mea culpa mea culpa,* but the words were impossible to my mouth and my eyes did all the speaking, his eyes spoke back and not only spoke but shouted and I thought that he might strike me but instead he kissed me brutally, I crushed against him, I let him strip me down to nothing, and I pressed my nakedness against him with all the ferocity of a demon straining for deliverance. I pulled him to the floor and pulled him into me, brashly, savagely, the first time. We made sounds like people fighting for our lives. Such pain, so round and swift, whirling through my body, carrying specks of pleasure on its back. I did not want it to stop, I wanted it to lash through me forever. Afterward, I heard him weeping softly. He was beside me on the floor, his face half-buried in my hair. I crawled over to the lamp to turn it off and then returned and cradled him in the dark until the tears were gone and he was limp against me, wrung out, open. Then, gently, we began again.

We kept on for three more years. We were pulled to each other again and again, we breathed each other's air, there were nights when it seemed the rest of the world with all its rage and nightmares could fall away and leave us to the savage joy that spilled from us when we made love. On those nights – this may seem mad, but I must tell you, of all people in the world I must tell you, even though you won't understand what I am saying – I could have sworn that the world was being born again in the rocking cauldron of our hips. Lust as cleansing force, not only for us, but for the wounds that haunted us.

But it was not always like that. We also fought like dogs. Gabriel attended HIJOS meetings, he protested outside the homes of accused members of the former regime, he spent hours between midnight and dawn at bars with other people who gladly rode the rapids of political discussion with him. He engaged in similar discussions with his parents, or so he told me. His mother in particular was proud of his work. She was passionate about the subject, so much so that *The Official Story* had become her favourite film. She never tired of watching it. It wasn't particularly original of her, of course, to love that movie, which was a source of pride to all of Argentina (those were her words about it) ever since it won the Oscar for Best Foreign Language Film. And a pride to the world, really, since it wasn't just the first Argentinean film to win the prize, but the first film from any part of Latin America, can you imagine that! And so, she would say (and Gabriel was an expert at impersonating her exaggerated fervour), it has made history. But more important, she'd go on, Norma Aleandro is an abso-lute genius, perfectly cast in the starring role, she makes you feel exactly what it would be like to be in her shoes – that is to say, in her character's shoes – discovering your adopted child was actually stolen from the disappeared. Gabriel found all this amusing, but it made me dread ever accompanying him home. I tried to stay distant from his work, and though in the past this had relieved him, now he found it irritating. He wanted to learn more about my family; I could not stand the notion. I avoided spending time with his friends, who, it seemed to me, might appear any day at my own doorstep. I often imagined the scene, the angry faces, our curtains drawn, Gabriel outside with them unable or unwilling to cross the lawn to see me, or even yelling *Won't you come outside and join us?*

'Understand,' I told him, 'that I hate who they are. Who they've been.'

'Have you told them that?'

I hadn't, I couldn't, I couldn't explain it to him. Not the fear, nor the guilt, nor the love – least of all the love. 'I know you're ashamed of me.'

'Look, I keep asking you to come with me. You're the one who won't meet my friends. I'm not the one who's ashamed.'

'Fine. I'm ashamed. Of course I'm ashamed.'

'Perla.'

'But you don't understand them.'

'If you understood them you wouldn't live with them another instant.'

'Go to hell, Gabo.'

'Why won't you bring me home to meet them?'

'You don't want to do that,' I said quickly.

'What if I do?'

'That's impossible.'

He turned away to heat more water for our *mate.* 'You know

what's impossible? This. We are. We're impossible.'

I never told my parents about him. It may seem strange that I could hide such an important relationship for four years. I'd love to take the credit and say it's all because of my expert sleight of hand, but that's only partly true. At the end of the day, people will believe what they most want to believe. And my father, in particular, preferred to believe that I was too engrossed with my studies to take any boys too seriously.

That didn't mean he didn't ask.

'So,' he said over dinner, 'you're going dancing tonight.'

I shrugged, casually. 'With my girlfriends.'

'But you're not going to be dancing alone.'

'I don't know yet, Papá.'

'A gorgeous girl like you? The men will be all over you.' He waved his fork in a mix of worry and pride. 'Be careful.'

'Ay, Héctor, leave her be. She knows how to take care of herself.' Mamá smiled at me. 'Right, Perla?'

'Right, Mamá.'

'And if there were anyone special … anyone worth mentioning… well, you'd tell us that too, wouldn't you?'

I nodded, somewhat impatiently, as if the answer were too obvious to say aloud.

'Well then, in the meantime, let the girl dance.'

After dinner, though, as we were clearing the dishes and Papá had retired to his study, my mother added, conspiratorially, 'It's too bad it didn't work out with that Rodrigo fellow. Is he going to be there tonight?'

'No,' I said. 'Thank God. I don't ever want to see him again.'

She sighed in commiseration, though I also sensed a pinch of pleasure at being in the know. 'You'll find someone else,' she said. 'Just wait.'

I felt guilty, then, unworthy of her compassion and encouragement. As far as my mother knew, my dating life was riddled with these fitful starts and stops, young men whose names I had to keep careful track of so as not to confuse my stories. They never lasted; they were never worth bringing home. Sometimes, it was nothing more than an interest, a spark with a classmate that I'd drag on for months without it going anywhere. And she'd coach me: have you given him enough clues? Do you think he's shy? I'd answer in two or three words, and she learned quickly not to press me for too much information so as not to break the fragile shell of our confidence. It delighted her that we shared this mother-and-daughter talk, and that she knew things about my life to which my father was not privy. She never told him a word of it. She almost seemed to revel in the notion that there was something Papá and my secret club could not contain – especially something like this, that gave her vicarious access to the dating life of a young woman, something she herself never had, having shut so many doors at a young age. She seemed to imagine my romantic prospects as a limitless horizon to be savoured. After so many years of feeling far from my mother, I would have liked for this new closeness to be genuine, rather than a farce made up of one small lie after another. But I could not tell her about Gabriel without eventually telling her who he was, and bringing him home to meet them. Each day I felt more entrenched in a double life.

But what choice did I have?

Once, lying naked in Gabriel's arms, in the succulent warmth of half-sleep, I succumbed to fantasy and imagined the four of us – my father, my mother, myself and Gabriel – sitting around a table. We looked at each other and talked, and though I couldn't hear what anyone was saying, the scene seemed miraculously calm. Maybe such a thing could happen after all. Maybe the world wouldn't come apart at the seams. These were drunken thoughts, of course, steeped in the liquor of sex and love and hope. But then the vision changed: suddenly the table was strewn with dead geraniums, and the four of us stared at them in horror. I snapped awake. Gabriel had fallen asleep, his arm around me, his chest against my back. I lay in the dark for a long time. Outside, cars moaned through the insomniac city, a song with no solace and no end.

§

The geraniums arrived in droves, during my last year of high school. They invaded our house, shouting red, shouting orange on their way to a synchronised death. Mamá had read about geraniums in a magazine – *versatile, pretty, easy to grow* – and, after that, had seen them featured in the home of a Navy captain's wife. The wife had placed a few cheery painted pots near the windows, that was all. Not enough for Mamá. Her geraniums would be extravagant, unparalleled. She would have a fiefdom of geraniums if she would have any. She became possessed with a vision of a house flooded with flowers, accosting you with their bright colours everywhere you turned, drowning out the chairs and shelves and carpets, more flowers than any other house in Buenos Aires – so that when you enter, she said, you feel as though you're swimming through petals.

The notion ignited her and propelled her into motion. She spent a small fortune on elegant plant stands, imported flowerpots inlaid with mosaic, and armies of fully grown geraniums. She could be like that, my mother, given to sudden sprints of creativity. When she was young, she'd wanted to be an artist

– she had not yet told me the whole story, but I'd seen the single frightening canvas in the attic – and though that desire had long ago been strangled, occasionally its phantom escaped to attack the world, usually in a bout of shopping that yielded designer shoes and skirts and blouses which she combined into tastefully bold outfits for a few weeks until she tired of them.

I had never seen her take an interest in plants before, beyond providing general instructions to the gardener. The geraniums were different: they were not to be delegated to a mere professional. She repotted them herself. The operation took three days. She commandeered the backyard and transformed it into a flower factory, crowded with pots and plants and large bags of fertile soil. She enlisted my help, and we squatted in the backyard together, surrounded by the red and orange flowers (she had, I noticed, overwhelmingly chosen red), arranging roots in their elegant containers.

It was February, the ripe height of summer, and the sun cascaded over us in slow, humid waves. Mamá wore long gardening gloves over her manicured hands, and her fingers pressed soil into place with fastidiousness and even passion. She had bought me gloves too, but I refused to wear them.

'You'll get so dirty, Perla.'

'I want to get dirty.'

'Ay, Perla,' she said, shaking her head. She said no more but beamed with irritation. After all, my refusal disturbed the plan for how the geranium days should go, mother and daughter tending flowers and don't they look picture perfect in their matching gloves? Such interesting gardening gloves, with their violet fleur-de-lis, what a find! For half an hour she would not talk to me, but then she thawed, so engrossed in the execution of her project that she forgot my transgression, or perhaps for fear that I might abandon the project altogether.

She needn't have worried. I didn't want to leave. I had protested this chore, but only mildly; it was a rare chance to spend
time with my mother without the pressure of speaking to one
another. We could crouch side by side, our attention on the
plants, and I could taste the scent of her perfume and feel the
rhythm of her breaths without having to find anything to say.
We often struggled to find things to say to each other, beyond
the essential *good morning* and *here's your breakfast* and *what
time will you be home?* and *good night,* as though we were both
foreigners who'd stumbled into this house from utterly different faraway lands, and had only just learned the rudiments of
each other's languages. At that time, I still wanted to learn my
mother's language (though I would not have told her that), if
only to better understand her, and to increase the chances of
her understanding me. There was so much I longed to tell her
as I squatted beside her with my hands full of dirt, but I also
feared that, if I started, other matters might leap out that were
not meant to be spoken. Better not to risk the opening. Better
not to attempt too much speech with my mother, especially on
such flagrantly hot days on which it was impossible to rest your
eyes on anything but geraniums and geraniums.

They were hardy little plants. The blooms themselves were
bright and simple, relatively unassuming, but when gathered
in such plentiful crowds they seemed to acquire an almost hyp-
notic power. The roots were much darker than the petals, and
more twisted than the stems, a hidden half that exposed itself to
my curious fingers in the journey from pot to pot. Strange, the
body of a plant, with limbs never meant to be exposed to the sun.
Every once in a while, over the course of our three days, Mamá
hummed. The melody meandered, it was nothing I recognised,

but it soothed me. At night, I would close my eyes for sleep and see a great geranium with its root bared in all its gnarled intricacy until my hands arrived full of soil to cover it back up.

When all the flowers were ready in their decorated pots, Mamá spent a fourth day distributing them through the house, moving a wooden stand here and now there, there and now here, now this pot with the shell motif, now the other pot with the Spanish tile, until at last every geranium had moved into the house and she collapsed onto the sofa in exhausted triumph. Flowers lurked at every turn. You could not rest your gaze without encountering a geranium, two geraniums, hundreds of geraniums, and you could not walk without the feeling that geraniums were following you close at heel, bright mobs of them, crowding the air at your back. You could not help feeling vastly outnumbered.

For a week, Mamá was delighted. The geraniums gave order and purpose to her days. She spent hours watering them, tending to them, examining their petals in gently cupped hands, even whispering to them when she thought no one was looking. The flowers may or may not have whispered back, but they stood fresh and still and, in that first week, they thrived.

And then, as Mamá later put it, everything was ruined by Scilingo. He appeared for the first time on March 2, 1995. Every year thereafter, I would remember the date, an unnamed anniversary. It was not a live show, just a photograph and his recorded voice on television. Everyone knew about the broadcast. The ads had been running all week. I didn't watch it with my parents; this was for their private bedroom viewing only, and I knew this without having to ask. I went to my friend Amelia's house to watch. Don't worry, she said, my parents don't know. She didn't add *about your Dad,* but I understood and I was thankful. Amelia's father was an attorney, her mother was a housewife who made her own aprons. Her mother brought soda and cookies on a tray and we all sat down in time for the start of *Hora Clave.*

The famous journalist presented his story. This, he said, is not the first time we learn what happened, but it is the first time we hear directly from one of the men involved. He approached me of his own accord, in the subway, wanting the truth to be known. We met many times. It was extremely difficult for both of us. We recorded these tapes.

I stared at the photograph of Scilingo as the tapes played. He looked older than I remembered him, hair and mustache gray around the edges, eyes tired and plaintive, but it was him, Adolfo Scilingo, the same man who never came to my house without pulling a dulce de leche or apple candy out of his pocket for Perlita linda. That's what he called me: *Here you go, Perlita linda, just for you.* His face earnest, hopeful, as if he'd spent all day worrying about whether I'd like the gift. The candy was always warm from having travelled against his leg, slightly melted into its paper skin, and I always took it eagerly, put it in my mouth and sucked gladly with no thought of where the candy or the leg that warmed it had gone that day. So that, as a girl, whenever I saw Scilingo coming, my mouth would water in anticipation of something sweet.

The voice of the man on the tape spoke of requesting to be sent to ESMA, the Escuela de Mecánica de la Armada, to serve with the saviours of the nation. The voice did not work in the quarters where subversives were detained, but it did once stumble into the zone by accident and see and hear and smell more than intended. One day, a superior told the voice to take subversives on flights, assuring that these acts were sanctioned by the clergy as Christian and humane. He took part in two flights, casting thirty people altogether into the sea. How many others there had been, he couldn't say, but thirty fell from his own hands. The people were drugged and stripped, then thrown out of the airplane, naked and alive. Everyone had participated in such flights, as part of their rotating duties. There were times when the voice paused, broke, lowered, other times when it sailed through details as if reading a shopping list out loud.

Afterward, Amelia's mother stood quickly and turned off the television. A gaping silence filled the room. 'God,' she said. 'Oh God.'

The father rubbed his forehead as though it pained him.

'I can't believe it,' the mother said. 'All those people.'

For an instant the room filled with the watery breaths of thirty ghosts, burdening the air with their damp, ragged exhalations. Then they were gone. I could not feel my legs, my arms, I felt unhinged from them.

'The worst part,' the father said, 'is that we can't throw him in prison. With a confession like that!'

'I know. That men like him should get immunity.'

'That's politics for you.'

'I hope they all die a painful death and rot in hell.' Amelia's mother turned to me. 'Another cookie? Really, don't be shy.'

The late summer light fell on the plate of cookies. They were homemade, and the warm scent of their baking still lingered in the house. My own mother hadn't baked cookies in over a decade. I took another one, not because I wanted it, but to please Amelia's mother, or perhaps to feel like less of an intruder.

The next evening, at home, I sought and failed to find a

rudder in my parents. Why I looked to them for one, why any part of me thought it could depend on them to navigate a clear route through the dark, I cannot say. There was no reason to such a thought. But in any case, that fantasy was soon dispelled. They, too, were lost. Dinner was burned and too salty and no one said a thing about it. We ate our tough *milanesas* in silence. The silence was taut and ominous. I ate slowly, dutifully, though my stomach clenched and I had no appetite. Out of the corners of my vision I glanced at Mamá and Papá and attempted to read the emotions on their faces. They looked like refugees of an unexpected natural disaster: there was shock and fear – was that fear? – and also anger, especially from Mamá.

I looked for shame in their faces but could not find it. I looked for innocence in their faces but could not find it.

Mamá emptied a bottle of wine and opened a second. Her cheeks grew flushed. I had never seen her with such turmoil on her face. My mother, after all, was the consummate expert at keeping her poise, she was none other than Luisa Belén Correa Guzmán, known for a smooth exterior that some interpreted as coldness and others as graceful restraint. I admired this exterior, even tried to emulate it (though it was hard work for me, with so many inner fires to douse and douse), but I also cringed from the moments when the mask would crack and reveal the seep of molten forces mortal girls were not designed to withstand. A kind of heat pulsed from her, across the dinner table, urgent and amorphous. Sitting at the table in the scope of this heat, one could forget that my father was the one trained in the art of war. He seemed to skulk from her; the air grew tense between them; they explained nothing to me. They did not look at me. I pictured our feet under the table, forming an agitated hexagon.

Toward the end of the meal, Mamá tipped the second bottle to her glass, found it empty, and knocked it over. She watched it roll slowly to the edge of the table, fall to the floor, and continue rolling until it hit the wall. No one moved to pick it up. No one acknowledged its trajectory, or even its existence. The next morning, as I left for school, it was still there.

A week later, on March 9, I returned to Amelia's to watch Scilingo's live appearance on *Hora Clave*. This time, her parents had recovered from their initial shock and grown emboldened. They had had a week to let the revelations simmer, and they had plenty to say to the television screen during the show. It was clear that they still did not know who my parents were, and I was grateful to Amelia for this protection, even if she did it less out of loyalty than for reasons of her own. We had never talked directly about my father's profession, only in half phrases that trailed into silence. She seemed not to judge, or at least she seemed to pity me the way one might pity a cripple who cannot help her inability to walk, which stung, of course, but was far better than the alternative. Amelia glanced nervously at me as her parents hurled forthright insults at the television, but none of that mattered. I wasn't there for them or even to hear Scilingo's words, all I wanted was to see him on the screen.

He wore an expensive suit and had every hair in place and, at one point, to the contempt of Amelia's parents, wept. *I believe you,* I thought at him, *I believe your tears,* though I wasn't sure whether I could believe in whatever had impelled the tears, or merely in the fact of their existence. Tears seemed so simple, an obvious answer I had not yet managed. I envied Scilingo his tears. I wondered whether there was candy in the pockets of his slacks, what he would say to me if I could crawl into the television screen to meet him, whether he would take everything back, Perlita linda, it's you, I've been stuck in a strange dream, conjured by a curse, absurd lies have been pouring from my mouth, but no matter, you're here, you know who I really am. And I would curl up on that lap and we would rock, Scilingo and I, my body would shrink to infant size and his arms would be warm and we would rock, back and forth, forgetting planes, forgetting silences, forgetting the words that cut our minds.

'Monsters,' Amelia's mother said after the show. 'Those men are monsters.'

I nodded blankly.

In the week that followed, the tension between my parents deepened and expanded. They fought behind closed doors. I tiptoed to their bedroom door to listen. Sometimes there was nothing; sometimes there were scraps.

'Don't you dare call him.'

'He's not a bad man, Luisa.'

'He's a disaster. Look what happened to his career. He has nothing left but to go crying on TV.'

'He's my friend.'

'He *was* your friend.'

'Just a phone call.'

'A phone call is enough to destroy us. Is that what you want?'

'No, no.'

'Then shut up, Héctor.'

'Don't tell me to shut up – '

It went on, but I went to bed, and as sleep had long since abandoned me I stared out of the window and watched the moon hang in the sky and do nothing. I tried not to think, but the images came, my father on *Hora Clave*, my father on an airplane, my mother kissing my father good-bye on a Monday morning, *have a nice day, call if you're staying late,* my father in a dark room with naked bodies, my own self in a dark room with naked bodies, implicated, struggling for breath, unable to get out. My father in my bedroom, kneeling on the floor, begging for something incomprehensible in flotsam words. He was not there, his shadow not hulking in the dark beside my bed, but still I turned away to face the wall.

April came. I strove to maintain order at the surface of my life. I threw myself into the pursuit of excellence in two arenas: my studies, and drinking shots at parties. I was equally ruthless and equally successful in both endeavours. My grades were perfect and I gained a reputation for drinking even the most athletic boys under the table. All I wanted was to burn my throat with grappa while a boy floundered in his effort to keep up, until his eyes registered wonder and *Who is this girl still in control* and *Shit why won't she let me* and then I'd rise from the table with my head on fire and dance, dance, dance alone and not let anyone touch me, dance so hard the beats could almost bruise, dance my way through exorcisms no one else could see.

Another confession hit the television screens, this time a man notorious for his creative cruelty and high voltages, and he was neither well groomed nor repentant. His name was El Turco – or so, at least, he'd been known in the force – and he seemed to revel in the national attention. The immunity laws, after all, gave him a protected sphere in which he could speak of his acts with frank abandon and no fear of being arrested like a common criminal, for he was no common criminal, he was just a man who had carried out his duties to the state with special zeal. His appearance barely seemed to affect my parents, who were already caught in the gales of private skies. They didn't speak to each other, they glared at each other, Mamá seethed through dinner and afterward Papá disappeared into his study with his scotch.

The geraniums died of thirst. They turned brown and brittle and withered in their pots. You could not rest your gaze in the house without seeing the corpses of neglected geraniums unless you looked to the ceiling, steadfastly ignoring the sphere in which people move back and forth to inhabit their every-day lives. Because in that sphere, in the everyday sphere, the bright mobs of flowers had turned to dark mobs of putrefaction that crowded the vision so thickly and filled the nose with such a ripe, sharp odour that they created the illusion of also reaching other senses: your mouth could taste the decay, your skin crawled with the sensation of a hundred crumbled flowers, your ears were privy to the dying cries of potted plants that echoed through the air in fine high voices long after their demise. We were choked and crowded out by the geraniums' deaths. We were stranded, three lone humans in the botanical graveyard our home had become – a graveyard without graves, since no one bothered to clean anything up. The pots remained in place all over the house, offering up their stems like gnarled thin fingers reaching out of dirt. In an act of denial so prodigious it bordered on a marvel, my mother swung from tending the geraniums like children to ignoring them completely, as though she could make them cease to exist by barricading her own mind. She went about her days as if the flowers were invisible to her. She left them to die. My father seemed to notice nothing; his gaze was always reaching toward something just behind the walls. At times, I wondered whether I was insane, hallucinating dead plants that no one else seemed willing or able to see, while my parents lived God knew where, in some other house that occupied the same physical space but adhered to different rules of reality, impossible to penetrate.

After three weeks, I couldn't stand it any longer and I finally began to clear the flowerpots myself, filling garbage bags with broken blooms, stacking empty pots and plant stands along the edge of the patio. I filled thirteen garbage bags with dirt and plant remains. I stood among them on the patio and stared and stared at the bulging black bags and pots still laced with earth. I wanted to haul the bags up the stairs and spill their contents on my parents' bed so that dirt and broken roots seeped into their clean linens. I wanted to smash the flowerpots against the patio and use the shards as knives with which to cut my parents open, and myself as well, peeling back the skin as if the truth of who we were could be so easily laid bare.

There was so much to lay bare, so much hidden. Behind the locked door to the study, in the flowerpots, and in the stiff and bitter smile my mother wore like armour. The Hidden loomed among us, impossible to shrug off or deny. It claimed all three of us as its creatures. It thickened our nights and drained the colour from our days. I could barely stand to be in a room with both my parents. Even the smallest pleasantry seemed to throb with hostile undertones. My mother never said anything disparaging to my father – at least not in front of me – but she looked at him differently now, with an expression of vexed pity, as if he had crumbled in her esteem. She had married a man with a clean uniform and clean hands, a man of righteous actions and sure footing, and now that man was in danger of becoming something else, something unacceptable, neither righteous nor sure.

On some nights, dinnertime would arrive and Mamá would not be home. She neither called nor left a note informing us of her whereabouts. On those nights, I cooked pasta and heated a jar of tomato sauce, which Papá and I would eat at the table without talking. I never found out where my mother spent that time, though I imagined her wandering through her favorite boutiques, perhaps in search of outer manifestations of an inner wilderness, rubbing skirts between her fingers, stroking shoes, never purchasing a thing. One night she arrived home while we were still at the table. My father and I both looked up, forks in midair, at the sound of her key in the door. Her footsteps approached the dining room, stopping at the threshold. I turned to greet her but she didn't look at me; she was staring at the back of my father's head, which had not turned. He had resumed eating as though nothing had happened. Somehow, it seemed that anything I might say would only make the situation more awkward, so I faced my plate again. For a minute, the only sound was my father's fork against his plate.

'Who cooked?' she asked, surprise in her voice. As if she never would have imagined that we'd eat without her.

'I did,' I said.

She sighed. It was a protracted sigh, almost melodic, almost ennobled. I thought she'd walk away then, but she didn't. My appetite was gone, so I rose and took my plate to the kitchen. When I returned, she was still there, staring at my father's back with an indecipherable expression on her face. I wanted to slap her. I wanted to shake him. The scene seemed at once tense and ridiculous. But whatever it actually was, I was not part of it; I left the room and they remained immobile, as though my exit were entirely inconsequential.

I started to wonder whether my parents were headed toward divorce. Part of me wished they were, if divorce could ease this freighted atmosphere. I was seven months away from starting at the university and I tried to imagine what my life would be like when classes began, whether I would still live in this house, and if so with which parent. It would be a new life, more fully mine, or so I dared to hope. Wherever I lived, and whatever became of my parents' marriage, I would have something of my own, a course of study that would take me down paths they could not enter. And what path would I take? The plan, not devised by me, had always been to study medicine. But now I felt no interest in it, even chafed at the thought, as if it were a drab coat tailored for a very different body. I wanted to be excited by my studies; I wanted them to make the world more real to me, or make me more real to the world. The practical approach, which many of my peers took, involved making decisions based on sensible, orderly long-term plans. I could not see so many years ahead with the months in front of me so hazy and uncertain. Later, the professional trappings would come into focus, but when I first decided, I could think only of what studying the mind could open for me, a direct route into everything that dwelled inside me, and around me, unspoken, unspeakable.

I didn't tell my parents about this plan, knowing they would disapprove, and they were too distracted to ask. I tried to imagine living alone with my mother or my father. I could not imagine living without Papá, knowing that he was alone, especially if he lost the house and no longer had his study into which to disappear. All those long nights alone in his study. I wondered how many hours he was spending in there, what thoughts went through his mind, whether he turned on all the lights or kept the room dim, whether he paced back and forth or lay on the floor or sat in his chair with his eyes closed.

One night, I dreamed my father and I were in an airplane

over the sea, and the hatch opened and he turned to me and said *Shall we?* And then he smiled and pointed at a naked man on his hands and knees at the hatch, grabbed his hair and pulled his head back but the man had no face, it was an empty face. The sky whipped in and I could hear the distant sound of bleating donkeys. My father pushed the head back down and pulled it up with a face now, a girl's face, my face, with donkey teeth and donkey ears and my own terrified eyes, and the girl looked up at me as wisps of hair escaped my father's fist and writhed in the wind and she bleated and bleated and said *go on, push,* and Papá said *Perla, hurry up, the pilot has lost his way home.*

I woke in the dark and lay still for an hour, feeling the warm blankets, the pace of my breath, the air that hung still because it was not (was *not*) at the open hatch of a moving plane. I saw myself packing a hasty bag and running away into the night, leaving home and father and future university studies for the life of a vagrant, starved, vulnerable, free of conscience. I saw myself going to school tomorrow and denouncing my father to my class, my friends, reporters, Amelia's parents, *I am so sorry, I was just a baby, please forgive,* tears and rage and a family torn apart. I saw myself going downstairs to look for my father in his study, in search of truth, in search of understanding, in search of the man whose heart was full of things to show his daughter: love for her, suffering, perhaps even remorse.

I could not bear to do any of those things, that night. But the following night I got out of bed, went to the study, and put my ear to the closed door. I heard only silence. I did this every night for four nights, then slunk away and went to bed and tried to sleep. On the fifth night, I knocked.

'Papá?'

Silence. Then steps. To my surprise, the door opened.

I entered the wood-panelled room. It was lit by a single desk lamp, which illuminated a small sphere around it. My father had already sat back down in his chair behind the desk. His jaw was sternly set. I stood in the middle of the room for a while, searching for something to say. Nothing came out. I was not sure what I had come for, whether I aimed to reassure him or confront him or somehow push unspoken burdens off my shoulders, out of my body, into his hands. Whether to magically absolve or to accuse. I settled down on the floor, not too close to him, not facing him, not wanting him to balk at too much proximity. I heard him pour, lift his glass, drink, set it back down. Enough time went by that I thought he'd forgotten my presence. I almost started to drift to sleep, and then he said, as if picking up the thread of an ongoing conversation, 'It was war. It was a just war.'

He was silent for a long time. I didn't move.

'So it brings bad memories. Show me the war that doesn't bring bad memories. Hah? Just try it, you can't, there isn't one. That's war for you. Look, *hija,* even the church said it was just. God's work, they said. Separating wheat from chaff. The subversives, you know, they didn't believe in God.'

He went silent, as if waiting for a response, but I said nothing.

'Want a drink?'

I shook my head.

He poured himself another glass. When he spoke again, he sounded more at ease. He was quite drunk. 'We were the ones restoring order. For years and years this country had no order. You have no idea what a shithole this country was before. It needed to be saved, and people knew it, they even asked for it.

Now they criticise. Well, you know what – fuck them. They talk about the suffering of the prisoners, but what about our suffering? What about our sacrifice? Fucking bastards, the lot of them.'

He leaned back in his chair, away from the low sphere of light, his back approaching the wall of plaques behind him. I stayed very still, just like when I was a little girl and he would come into my bedroom late at night to stroke my hair and turn a bar song into a lullaby, with a voice as gentle and meandering as lazy waves on a warm day, his hand like raw cotton along my scalp, and I always feared that if I moved too much he'd go away and I'd be in the dark without his songs. Somewhere in the far folds of the cosmos, there might be a script that held the right responses to his words, the way a father confessor intimates the next lines in a penitent's dialogue with God. But I had no access to this. I was not a confessor and in any case my father had expressed no penitence. My voice seemed to have vanished from my throat.

'I just did my job,' my father said. 'I carried out orders, like anybody else.'

Then he wept.

At first, I did not recognise the sound, hoarse and stifled as it was. The sobs did not come freely; they pushed under the surface of short, heavy breaths. He sounded like a man with a fresh bullet wound, desperate to keep quiet, battling to contain the pain. I did not look over at him. I did not move. I could not have moved even if I'd wanted to: my legs had frozen in their curl beneath my body and there was no hope of running, not toward him, and not away. I did not cry. I felt as though I'd never be able to cry again, as though my father's and Scilingo's tears had robbed me of my own.

After a long time, the sounds abated. He blew his nose, once, twice. We sat in silence.

'Ay, Perlita,' he finally said. 'Then there's you. It was all worthwhile, because I have you.'

I strained to understand how these words connected to the rest of them. These words like tiny foreign bombs. Looking back, I should have known right then, except that something shut in me and left those words out in the cold.

He rose from his chair, abruptly, and turned off the light. I watched him walk past me, toward the door.

'Go to sleep,' he said, and then he was gone.

I stared into the blackness all around me, thick and dark like the inside of a great mouth, ready to gulp you into oblivion. The floor heaved like a bottom jaw. I sat for a long time, in the swirl of air and dark and whispers that were not to be deciphered, trying not to think too much, unable to stop thinking, my ears ringing with the sound of my father's tears, and also with sounds that were absent from the room, the soft *whooosh* of naked bodies falling and falling and falling. I felt sick. I almost fell asleep there, on the floor, but I feared what I might dream if I stayed. When I finally went to bed, I dreamed, mercifully, of nothing.

The next day, he found me in the backyard. I was standing in front of the flowerpots, restacking them in higher towers, for no good reason.

'Perla,' he said, and was silent until I turned toward him. His face had changed from the night before, closed up, a storefront that's been boarded and abandoned. 'I want to make something clear.'

I waited.

'There are elements in this country that are not to be trusted.

You've got to be careful. Especially now that you'll be at the university soon, exposed to more kinds of people.'

I looked into his eyes and he looked away from me, at the rosebushes at the edge of the patio, the tall stacks of mosaic flowerpots, the plant stands that held nothing but air. He looked exhausted, his skin lined in that manner that seems to etch the story of a life without revealing any secrets.

'You're never to speak to reporters. They're like vermin, they get in where they shouldn't and they're never any good. And in general, be careful of the company you keep.'

'Whom I speak to is my concern.'

'Perla. Everything you do is my concern.'

'It's not. I have my own life.'

'Because I gave it to you.'

I stared at him; he seemed startled at his own words. 'Fuck you,' I said, fully expecting him to shout or slap me for it. I'd never dreamed of saying such a thing to him before.

But he did not shout or slap. Instead, he said, 'Perla, listen. You have to listen. There are things you don't understand.'

He stared at me with an intensity that reached beyond his words, and in his gaze I read a plea that he would not articulate and that I should not accept, a plea that reached back to our conversation from the night before and asked for absolution or amnesia or, at the very least, for continued love. He wanted me to stomach his confessions and stand by him, his faithful daughter, an essential part of a united family that knew how to keep secrets from reporters, from the world, from their own selves. I should not accept the plea, I thought. I should spit in his face on behalf of a nebulous thirty thousand, or at least denounce him with brutal measured words, disentangling my own conscience from his deeds – but I could not. I would pay a price for this. It seemed a terrible crime to allow the threads of our connection to go uncut. I wanted to be a different kind of person, free to condemn the flights and other horrors with pure contempt. What a luxury, pure contempt. How very civil, how very smooth. Like Amelia's mother, and like so many members of my own generation, with whom I felt out of step, unable to join the full-throated recriminations without tearing myself in two. My father needed me. Only I had seen his tender places, heard his tears; if I abandoned him, in any sense of the word, he would surely wander lost and fragile and alone, without anchor, without salvation.

I wanted to run from him, from the crowded patio, from his gaze on me, from my own freighted love. But I did not run. I stood, paralysed, while my father walked away with the last word.

6

The Word Where

This is how it ended: they came in with syringes and he thought it would be lethal but it was just some kind of drug, to keep you calm, they said, while we transport you to a special station in the south. Bliss, relief, to enter the haze drugs gave him, like white gas piped into his mind. Then he was in a truck, an Army truck, the kind with a green canopy over the top, he couldn't see it through his blindfold but he could tell by the fabric he leaned against, the leak of air from outside. He was crushed against the other bodies, also drugged, all of them nameless with nothing but a number to identify them. He tried to recall where they were going: to the south, yes, that was it, they were going to a special station in the south. He tried to hold on to this with his sedated mind, grasping at the word *south* like an anchor, but it kept slipping away into white fog.

When the truck stopped, they were taken to an airplane, dazed cargo that they were, with legs that could not walk or run. They were half-carried, half-dragged, a guard holding his arm, holding him up, guiding his steps. The guard's body was young and lean, muscular, most likely he grew up on the edge of town, so many of the military boys of low rank grew up on the edge of town, meals without meat, not enough bread, not enough school, hard knocks, perhaps he'd been a good boy, was still a good boy now, the arm was strong and could be leaned on, faster, said the guard, come on, let's go.

At the door of the airplane two guards fought over their bodies. There isn't room said the guard right beside him.

Then make room, the other guard said. Pack them in.

What if they don't fit?

Idiot, then come back for the second load.

Strange, he thought, that they would argue in front of prisoners. Perhaps they were confused by their instructions. Perhaps they thought their charges were too drugged to understand. He was dragged into a hold and pushed against other bodies, stacked like odd-shaped boxes.

They flew.

They rose into the air, stuffed into their dark hold. He felt a woman's body crushed beneath him, a man's legs on his chest, felt the lurch and rattle of the machine. The air was scarce and fetid. He wondered where they were really going. The plane rumbled and groaned. It took a long time but there was no time, not anymore, it had stretched and warped so it didn't matter. He felt another needle in his arm, another prick, more drugs. From the flinches of bodies next to him he knew they were injected, too. More time passed. The fog inside him deepened. The hands returned and stripped their clothes off. He thought, The south, I'll never see it, not that I'd have seen anything anyway, but the south is not where we are going. The stripping seemed to take a lot of time. His sores opened as pants legs were removed, he oozed onto their hands. They wiped their palms off on his thighs, brusquely, still so much to do. Eventually his body pressed against other naked bodies, his thigh was in an ass, a hand pushed against his rib cage, no, it was a foot, twisting the skin, as though trying to get some kind of foothold, they were so close, the gas so thick inside his mind, skin is pliable, it melts, skin is made to melt right into skin, you can't escape it, their bodies seemed to blend into one writhing, liquid body. It was hot and hard to breathe. Suddenly the slide of metal, roar of air, and the hatch stood open to the sky. The bodies drew back from the open door as if they were one body. He felt the scuffling of many limbs, some of them his own, a slow and pointless stupor of a scuffle. A body was pulled on, pulled away, and he felt the ripple of its loss through the mass of them, the swirling human cumulus.

A guard-voice: Come on, push.

Another guard-voice made a sound, a sob, the kind of sob that cuts the throat.

You faggot. Fuck.

Another voice, deep with age: Take him to the cockpit.

There was confusion among the naked ones, they were too dazed to scream, some of them were pinned against unconscious bodies, the hatch was open, there were a few groans that rose and disappeared. He heard the guard who'd sobbed move through the groaning mass, away from the opening, away from the bare sky. From the hatch he heard a whimper, a whimper falling away, so far already, lost in the air. More groans now, grunts, whispers, quiet sounds of terror. Slowly there began to be more room. There were less of them and he was not so crushed, they were pulling apart into discrete bodies. Naked bodies were falling from the hatch. He swung an arm and it was caught by a firm hand that pulled him to the edge of whipping air; he didn't resist; he was so flimsy: he was on his knees at the lip of the hold and the push was almost gentle like a blind man being guided through the night and then he tumbled forward into sky.

His hands flew to his face and pushed his blindfold off his eyes. Below him was a sea of clouds, torn, white, criminally beautiful, blinding in their radiance, the moonlit water far below. They fell down, naked humans, puncturing the clouds. He is one of them, a drop of rain, it's raining humans, naked humans, naked drops, below him white, around him wind, the whir and whip of air, his mouth hangs open and he opens his arms too, as if to fly, as if to brace, he thinks he may be pissing on himself, he falls into the spray of his own piss, white, he falls through white, it doesn't break his fall and for an instant he is cloud and there were times when as a boy he'd lean back and stare at clouds and on his wedding day she came to him right down the aisle in her white bridal gown all puffs and lace and how he longed to touch her, he falls now through her skirt, her billowed bridal skirt, vast and white and torn by bodies falling and so soft so very soft it cannot hold him, cannot keep him, he grasps the air for threads but still keeps plunging, hold me, wrap me, where are you *mi amor,* I think I smell you, the musk under your skirts, strong, savoury, opulent, your deep scent; I want to stay inside the skirts but I am falling, down, away, he fell through all his memories of white, the clouds in boyhood, altars at church, paper silent underneath his hand, all those words he'd written, the words he'd never write, none of his words had white to land on anymore and he had nothing to land on also, he was below the clouds now in the black crystal air, his arms still out as if to embrace the sea, wind rushed against him, the water stretched below him long and calm, a thick dark mass now broken by a falling body, then another, naked bodies break the surface and the water twists and spikes and takes them in, ripples circle out around their landing, subtle wrinkles glistening beneath the moon, water slightly wrinkled by human bodies and the wind, he would not wrinkle, would not age, now it was decided, instead he would be swallowed by the sea as he was, young, smooth-skinned, rainbow-skinned, with red and blue and white and green and purple marks across his skin, it would take him and he prayed it wouldn't sting, he could face death if it only wouldn't sting no more stinging, water was close, an instant left and he said, God, where the fuck are you? where's my wife? our baby? though all that left his mouth was the word *where* before the water broke and swallowed him and cracked his bones and filled his mouth and didn't sting at all.

Memories exhaust him. They have wrung him like a rag. He would rather shut them out, at least for a time. He is alone; the girl has not returned; even the turtle has slunk off to the kitchen. The room is dark, lit only by dull blades of light from streetlamps through the window.

There is only one thing he wishes to remember, and that is Gloria's face. It hurts him, the empty oval in his mind, surrounded by dark hair. Other parts of her are vivid and exquisitely illumined – her shoulder blades, the way they jutted that last night in sleep; her ankles, thick and solid, surprisingly so for her slight frame; her shoulders tense and compact that last time he saw her, tied to a chair; her long fingers on his knee in the evening; her fingers the first time she touched him, the night they met, at 2 a.m. in the bookstore when, like an idiot, he asked her for the time, because she was beautiful, to start a conversation, and she said, I don't know, I'm not wearing a watch. She looked amused and glowed as her friends laughed at him, but she also brushed his wrist with her fingers, saying, You're the one with a watch, why don't you tell me? She looked up at him undaunted, waiting, as she would do so many times from that night on, and he longs to see but cannot see her face. It tilts blankly in his memory, a blur of erased flesh. She was small without being fragile, this he knows. She was bony and the bones of her cut into his mind, he wants their cutting, wants to be scarred by her protrusions, to carry their marks on this new skin. Most of all, he wants her face back, wants to recall her nose and eyes and jaw-slope in the fog behind his eyelids. If he can just see her face, he thinks, then perhaps he'll have her back, at least a scrap of her, no matter what's been done to her or what she has become, and then he won't be alone in this dark house.

He gathers all his strength and stares at the wall. He will conjure her face along its surface. The task is slow and arduous, but he is determined. It is coming. He will have this part of her back.

He works for a long time, in absolute silence.

Finally he has done it. Gloria's face is there. The forehead is hazy and there is fog where ears should be but the rest of it has been composed against the bare wall. Gloria's face, ceiling to floor. He could soar up into it, fly right up to the face, and lose himself there, open his head and press his naked mind against her lips, that's what he longs to do but he stays still because he doesn't want to lose the image. And so he concentrates. He stares unmoving at the wall, keeping his mind still, his mind a jar of splinters that must not shake, must not be jostled, every fractured shard of memory in its place. The face glows. The eyes are perfect. He holds the image of her eyes and they are wide and alert, his masterpiece of recall.

Key in the door. He hears it turning. The girl is home.

She enters and shuts the door behind her. She stands there for a moment, looking at him without turning on the light. He feels her gaze on him as he stares, intently, at the wall. He feels his body again, under her gaze – hands damp on the rug, the drip from his chin, bent knees. The light from the streetlamps mixes with the glow from Gloria's face. He stays still, he has to, the life of Gloria's face depends on him. The woman in the doorway walks toward the wall. She's in his peripheral vision now, and Gloria's mouth is large and voluptuous and opens slightly. He lets his gaze dart at the woman who has come.

You're still here, she says, with no trace of surprise.

He looks at her and her mouth is also open, slightly, in a manner that makes his head roar because it is so much like Gloria's – so very much like Gloria's – and then the face on the wall is gone, leaving sudden clarity in its place. The room becomes a vortex of stars that shoot fast circles around him, closer, closer, threatening to cut into his heart. He wants to make a sound that is unbridled, a sonic flood that rises but stays trapped inside his throat.

All he can say is, You.

He stands up for the first time, knees shaking, and reaches out to her.

The woman looks into his eyes and then she runs to the stairs and is gone.

TWO

7

A Map of Her

All night he has stayed up like this, eyes open and fixed on the empty wall. Now the knowledge is indelible, pressed into him, hard knowledge and his mind strains to form a new shape around it. He has recognised the girl.

He is stunned, dazed. Questions swarm him – how can this be? How did he find her? How did she arrive into this place? Should he tell her who he is, and where she comes from?

He longs to tell her. He cannot tell her. She cannot possibly be ready for such knowledge, having grown up in this house – and considering how she ran from him last night.

He wants something he can never have. A map of her. All the inner routes and shores and glaciers. He wants to know her better than he ever knew himself. She has been so many girls – she was a thousand days old once, and then a thousand and one – and the girl she was each day can't live again, can't re-happen, for all that he would scour the world to find them. He pictures all the versions of her he can never know: girl too small to lift up her own head, girl the size to lift up to his shoulders, girl hide-and-seeking in a kitchen cupboard, girl the size of hopscotch and of ribbons in the pigtails and the wind in pigtails and the pigtails in the wind, the shine of sun on pigtails never to happen again, secret girl discovering storms in her body, clenched girl finding reasons to fight, sharp girl with her weapons, growing girl alone, growing girl accompanied for better or for worse. Then woman. Somewhere, somehow, woman, with thousands of girls inside her. You can't go in there. It's in the past. You can't repeat the past even though he longs to, he longs to push at the river of time, force the current to run in the opposite direction, pushing upstream toward the girls that she has been. He could shout, he could explode out of his strange damp skin with his desire to see her childhood, to touch her delicate newborn limbs, to hold her when she was too small to walk, to brush her hair when she was too small for school, to send her off to school, to be there for her first step and first word and the first time she ever spelled out her own name. To recognise her name as something he himself had given, the gift of syllables in his mouth, in hers, in the mouths of the world, *may this name become your home.* Such intimacies, such ordinary joys, the only ones that mattered. He tries to plumb toward them with his mind, tries to seek the past and thrust his way toward it, it was stolen and he rages to have it back, but he cannot find his way, he has no map and time is cruel and does not care about his losses, not the loss of his body or his senses or his eyes or days or life or this, the loss of time with a girl before she became the woman who has stood before him, large and young, as large and young as he was when he disappeared.

How beautiful she is. How very much she carries in her skin. How much of her there is to get to know; he has so much catching up to do, it seems a task that he'll never fully accomplish. But he must try. There is no boundary left for him between knowing the girl and knowing himself. She is the road to his own heart, to what remains of it, to what survived und-rowned. He wants to believe that the link between them has remained, indelible, coded in her blood as it whispered through her body, as it kept her vital and alive, spilling occasionally with the scrape of a knee or the seal of a childish promise *best friends forever, I swear,* she never guessing that her true origins lay ciphered in each drop. She learning how to climb a tree and fall and how to make promises and break them, and he not there to catch her, to believe her, to clean the wounds carefully with both hands. Ten minutes, he thinks, I want the whole of life with her but all I ask is to be transported to her childhood for ten minutes. He knows just how he would spend them: alone together at a riverbank, where he could watch her fingers dive into the dirt, memorise the contours of her face, listen to her words or laugh or silence.

He closes his eyes and strains; it does not happen. He cannot return.

He looks at all his losses – everything the water swallowed – and this is the least bearable. Time that can't be spent with the small girl.

But he should not be ungrateful. Because now he is with her, she is here in this home and he has a chance to get to know her as she is. He cannot let grief subsume him. He must wake up. The little girl is gone but he has precious moments now with the grown woman. He does not know what star or god or crook of fate he has to thank for his collision with her world, for this time they have together, but he rapidly thanks it. Whatever it is he came to do, he must still do it, for himself, for the girl, and for Gloria.

Gloria. She came out of you, she lived, how did it happen? Did you survive as well? Where are you? Whether you lived or died she was taken from you, brought to this house. How you must have keened for her. But Gloria, she's alive, I must tell you that she's utterly alive, and also beautiful, more than I could ever have imagined. A creature with a mouth like yours.

A mouth like yours, God help her.

It is morning, swords of sun in him, he is ravenous.

Because the morning that loomed over me appeared so harsh with light and breadth, and because the guest's terrible *You* from the night before still burned at the centre of my chest, I could not get out of bed for a long time. I thought of many things. I thought of the attic, hidden just above the innocuous ceiling. Once, when I was eight or nine years old, I went upstairs into the attic to look for costumes for a school play in the trunk that always stood against the wall, old and heavy like a pirate's chest. I had seen that trunk up there before but never looked inside, and always pictured it full of pretty silks and pearls and gold medallions. I climbed the ladder to the attic alone for the first time. Dust idled in the single beam of sunlight from the window. The trunk was locked. I pulled at the ornate metal lip but it stayed locked. It was hot and stuffy and I shouldn't be there, I hadn't asked permission, I could get into trouble. My body flushed at the thought of trouble. Behind the trunk loomed the painting, the only one my mother had ever made, when she was seventeen: an enormous garish canvas gathering dust, its furious billows of black paint roiling over crushed mounds of dark purple and maroon. The billows seemed about to seethe from the huge canvas and drown me. I feared the painting, but I also longed to leap into it to search for Mamá, the inner storm of her that almost never broke her smooth exterior but had escaped her brush when she was young, and that still waited in the dark curls of the painting, potent, brooding, formless. The painting stood still and could not be plumbed and revealed no secrets. I thought of that Alice girl, the one who fell down the rabbit hole and tussled with a Queen of Hearts who wanted to cut off her head. How blind Alice must have felt while she was falling in, spinning, exhilarated, lost. And then, when she arrived: sight. Too much sight. Danger. There are worlds you long to enter and worlds you should not touch, and some worlds were both of these at once. Even so I stood in front of the painting for a long, long time. In fact, even now, as a grown woman, I couldn't recall how I left the attic, how I ever broke the painting's spell.

Another time I went to a forbidden place: once, at Gabriel's house, I took down his copy of *Nunca más*. He was in the shower, and I did it before I could stop myself or ask myself why. It was a thick red book, impossible to miss on any shelf. Of course I knew about it – everybody knew about *Nunca más* – but I'd never actually held it in my hands. I traced the cover's worn edge with my fingers. NUNCA MÁS, IT SAID, THE REPORT FROM THE NATIONAL COMMISSION ON THE DISAPPEARED. The commission had been created by the president in 1983, when democracy returned, to find out what had happened to the missing. They gathered thousands of testimonies. This was their summary. When Romina and I were still friends, she referred to it as the Terrible Book, the one everyone had to read but no one could finish. Needless to say, *Nunca más* could not be found in my house.

I opened Gabriel's copy. I read until I heard the water turn off in the bathroom, roughly five minutes, after which I put the book back on the shelf, as if it had never been moved. I closed my eyes. I listened to Gabriel shuffle around behind the closed door, electric toothbrush, comb, cologne. In the pink-dark behind my eyelids I saw hooded bodies naked in a cell, a steel rod, spread legs, toes clenched against a bloody floor, an empty kitchen with the chairs overturned and then my father's hands on our polished dining table and his feet marching into an office and his silhouette at my bedroom door at night, broad and strong and black, blocking out the light from the hall.

Gabriel emerged from the bathroom, and I smelled the sweet peach of his soap and the sting of his cologne as he came up behind me and kissed me on the exposed nape of my neck and, when I leaned into him, his hands reached around to my breasts, easily, greedily, he was not, at that moment, thinking of hoods and rods and planes, though of course he knew all about these planes and rods and hoods, they ricocheted between us all the time and kept us adrift from each other, pushed by the storm, unable to find a common harbour. I meant to stop his caresses so as not to mix the place to which my mind had fallen with his touch, but my body had other plans: it wailed for him; it demanded force, demanded nipples to be twisted until they bled (though he would not go that far) and the fucking to be hard (though he still said and said *my love*) as though only this could exorcise the flesh-and-metal sounds that had erupted from the book. Once climax had swept over us, I clung to him and would not unwrap my limbs and would not tell him why.

He never brought up the incident, for which I was deeply grateful. But on another night, not long after that, he said, 'I wish I could leave you.'

We were in bed, almost naked, and he said it with the tenderness of a love song.

'Then you should.'

He shook his head. 'I can't.'

'Why not?'

'I don't know, but sometimes I hate it.'

'And other times?'

'Other times I don't care. All I want to do is be with you.'

I burrowed close to his chest. It had been a hot day and he smelled of sweat and sun and cigarettes, his smell many times more palpable than his words.

'In any case, I'll wait for you.'

'Wait? For what?' I stiffened defensively but did not rise, did not attempt to look into his face. Gabriel stroked my hair and failed to answer.

I finally sat up. It was already eleven o'clock. I'd have to skip my shower if I was going to make it to class. And what a strange ritual that was, preparing to go out, the way emerging into the world and doing things that can be termed productive involves such small intimate rituals as the plucking of your eyebrows and the soaping of your thighs, the styling of your hair before the mirror, these rituals of looking at yourself without looking at yourself. This morning I was more likely to slip up, and look at my face as more than canvas for makeup and linger too long examining its slopes and features. I didn't want to see my eyes, nor did I want to see the arc of cheekbones or the way my chin came to a surprising whittled point. Where did this all come from, how did it get shaped, this thing I have called mine? My face. Was it really mine? Only gods spring fully formed from foam or godly foreheads. My face had sources and on this day I didn't dare to think about them. When I was growing up people would say You have your father's face. They never said I looked like my mother – my mother with the blue eyes and light brown hair; it was my father's dark weight I resembled, his coarse black Andalusian hair and thick eyebrows on a steep ledge above large and doleful eyes that, according to my uncle Joaquín, drew a lot of ladies in his day. Everything else was hard-set as for a good military man, but the eyes held the weight of a formless lament, a vulnerable layer beyond reach.

And what about the way my father sang? Drunk, in the dark, offkey and full of resonance, turning ballads from the bars into lullabies? For me. He sang for me. With naked emotion, which he rarely if ever exposed to anyone else. As if he loved his daughter so very much that he saved up his vulnerable layers all his life until he finally revealed them to her, and only to her, his light, his prize. As if he always knew that, when his pain became unbearable, the girl would be there, to hear him, to hold him, even to love him, because what human being was not beautiful when seen at such close hand? When seen through the eyes of a daughter? And that even in the face of the worst horrors she would never let him go. Because she was good, because she was his, because there was nowhere else that she could possibly belong.

As I rose and changed my clothes, I couldn't stop thinking about him, Héctor, the man whom I had always called *Papá*, his stern face and gentle hands and scotch-scented breath and the sound of him singing in the dark.

Steps sound on the stairs, and she descends. His skin thrills at her return.

Don't say anything. She holds up her hand. Not a word.

He gazes at her. She hasn't bathed, she's dry and still a little rumpled from sleep.

Hungry?

He nods.

Water?

He nods.

Obviously. She goes to the kitchen. She comes back with the pitcher and a glass. He cats and eats and water drips down his face and seeps inside him. When he's done he starts to thank her but she says, sternly, Not a word.

He leans forward on his arms, into the marshy rug. I was right, he thinks. There is no way I can tell her.

I don't know how you got here, or when you're going to leave. I have no clue what to say to you.

He nods.

Last night I wanted to throw you out. I almost came in here and dragged you to the street.

In the corner of his vision, he sees the turtle crawling away into the kitchen.

But I can't do that. She sinks into a chair. Not today. In fact, if you left today I couldn't take it. You're not going to leave, are you?

He cocks his head.

Now you may talk.

No.

I can go to class? When I get back you'll be here?

I will.

How can you be sure?

I can't be.

Then how can I trust you?

No one is ever sure of anything.

Some people say they are.

They're liars.

She smiles wryly. Maybe so.

She leans back in her chair, into a ray of sun, and glitter briefly fills the chaos of her hair.

8

Nectar and Venom

I meant to go to class. I really did. But in the end I couldn't bring myself to leave the house. I couldn't even bring myself to shower. I cooked Lolo's squash and returned to the living room. Cigarettes for breakfast. I was low on smokes again. How had that happened?

The living room rug was ruined. It had soaked through with the strange waters of my guest, and smelled like a decomposing orchard. I saw myself attempting to explain this to my parents on their return: I'm sorry, your fine Persian is gone, it's just that I had a phantom over, or rather, one of the disappeared who reappeared. Yes, I know, who could have imagined it – but then again, isn't there some logic to the reappearance of what disappears? Isn't that what keys and socks do? If you can't explain how something went away, then why should its return obey the laws of reason? And what is reason anyway, hasn't it been used to exploit the – yes, yes, I'm sorry, let's not fight, we were talking about the rug. Your rug. I'm afraid it's gone. You might say it's disappeared.

That would be the easy version, the one that might conceivably occur if the guest were gone when, four days from now, my parents came home. But what if he was still here?

He showed no signs of leaving. I had no idea how to explain his presence, or, more important, how to keep my father from trying to slaughter the ghost. I could see him now, the look on his face, the kitchen knife or what he could do with his bare, well-trained hands – though surely he would not succeed since ghosts cannot be slaughtered. Who knew what would come of such an attempt? It was a mystery. The whole future was a mystery. I had no plan for what to do on my parents' return. I tried to picture the moment but I could not bring it into focus. Two blurred figures would hover at the edge of the living room, their faces inscrutable. Then a sharp cry from one of them, followed by a garbled stream of words in which I could make out only *Perla* and *our house* and the high rise of a question mark at the end. Then it would be my turn to speak, to answer the question I had not understood, but I could not imagine forming any coherent words, I saw myself opening my mouth to speak and spilling out water the way the ghost had when he first arrived.

These were, of course, ridiculous imaginings. They did nothing to move me closer to a real plan, which I needed, of course, but which I could not bring myself to make. The pragmatic part of my mind had come undone, its order dismantled by droves of thoughts that clamored to be noticed, to be touched, to be seen. I could not touch them all at once. I could not address the future when I had barely begun to address the crowded past. The mind is elastic but not infinite, it can only pull so far at once before it starts to break apart, and Time, it turned out, was not a river at all but an ocean, spreading in all directions, disorderly and vast, swirling with spiralled currents. You never knew where you might drift, or what would become of you along the way.

Such thoughts rushing through my mind. More than enough to drown in.

The rug. I stared at the rug. There was nothing left but to get rid of it, stow it somewhere out of sight. Gently and with great effort, I pulled him over. He didn't resist, but it was still difficult, as he barely had the strength to stand up on his own. The feel of him startled me, it was so ordinary, like any human being just risen from water, from cold water, perhaps on a dark winter's night. I rolled up the rug and stowed its damp remains in the basement, then returned to him.

'There. You're dry now.'

'Am I?'

I looked at him. He was dripping. 'You're drier. You have a dry place.'

I moved him back to the centre of the room and arranged towels around his body, to catch the moisture as it emerged from him. He was curled up on his side, so I gently lined his back with towels, and draped others along his legs and hips, white towels against pale skin. I covered his groin with another towel, a kind of loincloth, even though I was accustomed to his nakedness, and no longer had to consciously avoid his genitals with my eyes. I'm not sure why I covered him. Perhaps I was thinking of the lepers in the Bible, their supplication, the acts of charity and grace. I wanted to minister to him that way, not out of selflessness, but for more complicated reasons. There was something for me in it, a kind of expiation, or perhaps a restoration, but of what exactly, I could not say.

I was still telling myself that any moment I'd leave for school, but as I draped the last towel around his knees I realised that I would not. I could not leave. I'd always been the girl who felt the sky collapse if she arrived in class a few minutes late, but now I thought, To hell with it, the heavens can buckle and fall if they must, the grades can plummet if they must, I don't care, I can't care, I can't leave. Everything that matters is here, in this room, in this strange unfolding story – once upon a time there was a turtle and a woman and a man or not-man and they spent many hours together as if their lives somehow depended on the spending, or on *together*, or on how the hours slowly sank into their skins.

We were quiet together. He stared at the ceiling. I was free to examine his nose, ears, eyes, the way his jawbone jutted an angle at the edge of his face. He'd be handsome if he weren't so blue and soggy. I wished I could see the way he looked before he died. He would have been a young man then, just venturing into adulthood. I imagined that, back then, he had a fresh clean face and a lithe body and that love came to him like an act of grace. The world rolled out before him in all its shine and possibility, entreating him to come and rove and touch it, and he surely would have if he hadn't disappeared.

I couldn't stop looking at him, couldn't stop straining to imagine his features on a living man.

By evening he had soaked through the towels. I replaced them with dry ones, knowing they wouldn't last long.

'Do you want to move to the bathtub?'

He shook his head. This had become his room.

Later, as I brushed my teeth, I thought of the pool. I found it after a long rummage in the basement. It was packed neatly in a cardboard box, labelled with my mother's handwriting. Mamá was the most organised person I'd ever known. She thrived on the maintenance of order, as if assembling boxes and arranging shelves pushed back the dim unpalatable chaos of the world. How did I marry a man who can't even find his keys? she would say, smiling at her husband. Didn't they teach you anything in the Navy? Her husband would smile back, genially: Who needs the Navy when I have you? Those were their good days, the days I would call up in my mind during less hospitable times.

I opened the box and pulled out the deflated red plastic. Holding it, I could smell the fulsome warmth of summer grass, see the red tint of water captured in red walls, and hear light splashes around my body, which was lithe and small and supple once again, the shape-shifting body of a child; now I was a princess, now a dolphin, now a fusion of them both, a royal animal with gemstones draped along my fins. The sun leaped and shimmered in the water. I flapped my feet and the crowds – fish and seahorses and octopuses – shivered in delight. They bowed to me, to Princess Perla, and the salty currents sang my name, Perla, Perlita, swim for us, stir the waters. I laughed. I swam around my tiny sea, utterly alone, pretending I was not alone, never thinking about the breath from my father's lungs that had created the pool and that held its walls in place. Sometimes my father came to squat nearby and watch me play, with a look of baffled tenderness, as if he could still scarcely believe this good fortune, a princess in his midst, or so I imagined his thoughts from the perspective of my subsuming game. And I would think, I will tell the seahorses to carry him a gift (a rock, a whisper, a rare bone), the poor man, so tied to the land, incapable of experiencing our sea. In the context of my game, he was of a different species, a lesser one, unequipped to learn the ways of water. He was foreign to me, and though he didn't know it, the imaginary animals around me did. The seahorses would not want to carry gifts to him; the octopuses shuddered with mistrust; the fish swarmed around me in defense. I had to placate them, sshhhh, don't worry, be kind to him. He's not a bad creature. He just doesn't understand our world.

I returned to the living room and inflated the pool. He lay on his side, limbs limp as always, watching me do it with those eyes that seemed to look right into me, wide, clear, indecipherable. A man with limp arms and weak legs and the most vigorous eyes. I put the pool down in the middle of the floor and helped him into it, propping up his body as he swung one leg in, then the other. We're getting better at this, I thought.

He looked like a child in a plastic crib, limbs curled into its confines. I didn't know what to say to him, but then, he didn't seem to be waiting for me to speak. He seemed immersed in staring at the porcelain swan on the bookshelf. I read on the sofa, a Saramago novel I'd left unfinished months ago, about a city thrown into chaos because everyone sees white, nothing but white. I read until the words began to blend and lose their meaning. I fell asleep with the book open on my chest.

In the morning, the water level had risen; the pool was a third full.

'Good morning. You dripped a lot.'

'I remembered a lot.'

'You drip when you remember?'

He shrugged.

I got a tall cup and a bucket and began to empty his pool, slowly, cupful by cupful. I watched the water pour from cup to bucket, catching the early morning light. It looked silty, slightly opaque, like river water, but otherwise quite normal. 'So are the memories in the water?'

He didn't answer.

'I'd like to know what you remembered.'

He looked doubtful.
'You don't believe me?'
He shrugged again.

He remembers that when he was in the water, the water ate him, ate his body, and as his body decomposed his consciousness was freed into the sea. Consciousness – death showed him this – is a supple wide translucent thing that can gather and disperse, stretch and shrink, be thin or viscous, roil or remain still. Let loose from the body it becomes a free amorphous haze of presence. He was untied, loose, he had no static bulk or density, he simply interpenetrated water. Objects with life or bulk could move through him with ease: currents, silt, the deep-down cold, the dance of starfish, coral fingers, tentacles, fins slicing their world as they passed by, the shake of sun, gentle knives of moonlight, bones down in the sand, things he could not name, and there were no names left, only the plumb and swirl and hover glide pour open close of being.

The sea, the endless breadth of it, long push of unhemmed waves, the sea, the sea, dark and wet and dirty, he was not alone there, the sea was full of presence, including presences like his because his living body did not fall alone, other bodies came undone inside the water, other clouds of consciousness glided too, and it is an illusion to be one and only one, especially once the body breaks apart: then communal truths reveal themselves; he blended with the others and what a searing joy to mix with them, complete the merging their skin had begun during the flight. Now without skin it was so easy, there were memories in the water, the water was marvellously cold, the memories were points of light that shot through them, shot through the schools of fish that pierced them, shot through their water, iridescent flashes of their collective past: someone ran through wheat stalks on naked feet, someone opened naked legs on the kitchen table, someone's wrist blistered under shackles, someone watched sausages blister on a grill, someone writhed tied to a grill, someone lay between two men who writhed in sleep, someone woke up to the wail of a tango from the piano, someone danced on a crowded balcony, someone hid in a bare basement, someone smelled shit, someone smelled fear, someone smelled night-blooming jasmine, someone kissed a woman beside night-blooming jasmine, someone kissed the toes of a child, someone was a child, someone was afraid of the dark, someone prayed in a clean cotton nightgown, someone heard a bedtime story, someone heard a gun, someone wept, someone sang, someone opened empty palms, and there were no more someones, all the memories were shared, everyone remembered or not so much remembered as shared a single consciousness infused with memories; the memories shimmered in the mesh of them; the mesh of them expanded and contracted, together, a heaving underwater lung.

Others came at first. They fell into the water just the same way, in clusters, thrashing against the sea. The vast collective lung inhaled them and helped them decompose, sshhhh, sssshhh, here you go, take off your flesh, take off the pain, open to the water, let your body fall apart, let us absorb the rest of you like oxygen. Water rocks and breathes and in the water there are things that awaken. In the wetness there are things that sink away. And then there is this, the merging of things, the sloshing permeability of consciousness, shot through with bright darts of memory that belong to the currents, the breathing, the seaweed and the silt and the sharks – and so inside this liquid haze all things belong to each other, the seaweed belongs to the light that illuminates its fronds, the breaths belong to the silt itself, the memories belong to sharks that belong inside the drenched collective lung.

And the sun, the sun pulsed through all of it, slow and golden, pouring its heat into the water. Unmeasured years of underwater sun. The mesh of them drifted out to the vast ocean, kissed the roots of hot islands and cold icebergs, but they returned. They reached the shore of their own land again, hovered at the wide river's mouth. The river yawned to welcome them. It unfurled fluid claws. It pulled them in and they rode its rich waters, riding against the currents, into the bay between two countries that burst with human life. The claws of the river drew them, hooked into them, seemed to know them and want them close. And they, for their part, permeated the river with ease and gladness. It was home. They were close enough to the lands of their beloved living ones to almost taste them – their morning musk and piquant sweat and bitter sadness – in the particles of soil that browned the water. The almost-taste of their beloved living ones kept them in the brackish bay. Meanwhile, the two cities on either shore hummed on, unaware of the third city, the liquid city, that hung underwater close by, mocking their solidity, challenging the arrogance of steel and stone, *psshhh we are also here and also real,* breathing in the great wet space between two nations, between saltwater and fresh, sea and river, true life and true death.

He knows his story now, the essential arc of his own genesis. Once he rained into the sea and died. In death he merged with others. And the memories keep welling up, that's why he's here, why he's back – to let the memories froth and rise and splatter out of darkness into sonorous light.

For that, and for her. His return would have no meaning without her.

The water looked as red as the pool that held it. He created his own red sea. When I drew the water out with a cup, it lost its tint and became plain and transparent, with its traces of silt. The guest watched me pour water into the bucket, watched my hand as it dipped back into his pool to take more water. He looked up at me, his gaze unblinking.

I smiled at him.

He smiled, a little, for the first time since he arrived. I waited for him to speak, to tell me about his dreams, to ask me a question, but he said nothing. Now it was he who was reticent, and I who wanted to talk, the silence around us a palpable thing I longed to break into small pieces.

'Are you comfortable?' I asked.

He looked at me as though it were the strangest thing I had said so far.

'I mean, in the pool?'

'It is good, yes. Thank you.'

'If you need anything else …'

'You do too much for me.'

'No.'

'You must have other things to do.'

I shrugged. 'They can wait.'

He leaned forward on his arms, in that pose that reminded me of a dog. A stray dog just starting to ease into the comforts of human housing.

I lit a cigarette, sat down, looked out the window. It was later in the morning than I'd first realised; the sky was strong with light, though covered with a smooth sheet of clouds. I hadn't looked at a clock or brushed my teeth. I didn't want to brush my teeth, wanted the stale taste in my mouth to mix with the morning tobacco, so that my mouth would taste the way I felt, unpresentable, reduced to urge and impulse. 'Are you sure you can't tell me what you remembered?'

'This time, it was about the water.'

'What about it?'

'How we blended in the water, when our bodies were gone.'

'We?'

'Many of us fell at the same time.'

'From where?'

'From the sky.'

'From an airplane.'

'How did you know?'

I kept my gaze over his head, at the bushes in the patio, which were perfectly still, there was no breeze. 'Some stories have been told. Parts of stories.'

'About airplanes.'

'Yes.'

'And how we fell.'

'Yes.'

'Are these things still happening?'

'No. Not here.'

'In other places?'

'Who knows?'

'Do the stories scare you?'

'No. I don't know.' The cigarette was gone, too fast, reduced to a stained filter I crushed in the ashtray and abandoned. The taste lingered bitterly in my mouth. I forced myself to look at him. He was staring at my parents' wedding photograph on the bookshelf. His cheekbone jutted toward them like an arrow.

'Tell me about them.'

The room seemed suddenly deficient of air, a hostile place to breathe. 'What about them?'

'Who are they?'

'My parents.'

He didn't move and didn't soften. 'Yes. But who?'

'Their names?'

'Who.'

I wanted to shake him, shake the edge out of his voice, a new edge I didn't want to understand. 'They met at her cousin's wedding. They're both from Buenos Aires, although her family has land in the north.'

'And?'

'And … he was already an officer. She wanted to be an artist, a painter, but she had given it up by then.'

'Why?'

'Why did she give it up?'

'Yes.'

'I don't know. I think her father forced her.'

'How?'

I tried to tell him the story, the version I had cobbled together from my mother's furtive slips and sharp explosions, and he listened intently with his gaze still on the photograph. This young woman, the woman in question, this Luisa, grew up in a family that had owned cattle ranches for five genera-tions, and in which there were two constants: rules, and money. These two entities were ubiquitous, unquestioned. From what I could gather, the father never raised his voice and never bent his will for anyone, and the mother was an elegant socialite who glittered on her good days and glowered on her bad days until, finally, when Luisa was nine, she left for Rome and never returned. Luisa grew up as a goodgirl, obediently Catholic, obediently quiet, with all her ruffles and smiles in place, though no one knew what churned and curdled under the surface. Then, when she was seventeen, she spent the summer with an uncle in Madrid, and in that summer, the summer of 1969, she found the nub of rebellion within her and made it unfurl. This was the period that fascinated and bewildered me, the brief version of my mother I could not comprehend, and longed to see. This version of my mother parted her hair in the middle, wore long peasant skirts, and in a single month discovered both marijuana and Salvador Dalí. She confessed all of this to me right before I graduated from high school, the only night she ever told the story, the two of us alone on my bed. She curled in close to me. She had had more wine than usual at dinner and I had had two glasses myself. My leg fell asleep beneath me but I did not dare stretch it out to relieve the numbness for fear that, if I did, Mamá might wake from her storytelling trance, interrupt herself, and leave to begin her nightly rituals. I did not want to move and shake the warm, fragile portal that had opened between us and through which my mother's stories now poured. You may as well know, she said, you probably think you're the only one who has had big dreams, that's how it is when we're young, we always think we're the first to taste whatever it is we're tasting. Well, you should have seen me, that summer in Madrid. She propped her elbow against my pillow, her legs tucked under her like a daydreaming girl, as if the intervening years had somehow fallen away in the comfort of this night and she were not a mother on her daughter's bed, but a teenager spilling confessions to a friend. (On that night, I felt delicious hope that we'd stay like this now, mother and daughter, woman-friends, sharing secrets and delights. It seemed attainable. It was probably the wine.) In Madrid, she said, the marijuana had made her too paranoid for her liking, made her feel like a rapidly spinning steering wheel, and so she soon abandoned it. But the Dalí sank into her bones and lit them up: naked women with roses bleeding on their bellies, ants erupting from bare hands, heads peeled open like an orange – savage truths, relentless vision, the human mind turned inside out. She glutted herself on trips to the city's museums, spending hours in front of a single work by Dalí or Picasso or Goya or Velázquez or Bosch. She was most moved by the famous paintings, the ones that drew throngs of tourists to gape and gaze and forget the time and place in which they stood. All that attention, across time, on a canvas painted by a single mortal man. One day, standing in front of *The Garden of Earthly Delights,* watching naked men and women fall in ceaseless anguish through the guts of a beaked monster in hell, she decided to become an artist. She would spend her life creating images on canvas, painting shapes and creatures into being that did not exist anywhere else, that would never have existed if it were not for her hands. When she returned to Buenos Aires, she had two notebooks full of sketches and a print of *The Persistence of Memory,* a painting she'd never seen with her own eyes since the *yanquis* had stolen it away from Spain long before. She bought herself paints, brushes, a palette, and a single enormous canvas. Once she had these items safely in her room, their presence irrefutable, she went to her father and said, I want to be an artist, I want to go to art school.

Perla, she said the night she recounted the tale, *you have no idea how my hands shook as I was speaking.*

Luisa's father laughed, and then, when it was clear that she was serious, spat into a nearby rosebush. He walked away and the subject never arose again. Luisa went to her room and stared at the canvas, the paints, the notebooks full of summer sketches, evidence of the girl she had discovered oceans away from Argentina. She refused to eat for three days, but her father didn't seem to notice. On the fourth day, she locked herself in her room, blended all her oils in chaotic swirls, and created the only painting of her life, an abstract monstrosity of black and brown and maroon rage, piled thick in sweeping strokes that loomed and protruded from the canvas, hideous and heavy as a storm. She burned her notebooks, gave away her brushes and palette, and slept under the shadow of her huge painting because there was nowhere else to put it. She vowed to escape her father's house as soon as possible, and succeeded two years later, when she found a young Navy officer called Héctor who wished to marry her. By that time, the girl who had prowled the Museo del Prado was gone, her only vestige caught inside an awful painting that moved into the attic of their new house.

'He didn't force her,' the guest said.

'What?'

'Your grandfather. All he did was spit.'

'But he forbade her.'

'Did he cut off her hands?'

I was startled by the question. No, I wanted to say, he didn't cut off her hands because he didn't have to, he had cut them off long before, with years of keeping all authority in his own palms, all the rules and all the power and all the answers emanating from him and no one else. And if you don't understand that, if you've never been in such a family, then you can't know the way the mind shackles itself and amputates its own limbs so adeptly that you never think to miss them, never think that you had anything so obscene as choice. But how could I say this to someone who perhaps had seen the cutting, the real cutting, of real hands or toes, and felt shackles of real metal against real skin? How did a rich girl's thwarted desire to paint look through the eyes of a person like that? 'No. He didn't cut off her hands.'

'Then she could paint, she was free.'

'But she didn't know she was free. She couldn't possibly see that. Doesn't that make her chained?'

He shrugged, unconvinced, and a veil seemed to fall over his face to make his expression indecipherable. I felt a need – and this surprised me – to defend my mother, to convince the guest that she had been the victim of a subtle yet brutal psychic force, that she was a complex woman with wounds and flaws and a tenacious will that could be bent toward good things, like the protection and enfolding of a little girl. I said none of this, held it close inside, suspecting that the guest would not want to hear it, or would not receive it in the manner it was meant. I myself was not sure how I meant it, or what I actually believed. My head hurt. He, too, seemed taxed by the conversation: his skin was dripping copiously, as if he'd just risen from a plunge.

'And he?' he asked, eyes on the photograph again, on the man beside the bride. His voice was low and throaty. 'Who is he?'

I should have known the question was coming. 'A confusion.'

'What do you mean?'

'I don't want to talk about him.'

I waited for the guest to recoil from me, as I'd already said before that my father was an officer and surely that is more than enough information for repulsion; I had seen that look before, in Gabriel's face, in Romina for years at school and in so many other faces that I knew exactly how to shield myself, make the surface impenetrable, the face composed, the subject of conversation changed and the stain of wordless crimes buried and hidden. Though no matter what I did, I still felt my inner reaction keenly. Shame was ready at the base of me, would rise to choke me any moment at the slightest flinch of his body or mind. But he did not flinch or falter. He only looked at me with an open face and something in his eyes that I'd be tempted to call tenderness if it weren't so ferocious and if tenderness, in this exchange, weren't so absurd and impossible. Outside, it was raining; I hadn't noticed until now. The window caught the weeping shivers of the sky. We stared at each other and listened to the sound of the rain.

'And you?' he said, very softly.

'Me?'

'Who are you?'

'About that, I don't know anything at all.'

He tilted his head and held my gaze, and I had no way to comprehend it, no theory to encompass or articulate this hunger, this need to be with him, to lose or find myself in his dark, fathomless eyes.

'No,' he said. 'No, no. You do.'

No one, on meeting my mother, Luisa, would imagine she had once been that earnest and ardent young woman, bent on becoming a painter, prowling the museums of Madrid. Even I, growing up in her presence, could not have imagined it. My mother the mystery, my mother the masked woman.

Once, only once, I saw my mother's naked face. It was an accident, a slip, the result of a grave mistake. I was about to turn eight, and it was time for bed, but my heart was full of brightwarm colours because, the following day, Mamá was going to take me to the zoo for my birthday, and I would see the giraffes again with their slim legs and fluid jaws and serene eyes. Everybody thought the necks were what made giraffes special, but no, it was the eyes, I knew this because the last time I had met the gaze of my favorite giraffe our souls had spoken to each other for a long instant before the animal had turned back to her leaves. Eyes so far apart they seemed prepared to catch the whole world in their vision. Eyes that gave me the sense of floating high high above the ground. And now I was going to see them again and, since it was my birthday, perhaps Mamá would let me stay with the giraffes extra long. Ice cream cone first, then the giraffes – that, I realised as I brushed my teeth, was the best way to do it. And once I was finished with brushing my teeth and hair, eager to share my plan, I barrelled to my mother's bedroom door and opened it with so much haste that I forgot the strict rule of knocking first.

Mamá was removing her makeup. This was a solemn, private nightly routine, conducted on a cushioned seat in front of a table and mirror surrounded by eight little bulbs of light. I had glimpsed moments of it in the past, though in general the ritual took place behind closed doors, and bore a shroud of mystic secrecy. A mound of dirty cotton balls lay on the table, between the jewelry boxes and vials of perfume. Mamá was half-finished: one of her eyes wore a perfect mask of black lines and blue shadow, while the other was naked and sunken, bereft of paint, staring wearily at its own reflection.

'Mamá,' I said.

My mother did not move or blink, but the eye grew strangely hard. It continued to look at itself. I waited, wishing suddenly that I could erase my actions, unmake my entry, wait until the morning light to talk about the zoo. After a long moment, Mamá's reflection stared at me without smiling.

'What do you want from me?'

She said this in a voice I had never heard before, the voice someone might use toward a stranger who is not to be trusted. The mirror reflected a single naked eye, cold, aggrieved, and utterly foreign.

'I should have knocked,' I said. 'I'm sorry.'

'Stupid girl. That's not what I'm talking about.'

I hovered. I could not imagine what else my mother might be talking about. I tried to think of what else I'd done wrong that day, aside from the transgression of bursting through this door, but nothing came to mind. It had been an ordinary Friday. I had done all my homework and helped set the table for dinner. It must be something else, I thought, something much larger, a failing that transcends time and defies correction. Defining it seemed like a Herculean task – big and impossible and essential to survival; I could not face it. I felt so small.

I heard her sigh, long and slow. I stayed, frozen, until finally, to my relief, Mamá spoke again. 'You know what?'

'What?' I said.

'I wasn't made to be a mother.' She said this in a tone at once resigned and vaguely ennobled by her own sorrow. 'I often think you shouldn't have come.' The naked eye gazed at the reflection of itself, intently, as if searching for something hidden. All I could think of was the painting in the attic, the thick strokes of black and violet, threatening to leap into the room.

Then she looked at me, through the mirror, and her gaze was so raw I wished I could look away. 'Perla. Let's forget this.'

She spoke very quietly. 'Go to bed and let's pretend this never happened.'

I retreated to my room without a word.

That night, I dreamed of doors and doors and doors.

The next morning, I felt afraid to see my mother, but when I came downstairs for breakfast I found her with her mask whole again, immaculately applied: powder, lipstick, bright smile. She served me toast and milk and glanced at her watch. 'Ready?'

I nodded.

'Well then, let's get going,' she said. Her face was warm and steady, so much so that I briefly wondered whether I'd invented the encounter of the previous night. I might have come to believe this if it had not been for the way her gaze lingered on me, searching for confirmation of a pact that would never be spoken. A pact that encircled me in that moment and that I knew I would not betray. She would wear her mask and I would wear mine and as long as neither of us let them drop, everything would be all right, she needed this from me so I had to help her, and I needed it too, didn't I? It lasted only a few seconds, the lingering gaze, and then she nodded in what seemed like satisfaction. 'Eat your toast, Perlita.'

I had no appetite, but I ate anyway, and even managed a false smile.

At the zoo, I received my ice cream cone and my hour with the giraffes and I licked the cold vanilla slowly and most carefully as I gazed and gazed in silence at the beasts before me, with their famous necks and graceful jaws, but no matter what I did, no matter how long I stood there, no matter how I shouted with my mind, this time I could not make them meet my eyes.

It rains. Small drops torn from the body of a cloud announce their fall in wails and moans. He hears their trajectories through the air outside, gray, blue, violet, streaking the inner lining of time's cloak. They are pure colour, pure substance, pure sound. Only rain is pure in this strange world, collapsing toward the thirsty chaos of the earth.

She is in the kitchen, making lunch. She will bring him more water soon. He is hungry for it, ready to grind it wetly between his teeth, to feel it enter him and give him substance, fortify his presence and veracity with its whisper through his insides, *you belong here, wshhhh, this world is yours as well* – but he won't ask for it, she's coming, he knows she's thinking of it. It is easier every hour to sense the rhythms of her mind. Her mind is a wary forest creature, a deer perhaps, elegant, light-footed, expert at disappearing into dark folds of foliage at the slightest rustle of alarm. Not a simple creature to approach, let alone touch. If he is to touch her mind, he must be patient. He must circle and circle and also be immensely still. Above all, he must not let her see what rises up in him when he thinks of the two in the photograph, the other denizens of this house – the sour flood that makes him want to howl. He will not shake, he will not howl, he does not want to scare her and in any case he needs to bear the truths that have filled this house and taken possession of the girl. Because he hungers for the truth, however poisonous the draught of it. Without the truth he cannot truly know the girl. And you, Gloria, I do this for you: if I should ever find you, if I can hope against all hope that you might come here again, one day, one night, appear as I appeared with seaweed in your hair, or earthworms or bullets or flames – if I should find you in the curved road of the future that surely arches back into the past, and if we are unbroken enough to speak to each other or to meld as I did in the water, I know that you would reach into me for each follicle of knowledge of the girl, and I would give you everything, the nectar with the venom, the stars with the abyss, all the sights and scents and sounds of her that will quiver and break you, all the truth that I could gather, all the truth I could bear to imbibe.

And I would want to know your truths as well, the story of what happened to you after I disappeared. There are still so many questions.

He looks for Gloria's face in the room, but this time cannot find it, cannot re-create it in its entirety against the backdrop of the wall. The room is too alive now, noisy with the breath of shelves, the hum of books, the howl of rain, the constant sound of clouded light careening through the air. And there is the pool he now inhabits, that holds his fluids warm around him; this also sings; his mind is full of the slosh and buzz and glitter of his own little sea that came from him and now sustains him, surrounds him, holds him in its malleable embrace. It pains him – Gloria, the lack of Gloria. He gathers his mind by force and tries to focus. She comes in glimpses. He can see her if he lets go of the need for a coherent whole. Fractured Gloria, scattered shards, bits of Gloria protruding from the objects in the room. Gloria's eye, lashes and all, blinking on the tip of a pencil in a jar. Gloria's hair draped over the back of a chair, a pinewood slatted back that holds the tresses up like hallowed things. Her nose protruding from the spine of a novel. Her neck arched in the minuscule motions of the curtain, lithe and supple, ready for a kiss. Gloria's breath in the slow darkening of the day. Her thigh, without knee or hip to join to, thrown against the sofa in seduction, only there is no body to seduce him toward, no whole woman to laugh or arch or pull the skirt up and say *come.* Her sex appears only at night, in the shadows of the far corners, in many of them at once, the floor the sill the ceiling opening in the darkness to become her, Gloria, Gloria, damp and rich and potent. You are here, Gloria, and I accept each piece of you, I revel, I drink the sight, every single hair and toe a benediction. The eye watches, the neck turns, the hair quivers, the thigh awaits touch. He wants to tell the girl about Gloria's presence, tell her how Gloria's fragments haunt the room, but, as with everything, he battles vainly for the words. And anyway, the girl – though he loves her, though he hungers every moment for proximity – is not like him. She is alive. And the living may not understand; they may not find beauty in a broken woman flung across the house like shrapnel.

I came out of the kitchen with water for him and toast for me and saw him gazing at the painting, Mónica's painting, of ship and sea formed out of the same blue brushstrokes. He was riveted, as though its contents were in motion, unfolding a tale of homecoming or escape. I wondered what had gone through Mónica's mind as she painted, whether she was thinking of escape or homecoming, the urge to forge a home or flee from one. *Remember,* hummed the painting, *turn me in the light,* and the air itself seemed to brandish the shattered partial accounts of my aunt Mónica. Many of them were filtered through the lens of Mamá's disdain. Though surely Mamá's own repressed desires helped explain it: all her longing for the brush and palette compressed into that sharp knife of hate. *Your sister,* she once told Papá, *is the only thing about you I despise. A silly woman trapped in Picasso's blue period, no talent at all, who lived like a whore and shamed her family.* Words that stung Papá enough to make him glare at his wife as though he wanted to hit her, a rare response from him, but Mamá showed no trace of surprise and even seemed to hold her chin up as if to say, I not only stand by what I've said, I glory in it. It must have been unbearable to her, as a new bride, to watch Mónica painting away in direct defiance of her father and God's supposed unwillingness to bless her with the gift, and not only painting but hanging her work in little galleries across town. Free, flagrant, terribly shameless. At that time, Mónica lived in a run-down apartment in San Telmo with a girlfriend, and then, everybody knew it, she got involved with politics – that is to say, with the subversives. It was believed that she became part of ERP, that guerrilla group whose acronym always sounded, to my child-ears, like the imitation of a burp.

Of course, it was also possible that she'd joined a different group, not ERP at all, since in that time there were so many factions and so many strains of leftist underground movements; those subversives, Mamá once said, they plagued Argentina like cockroaches in those days, in the early 1970s, you have no idea how bad things got, the violence, the kidnappings, nobody was safe anymore, let me tell you, some people talk badly now against the military but something had to be done. Of course, she didn't mention the violent right-wing groups, like AAA, whom I learned about much later on my own. Growing up, my sense of the era before the dictatorship was one of utter chaos, of danger around every corner, of young people corrupted by bad people, of wanton violence in the name of revolution. It amazed me that a relative of my father's – his own sister! – could have become one of those people. It seemed impossible, though of course it wasn't. She would not have been the only guerrilla to come from such a family.

In any case, from what I could gather, Mónica did not deny the accusations when they were cast her way, though she did not admit to anything, either. She fled to Spain before the generals took over. Rumour had it that she landed in Madrid – how Mamá must have seethed! That woman, that supposed whore, in her own beloved estranged mecca! Twenty-five years now, and we had heard nothing of Mónica, she could be living in Madrid or any other part of Spain or of the planet, or not living at all. She never wrote, never called, and though Mamá always claimed that the family had spurned her, it had always seemed to me that it was Mónica who had spurned us. Mónica, the Girl Who Got Away, Mónica the aperture, the cautionary tale, the exile, the embarrassment, the wild card. She was rarely mentioned by name in our house. I had met her only through photographs older than myself – a serious young woman with a mournful yet defiant stance, even in her first communion dress – and through the single painting of a blue ship that I sometimes caught my father staring at, searchingly, almost expectantly, as though the ship might at any moment turn its course or cast its anchor down in a long-awaited gesture of arrival.

And there it hung now, the ship, neither reaching its destination nor abandoning the attempt. I stared at it as I gave the guest his water. If Mónica could come into this house right now and see who was here, what would she say? Perhaps she'd gape in amazement at this red pool and its contents, or perhaps she'd just want to turn and leave, *I left all this for a reason, don't drag me in,* or perhaps she'd sit down and open up her stories of where she'd been and who her brother was and who her father was and after she had emptied herself of all those keys and tales she might ask the impossible question that the ghost had asked and that still hung unanswerable in the air, *And you, Perla? Who are you?* And I would still have no tenable answer. There would be no words on my tongue, nothing but air.

The ghost devoured his water. He was so grateful (I could tell from the softening of his eyes) for a simple cup of water. He seemed to feel its secret texture, making it crunch and shape-shift between his working jaws.

His pool was already half full. He looked like he was bathing. I brought over the cup and bucket and began to empty it out. I thought, there is no end to his dripping, he will never be dry, for the rest of my life I will scoop and pour this pungent water that possibly contains the liquid essence of the nightmares my guest endured before he died. Who could have imagined it, such memories distilled in pungent water, what does it taste like? If I drank it would I absorb his memories, and if so how could I stand it? I was hypnotised by the pour of it, the gentle rush into the bucket. How easily water returned to itself and took the shape of anything that held it. It was clear and supple; it revealed nothing.

It should have felt like a burden, the edge of madness, this need to kneel beside his pool and remove the water he'd secreted. But it did not. I was too far gone to care about madness and its edges; it seemed to me that I had crossed them long ago and all I wanted was to stay close to this guest forever and not think too much and let his presence filter through me, through the air, this house so full of hieroglyphs and shadows, this house that had been thirsty for so long. It saturated me, woke up my empty spaces and made them roar. I felt dissolved and expanded, all at once. The regular world seemed far away, a strange realm whose language I was steadily losing the ability to speak. I thought of the city out there, full of people, full of rain: students ducked into class with dripping hair, professors closed the windows and noticed or did not notice my absence, taxis skidded dangerously on wet streets, coffee poured into demitasses in cafés crowded with bodies demanding warmth, umbrellas staved the rain away from small, lurching circles of dry space that people make around themselves, marching, purposefully, or pretending to have clarity of purpose. As if everybody knew where they were going and why. The city was an exhausting place, with all its charade of normalcy, its real and invented purpose. Tomorrow I would have to face it – my provisions were starting to get low – but not today. It was no place for a girl who was steadily coming untied, no place for a mind so unmoored.

The doorbell rang and startled me out of the long gauzy tumult of my thoughts. I wasn't expecting anyone, and there was no one I would open the door to, no one I wanted to see or was willing to let into this world. I decided to ignore it, pretend I wasn't home, let the person go away of his own accord. The bell rang again. The guest cocked his head and looked at me with wide eyes.

I heard a key turn in the front door.

It was Thursday. Carolina came on Thursdays, to clean the house. She always rang first but she had a key. I ran to the foyer. Carolina had begun to crack the door open, and already her face was crunching with confusion at the smell.

'*Hola,* Carolina.'

'Perla, what – '

'I'm sorry, I can't let you in.'

She looked offended. She was my elder. She had been coming into this house for years. 'What?'

'It's not a good time.'

'But I promised your parents – '

'I know, not today. Not until they come back.'

She sniffed the air, as if to corroborate her first reaction. 'Perla, what's going on?'

'It's hard to explain.'

'It smells like something's rotten.'

'Exactly. It's my problem, for me to clean up.'

'I could help.'

'No.'

'Did you spill something? Take home a beached whale?'

Something in between. I said nothing.

Carolina stared at me as though I'd grown into a strange beast, feral, roaming past the edges of acceptable behavior. She tried another tactic. 'Your parents have already paid me.'

'They don't have to know. I'll never tell them.'

She folded her arms and stared at me.

'Just take the day off.'

She didn't move, but she was listening.

'Please.'

'And what shall I tell your parents when they come back?'

That's when I finally realised, with the alarm of a person waking from a reverie who finally sees the obvious, that they were returning in three days. 'Nothing.'

Carolina pursed her lips.

'Everything will be back to normal,' I said, with a confidence I did not remotely feel.

Carolina sighed in surrender, and walked back to the door. I was about to close it when she turned around to face me. 'Perlita, what has happened to you?'

I smiled weakly and closed the door.

As I stood listening to her steps down the stone path, the question rang on in my head.

9

El Grito Sagrado

I awoke on the sofa, in the pale early morning. I had fallen asleep downstairs again, but I had not brought down a blanket or pillow because I'd told myself that I was just resting my eyes, that any moment I'd go upstairs to bed, that I was not camping in the living room out of a deep urge to stay close to the guest. Lying to myself, as always. How very many lies.

Darkness pushed up against the bottom of my mind, rising from my rib cage, threatening to expand and consume me. My whole body thrashed and railed against what I knew, what I fought to deny.

You can't win this.

I can't let it in.

You have to.

It'll destroy me.

So will the lies.

A dog barked, outside on the street, a pained and plaintive sound. Outside, the rain had abated, though the sky was still a delicate gray, as if wrapped in thin and somber silk. The rosebushes in the yard glittered in the glory of their dampness, all leaf and thorn, devoid of blossoms. The guest lay in the pool with his eyes closed. He looked peaceful, almost childlike, in his sleep.

I knew then that I couldn't hide anymore. Not because I didn't want to, but because there was no room left, no corner dry enough in this house.

I stood up, and to my own surprise my feet were firm and steady. In that moment, I began to say goodbye.

⚜

The memory that comes to him begins with beauty, it was a beautiful day: blue skies, loud streets, a victory for Argentina. The World Cup had come to Buenos Aires, it was 1978, the whole world had turned its eyes to them, and they had won. He felt an electric flush of vindication, he couldn't help himself; he certainly had his scepticism of nationalistic fervour, but still – the world was watching, they stood at the zenith of the world, and even if he balked inside at patriotism in these turbid times he could not deny, could never deny, his great passion for soccer. He had watched the game with his whole body taut, leaning forward from the chair, his legs thrilling with each flex and run and glorious kick. His head felt the thump of the ball, the shouts of the crowd, the hair slick with sweat and wind and motion, as though he himself were on that field writing his nation's name into the books of history. He cheered and groaned and tensed along with all his fellow countrymen in the stands and also home in front of television sets, like him, separated by walls of plaster and ideas but united, for today, in the throbbing nexus of the game, and when they won his fists shot up, his body leaped, his lungs were bellows pressing out the orgiastic *GOOOOL* that shook his body and the city and the world, the whole damn amazed circumference of the world, and now, an hour later, the television still roared. The street outside his open window roared as well, rife with sunshine and throngs and blue and white flags, honking cars, radios, chanting, *ganaa-mos, ganaamos, we won, we won, we won.* On the television, more crowds, even thicker crowds, and you could see the wide mouths and the fists high in the air, and General Videla among uniforms, shaking hands with Henry Kissinger, who came thousands of miles to witness the event and salute the Argentinean nation; he was in the stands to see their strength and victory, a not-so-tacit approval of the coup, of course, the U.S.A. all smiles with the generals but by the glow of the World Cup even this fails to disgust him. The cheers from the street erupt in polyphonic splendor and he feels them in this body, he wants to descend, to join them, to merge with these streets that are his streets after all, the people's streets, streets that can be danced across despite the rumours of these times, he is only waiting for Gloria to arrive, any moment she'll be home and they will plunge into their fomented city.

Gloria arrives late, her coat flung open, the buttons have long stopped closing around her pregnant belly. She bursts in with coat and hair and eyes loose and wild and she glares at the television as though it were the worst kind of perversion and says, Turn that shit off.

He stares at her from his perch at the small balcony.

Turn it off!

He comes in, turns it off, and tries to calm her with his hands along her shoulders, but she will not be calmed. She wrests from him and paces, a caged animal.

My brother's gone.

Gone?

He disappeared. Yesterday. He went to work and never came home.

He reaches for something to say, but can find nothing. Outside, the elated voices, *We won, we won, we won.*

My mother hasn't stopped weeping, I tried but I could not make her stop.

She looks up. The blankness in her face terrifies him more than her words.

Gloria.

I don't know what to do.

Could he have been a Montonero?

It is the wrong thing to say; she turns away from him. Should that permit them to do whatever they want with a man?

I didn't say that.

I don't know what he was, what he wasn't.

I'm sorry.

Mamá's taken out her kerchief, she's joining the Madres.

He thought of Gloria's mother out on the Plaza de Mayo, carrying a photograph of Marco. That's dangerous, he said.

She doesn't care. She says we should be careful.

Us?

She nods.

We haven't done anything.

She flares up, bares her teeth. What does that matter? Can you tell me what Marco did?

Of course not.

Can you? Can you?

Gloria, calm down.

She says nothing. A wave of trumpets rises through the window, buoyed by the sound of honking cars, the opening lines of the national anthem played on brass and sung along to by the exultant mob, *Oíd, mortales, el grito sagrado, libertad, libertad, libertad.* Listen, mortals, the sacred cry, freedom,

freedom, freedom. He should be thinking of her brother, her *hermanito* as she still called him even though he towered over her, with his eager lean and stubborn streak and shaggy hair and au courant mustache that belied his age, but he can only think of Gloria's belly, the baby inside, only three months from bursting out into the world, and his task as protector that has already begun, he must defend the baby (wild creature who kicked against my palm last night) from all dangers, including the danger of a womb receiving panic from the woman it inhabits, the chemical reactions of despair, he wants to calm them, smooth them out, surely all will return to balance if only Gloria will be calm.

Perhaps they'll release him soon.

God, you're such an idiot. You still don't get it.

He can't stand the distance between them, longs to close it. He says, I'm sorry.

Mamá thinks we should leave.

The country?

Yes.

Is she leaving?

No.

What do you think we should do?

I don't know. I don't know. She rubs her wide belly and weeps without making a sound.

He wakes. There is no national anthem and no Gloria, only the pool and the room and the girl, who kneels on the floor with a cup of ready water. Her hair is wet, she has bathed, and there is a strange expression on her face, something he hasn't seen before and can't identify. She offers him the water, and he leans forward to the cup, eats from it, chews the incandescent liquid and feels it suffuse him, augment him, give him strength. He watches the girl bring the bucket and begin to empty his pool and thinks, *Once again you give me life.* The thought makes him want to weep, how can this be, that she should give him life, the young to the old or the child to the father or the living to the dead rather than the other way around, it seems to have no logic and yet it's right and true. He accepts it though his mind could crack under the weight of his gratitude. She is so magnificent, every microscopic hair a revelation, how did all this emerge from Gloria and the seed of him? And also good, she is so good, her kindness with a being as strange as what he has become and the sudden intrusive chaos he has surely created in her life – her kindness has no reason, no sense. *Don't ever succumb to sense,* he thinks to her.

I have to go out, she says.

He nods.

I'm not sure what time I'll be back.

He holds her gaze and he could swear that there is something she longs to say, a kind of pursing at her mouth that suggests words striving to escape before the mind will let them, and her eyes, they are awake, alive, familiar – he has seen them years before – they are just like his own eyes, he remembers them, their stare in the mirror, eyes of intensity, eyes full of night.

Where are you going?

Various places, she says, and before he can gather his thoughts for something else to say, she rises from the floor and is gone.

The memory offers up a melodious coda: on the night that Argentina won the World Cup, Gloria fell asleep to the sounds of a drunken city. He lay awake beside her, wide-eyed, restive, his wife's pregnant belly bulging beside him like the corporeal voice of fate. She was so big now, vulnerable for all her fierceness, she had wept a flood of tears over her brother and collapsed into sleep exhausted by her own helpless rage. She wanted to leave the country. She did not want to leave the country. No matter what he answered, he was wrong and she was right and she fought him like a panther. How to protect a woman who tried to claw you to shreds each time you approached? And yet he had to protect her, it was his duty, the most solemn vow he'd ever taken in his life. Other men might mock him for taking marital vows so much to heart, to have and to hold, God you're so earnest, how very quaint, and perhaps it was indeed quaint and earnest – they were well into the 1970s, after all. But he didn't care, that was how he felt. The promise to protect her was the most serious one he'd ever made at an altar. He had never dreamed it would come to feel so difficult.

If only they could be as they had been, two years before, in the simpler era of their engagement, when marriage sweetened the horizon before them like a nectar they had yet to taste. When he thought of that period of their lives together, he always returned to the day they came home from a visit to Azul, driving through the golden wheat fields of the pampas. He had just proposed to her in the plaza of the town where she grew up, on his knee the way he'd seen it done in films from Hollywood, and she had blushed at the ogling passersby, smiled at their applause when she said yes. Now, hours later, they were quiet together in the car, listening to the poignant songs of Sui Generis at the highest volume their old cassette player could muster, and as he watched the stalks and stalks of wheat pour past the windows, the land and music seemed to blend together, Argentinean rock music, Argentinean land,

and he thought, I am part of this, part of the dirt that makes these stalks grow and part of the muse that fuels these songs; the hurtling stream that is this nation contains me too: and surely there are still good things in this nation even in these insane times, despite the kidnappings by the extreme right and by the extreme left, despite the death of President Perón, despite the wife he left to take his place, Isabel Perón, she has no idea what she's doing, how overwhelmed she is, how corrupt it all is, what a mess we are in, exasperating, perilous, who knows where it's all going, but here on this road I can see the best of Argentina and thank God it's still here, the wheat fields, the rock stars, and Gloria, yes, her too, the woman at the steering wheel, the pinnacle of what this country can produce, and I am going to marry her, I may not till our soil or sell any records but I am going to marry the most beautiful woman in the nation, she has said yes, and surely that is something, makes me part of the greater fabric of land and song and meaning, we will be inordinately happy and she will bear us many children who will carry on the Argentinean story, whatever shape it takes, our children's children's children will know our names. The blessing almost seemed too great to bear. Before he could stop himself, he asked her why she had accepted.

What are you talking about?

Well, why me?

She laughed. She pulsed her fingers lazily against the steering wheel. She liked to drive, and he let her do it even though his friends had teased him about it, *you give your woman the wheel, next thing you know she'll want you to piss sitting down.* Because you asked, she said, her eyes still on the road.

No really, he said, I mean it. Why? You could have any man.

Her face softened, then, in the way it sometimes did when

he stroked her breasts, and he wanted to do it right then, lean over and run his hands across her blouse even if it meant careening off the highway.

I don't want any man, she said. I want you. You have the face I want to watch grow old.

She said no more and he did not pursue the subject, did not dare upset the delicate grace of the moment, her words in the air, her breasts ripe against her blouse, his hands hungry to touch them and the rest of her as one day soon they would, the sun drenching the fertile fields, the highway long and straight, surrounded by the promise of fresh wheat. The cassette player crooned 'Quizás Porque,' one of his favorite songs, in which a man confesses that he's not of noble birth, yet dares to call his lover queen and princess, offering her a cigarette paper crown. He waited for the line and let it ripple over him. What a poet, that Charly García. He even says in the same song that he's not a good poet, then there he is turning cigarette paper into a crown. The transubstantiation of love. I would like to make a crown for Gloria out of – what? – out of this song, out of broken bits of the plastic cassette that holds this song. He imagined Gloria walking down the wedding aisle in a crown of his own making, cigarette paper and crushed cassette and stalks of pampas wheat. That would be perfect. He felt drunk. He was full of hope, like air in a balloon, almost enough to buoy him into the sky.

In bed beside his sleeping wife, plagued by the shouts of inebriated patriots outside, anxieties settled on his chest like harpies. How quickly, he thought, a life can become burdened; from one instant to the next, worries flood in, and the body itself feels old. He worried that he would fail in his duty to protect Gloria, to shield her from the stresses that could weaken the development of their child. He wanted to erase her sadness, and could not. He worried that all the weeping would make her sick, he worried that she would stay this way until her brother came back, which could be weeks, even months, and he worried about the question of whether to leave the country before the baby was born – was it really necessary? What would happen to his or her citizenship? How would this rattle their child's future? And what would they do for work in another nation, where would they land, how immensely would they miss Buenos Aires, what would they do with all their home-sickness, the three of them adrift in a strange place? It seemed a monumental sacrifice, the flight to exile. He touched his wife's taut belly in search of signs of life, but it seemed that the baby was asleep in her amniotic sac. There were no kicks or jutting elbows. I don't know what we're going to do, he whispered, speaking to the baby, what do you want us to do? There was no answer. He kept his hand on Gloria's belly and lay quietly, as the crowds on the street sang on and on for Argentina, an entity he had once loved blindly and that now seemed dis-torted beyond recognition. What is this Argentina they sing for? And does it even hear their cries? He thought this as he stirred and stirred the worries through his mind, not imagin-ing – never imagining – how small, how absurdly palatable, even how enviable such worries would soon seem.

Buenos Aires gleamed. After days in the house with my guest, I felt dazed by the brightness of the city. Rain had cleaned the buildings and made way for a bright blue sky to hang over them, a shining tarp. Tourists bustled past me, obvi-ously relieved at their change in fortune, smiling into the sun, wearing backpacks on their fronts because they'd read all about the pickpockets that roamed this city that, despite its legacy of old grandeur, could not escape the destitution of the Global South it still belonged to. Their legs were exposed below the hems of shorts, terribly pale because it was the dead of winter back home in Europe or the United States of America. I wondered how the city looked to them, whether they saw the lush majestic detail on the façades of old buildings and not the way they mouldered from neglect, or whether they saw the moldering of façades and not the lush majestic details. I could take you home with me, I thought, and show you a hidden face of Buenos Aires, something that is sure to, ahem, make a splash; you won't find it in guidebooks, it's off the beaten path, as they say, or rather on a path that has sustained an entirely different kind of beating. I walked on. At the university, I sped up my pace, taking detours down longer halls so as to avoid the classroom I should have been sitting in at this hour, and the offices of professors who might stop me and demand an explanation, *Perla, where on earth have you been?*, or perhaps they would simply look at me coldly and let me pass, or be too wrapped up in their own research to recall my days of absence. I couldn't decide which was worse, to be shut out or forgotten or pressured to come back in.

I made it to the library without incident. I thought – perhaps I hoped – that it might be difficult to find what I was looking for, but the computerised catalog instantly pulled up three titles that were all relevant and all available. One, I thought, I can stand only one. I wrote down the titles and numbers and carried the slip of paper into the stacks, held in front of me between ginger fingers as though it were a delicate grenade. When I was a girl, my mother would take me to the public library on Saturdays, and the stacks seemed like halls of hallowed knowledge where I'd pace randomly without a plan or any numbers jotted on slips of paper, emerging, to Mamá's consternation, with piles of books captured in forays to the shelves for adults. A history of China, eighteenth-century French verse, a survey of the botanical wonders of the Amazon.

'What on earth do you want with these books?' she would say as she leafed through them, examining each one to give her approval.

'I'm curious.'

Mamá frowned. 'About China?'

'Yes.'

'What is there to be curious about?'

'It's a very big country.'

'Yes. But it's full of Chinese.'

'I don't know anything about the Chinese.'

Mamá sighed. 'It's good you want to learn so much,' she said, though she still tried to steer me back to the children's books, which, she pointed out, would be easier to understand, and which were less likely to be riddled with lies.

'What kind of lies?'

'Various kinds. You have to be careful in the adult aisles; books for grown-ups have lies buried in them, like hidden fangs.'

When she said *fangs*, she aimed two crooked fingers at me, as if to emphasise the point. This only deepened the power of the image in my mind – if Mamá said it, it must be baldly true – and for years after that, while reading, until I began to read with Romina, I always felt the presence of those wild teeth between the lines, white fangs that concealed themselves in white space, chameleon fangs, ready to leap and sink into my skin if I wasn't careful. They lent a layer of danger to the act of reading: you could be innocently tracing the shapes of black letters and suddenly the lies might rise out of the whiteness, a flock of small and deadly jaws, disembodied from heads or faces, ready to sink into you with force – they would leap first at the eyes – and destroy you in a rabid white swarm. Of course, this never happened. By the time I was in high school, by the time of my mother's failed geraniums, I had discounted the whole notion of lies hidden in books as my mother's attempt to keep a girl away from pages that could intrude on the fragile reality of a house. My mother did not want to see, nor for her daughter to see, certain things that could be written about in books, such as, perhaps, the years when I was small and the nation full of quiet. *She didn't know. She knew. She knew. She struggled each day to not-know.* I had no way of discerning which it was. She would never tell me the true version, and even if she could I wasn't sure that I could bear to hear it.

I found my book in the stacks and turned it over in my hands, once, twice, feeling the weight of it, the creased binding, a book purporting to be as ordinary as any other. On my way back downstairs, I pulled out two generic history volumes at random, to stack on top as I handed the books to the librarian, whom I knew and would have to face in the future. I pictured her looking up from the last title and staring at me, eyes softening in pity, or hardening in alarm, but she did neither. She was impartial, dispassionate, she had many other important things to do and this was just another student with just another project or assignment or obsession, it's all the same, the books were stamped and waved through the machine and released into my care. I placed them in my backpack and walked out, toward the sunshine, their weight mauling at my shoulders.

I didn't know where I was going. I had nowhere to go but had to go somewhere, couldn't go home, couldn't yet face the melted clocks and thick damp air and contents of an inflatable red pool. I descended into the subway and took the first train. No one on board was smiling. A man read the paper with a mournful expression on his face. Another man, bald and hunched, stared out of the window as though he were watching trees, sun, houses, anything other than the black walls of a tunnel speeding by. A woman breast-fed an infant under her blouse. The child sucked greedily, surrendered to the pleasure of it, eyes rolled back under half-closed lids, legs kicking softly, fingers splayed in surrender. I was staring; I looked away. What is that like? I wondered. Did I ever do such a thing?

I exited at Plaza de Mayo. Upstairs, in the street, light stung my eyes.

I walked to the plaza. A breeze traced light and furtive patterns in my hair. Scattered tourists snapped photos of each other, while a vendor of ice cream and key chains looked on, sleepy, haggard, he had seen many days like this one. I didn't know why I'd come here but I stood, taking in the vast spreading presence of the plaza, which throbbed with pride or sun or history, its pink flagstones empty but still straining, surely, under the weight of all the steps that had traversed this patch of earth in the long years in which it had been a congregating place. I wondered what the flagstones knew: whether, for example, they still felt the blood that was shed here in the 1800s by Manuel de Rosas and his circle of assassins, the Mazorca, with their public destruction of all enemies, real and perceived. Violinists, the killers called themselves, for the long stroke of knife across throat, the music that surged from victims as they died. One throat after another, so that blood from dozens of men and women blended on one blade. And then their heads were cut off and placed on tall stakes here in the Plaza de Mayo for all to see and dream about, so even dreams could be scrubbed clean of thoughts of treason by the sight of severed heads, perhaps of friends or neighbours, slowly becoming unrecognisable thanks to the flies. All of this was long before the city was a sprawl of many millions, it lacked the cars and high-rises that wrap around the plaza now, but even then it was the centre of the city. The decapitated heads were on display for drivers of horse-drawn carriages, government officials, ladies visiting the shops. Now you could no longer see the flies and rotting heads on stakes, they were not here, unless we can believe that the past is always present in the place where it unfolded, still a phantom hiding in the winds of the current moment. If it were possible for time to collapse, for the great hulking curve of it to crash into itself, then perhaps I would see the heads on stakes sur-rounded by swarms of flies, as well as the crowds who faced the Casa Rosada when Evita Perón came to the balcony to speak, and the film extras who crowded here when Madonna came to the Casa Rosada to pretend to be Evita on the balcony, and also the countless afternoons and mornings they had come here, the Madres of the Plaza de Mayo, a small group at first, then growing, white kerchiefs tied around their heads to represent the innocence of their beloved lost ones, with their enlarged photographs in hand, walking around and around the plaza as if their bodies formed the spoke of a great wheel, *we want them back with life,* walking despite the governmental warnings and the nightsticks and arrests and *those women are crazy* and the threats, walking in the shade of the dictatorship and walking later in the shade of a democracy that still failed to cough up the ones they loved, *with life* – all the walking would compress here in the great collapse of time. As I stood and stared, I imagined how the various eras might melt into each other, how the women would march around the rotting faces eaten by the flies, flies would buzz around the kerchiefs of the Madres, the tourists who now snapped photos of the statue and the Casa Rosada just across the road would swat the flies away and say, It's so hot here in the south, the film extras would mingle with the masses waiting for Eva Perón, Eva Perón would gaze at Madonna as she gazed out at the Madres in their eternal circle of a walk, resolute, constant, women in their forties, women in their seventies, ageless as the sea, tattooing their existence into the flagstones and the earth below. And as for me, I thought, what if I'm seen here? What if one of the Madres could turn her head and see me, include me in the mad blend of epochs with a single gaze? The past has not disappeared, far from it, the millennium may have turned and placed us in the fresh new twenty-first century, but that does not protect us from the reach and clear-eyed gaze of the past.

Perhaps that was why I had come here, against the current of my own conscious mind.

To be recognised.

Even though nothing terrified me more than the notion of one of those kerchiefed women capturing me with her eyes, across the veils of time, opening her mouth to speak or weep or spit at the lonely, silent girl. I looked out across the empty plaza, where the invisible Madres walked with the dignity of people who know more of pain than fear. I was certain that I could almost see them; they, however, did not seem to see me. I stood at the lip of their world, small, separate. Never in my life had I felt so small.

The breeze had disappeared, leaving the humid press of

Buenos Aires air. There was a bench nearby, but I could not bring myself to sit. I stood and stood and stood.

Alone in the house. The room is quiet. The sofa has abated its attacks. The swan dreams but does not quiver. Even the books on the shelf seem to have forged a temporary truce with their pages. His mind goes to the girl. He would like to follow her with his consciousness, to see what she is doing, where she roams, what colours pulse through her heart. But he can't find her with his mind, and so he waits, watching the invisible dance of light and air.

Psshhht.

A voice from the corner of the room, from the shadows at the edge of the curtain, where he has seen Gloria's neck and knees waver in the semidark.

Psshhht, come.

Again he hears it, and he could swear it is not only in his mind, not just a memory, a sound as real as the voice of the girl or the rain. Could it be? It was not the turtle, who is across the room, in the doorway, eyes closed, unflapped. The room is still. He gathers himself.

Gloria?

Why won't you come?

Gloria. Gloria. I don't know where you are.

Water is timeless. Search for me.

The curtains quiver. The walls pulse. And now the light in the room is agitated, searing, bright with secrets, knifing into his mind; it can cut open anything, illuminate anything, he wants to call for her but is afraid his voice will break the spell and so he reaches out the currents of his mind to her, to Gloria, to the source of the voice inside the curtains. There is no more response. The curtains are emptied of sound. And so he reaches inward. His mind turns into a dense liquid that shimmers from within, it throbs with light and moisture, it can pour anywhere *water is timeless* and he closes his eyes and plunges into the dark glow behind his eyelids through which tunnels soar, he is soaring through them, slipping through gates of time and space, further and further until he is deep inside the caverns of the past and then he sees her. He is with her, Gloria, in a dark small place. The floor is dank and sticky and the smells are familiar, piss and fear and the metal undertones of blood. She is naked, there are bruises on her thighs and arms, her belly is like nothing he has ever seen, the most incredible protrusion of flesh, curved and taut and much larger than the last day he saw her blindfolded and tied to a chair in front of which he sank into a vortex of men, now the baby inside her must be planning its escape, must be torn between love for the womb and longing for more freedom than the womb can provide. Gloria let me enfold you, kiss you, save you from the spiralling abyss in your mind, but Gloria has not fallen down the spiral, she is distracted from despair, her body is too busy opening its ancient revelations, her eyes are closed, her lips are open, her hands do all the speaking as they glide across the expanse of her belly, slowly, fearlessly, her hands are lioness tongues, drawing on a thousand generations of beastly instinct to stroke and calm and cover what's inside her, Gloria calls out to a guard, he cannot hear the voice but he can see the motion of her throat muscles, the guard takes a long time to come and when he does he wears a face too stern for his young age (he looks like a boy dressed up in his father's suit, the ridiculous hanging sleeves) and Gloria mouths the words, *they're getting stronger,* the guard shakes his head, *we'll take you when it's time,* she says *it's time,* he says *shut up bitch* and then he's gone. Gloria is alone, but not alone, I'm with you Gloria, can you feel my ghost-hands next to yours? fluttering across your belly? slowly, warm sweat slippery on your taut skin, time is as brittle as reality – and reality can collapse into the nightmare of this underworld that you and I were cast into where humanity does not apply to humans; if reality can collapse then so can time; I have always been here in this moment of the past, a wisp of a man, disembodied but awake, carrying memories of the future. There are three of us in this room and one will live and one will die and one, you, Gloria, I still do not know, but for now, for all the dark stench of this place, I still can't help but revel in the joy of touching you again, of offering you the paltry futile comfort of my touch, the heave of your breath makes my fingers rise and fall, your body strains, another wave of contractions is arriving like a storm whipping the sea toward the rocks, a sea that will rage against the rocks and crash around them but will not – do you hear me, Gloria? – will not destroy.

I was still wandering the city, with nowhere to go, walking the streets that caught the light with wide and stony arms, slowing at a café to smell fresh coffee and hear the bustling clinks of cups against spoons before continuing on. I didn't want to stop. I didn't want to drink or eat; the smells and sounds and sights were as much as I could stand to imbibe. The brush of a man's perfume. A spike of laughter. A wave of car exhaust and radio blare, the gleam of sun on boutique windows, the silent mannequin alone in her boutique, a woman scowling at her watch under a dark red awning, the percussive beat of shoes on concrete and on cobblestones, a man talking to another man and gesturing angrily at the sky, a plaintive child-voice *please*

Mamá, the smell of fresh empanadas from a shop where the cook bustled as if all of Buenos Aires had been waiting impatiently for this, his pastries, his prize. How easy it was to drown your thoughts in the swirling streams of the city. How difficult to find a toehold for your mind.

I finally stopped on a very familiar street. Gabriel's apartment building stood across the road. *How did I get here? What are you doing, Perla?* I had had no plan of coming here, I was just wandering, it must be a coincidence that the motion of my feet had brought me here. If I were on the couch for any of my peers in the psychology department, none of them, not a single one, would let me believe such a thing. Buried desires, they would say, are the strongest ones, the ones that propel our unexplained actions and form the blueprints of our dreams. And as they said this they would look victorious, thrilled to see the theories brought to life, here, before them, in this tale of a woman's wandering feet. I had turned to textbooks in search of keys, but they only caused more problems: they made it harder to deny my own deep-sea urges and fears, without giving me the ability to escape them. I walked up to the door and rang the bell. His voice, wrapped in static, came through the grating. He was home.

'Hello?'

'It's me, Perla.'

'Oh.' Undisguised surprise. 'Hello.'

'I was just in the neighbourhood.' Right, of course – for what?

'Would you like to come up?'

'Could I?'

He answered with a long buzz to let me through the front door.

Upstairs, he was waiting for me in the open doorway. He smiled at me, though the smile seemed ambivalent and he didn't kiss my cheek.

'Come in.'

'I'm sorry to interrupt you.'

'It's all right.'

'Were you writing?'

He shrugged. 'I was.'

I glanced around his living room. It was full of stacks of papers that had always struck me as having the upper hand in the small space, like a strange and hardy species slowly asserting its dominion. The papers had not abated since my last visit; if anything, they had grown even more chaotic and triumphant. They ruled the kitchen counter, the coffee table, the edges of the floor. Gabriel had not removed the photograph of us from his bookshelf, the one where we beamed at the camera with our faces pressed together in the living room, slightly askew because he'd taken it himself with an extended arm. It still stood in its frame beside the larger photo of his family, the one I had studied so many times: the five of them, together in Montevideo, at an *asado* on the patio of their home. The two parents stood on either end, his father holding a plate of raw meat ready for the fire, his mother beaming with no makeup on, while Gabriel stood in the middle, one arm around each of his sisters. The close lean of their heads said everything. They looked as though they were that moment wordlessly hearing each other's thoughts. Gabriel loved to talk about his sisters. He was so proud of them. Carla was now a lawyer, though still living with her parents as she could not find enough work to get a place of her own. Penélope, the youngest, was at the Universidad de la República in Montevideo, studying chemistry. I had never heard a person say the word *chemistry* with as much tenderness as Gabriel, talking about his sister. She was five years younger than he, a gulf that surely made her seem a perennial child in his eyes. But she was two years older than I. I had brought this up only once, and Gabriel had laughed, but uneasily, and the truth was that it made me uneasy too. Neither of us ever brought it up again. I was moved by Gabriel's closeness to his sisters, but it also roused other emotions in me, a hot and sticky tar. For a long time, I didn't want to look at my reaction, know what was inside. Guilt was part of it. Look at that lovely family, and here I was, avoiding meeting them, refusing to join in the way he wished I would. Didn't he deserve the kind of girlfriend he could take home to visit without so much fuss? But after some time, I finally realised what plagued me most about his sisters. It was envy. I envied him – envied them all – for having siblings, for their miraculous trust and knowledge of each other, born at the very beginning of their lives, which gave them a lifelong antidote to loneliness that an only child could never hope to have.

Gabriel was waiting for me to speak.

'I had to see you,' I said, before I could feel the thought in my own mind.

'What's wrong?'

'Does something have to be wrong to want to see you?'

He held up his hands like a man under attack. 'I didn't say that.'

'I'm sorry. I don't know why you put up with me. The fact is, I thought you'd refuse to see me.'

'Why?'

'After the way I've treated you.'

He picked up a lit cigarette from an ashtray, and took a long slow drag. He didn't look at me. It was almost as though I'd said nothing at all.

'You should be angry at me,' I said.

'Should I?'

'Of course.'

'About what?'

'Come on. You know.'

'I want to hear it from you.'

I longed for a cigarette, but it didn't seem like the moment to ask for one, and he didn't offer. 'I shouldn't have hung up on you the other day. And, more importantly, I shouldn't have left you.'

He studied me. 'You're right. You shouldn't have.'

It was my moment to say the words *I'm sorry*, but they got trapped in my throat.

'I worried about you, Perla.'

'You did?'

'Why so surprised? You think when you run off and don't say where you're going and it's the middle of the night and you're far from home, people won't worry? Sometimes I wonder about you.'

'Sometimes I wonder about me too.'

That seemed to soften him. 'You could at least have left a note.'

'I just had to go.'

'Perla,' he said, gently, 'nobody ever *has* to do anything.'

'But they think they do.' The words hurt, thorns in my throat. 'I thought I did. I'm sorry.'

We stared at each other. Pain was naked on his face.

'Can I have a cigarette?'

He rooted around the clutter on the coffee table for his

pack, then gave me one and took another for himself. 'Here, have a seat.'

I sat down beside him on the sofa. We lit up and took refuge in the distraction of match, flame, inhale.

Then he said, 'But I've been thinking. About that night. It wasn't all your fault. I shouldn't have pushed you so far, and for that I'm sorry.'

I didn't know what to say. One drop and it could all come spilling.

'I missed you,' Gabriel said.

'Really?'

'Did you miss me?'

'What do you think?'

I had not meant it sharply, but he flinched.

'I'm sorry. I'm not myself these days.'

'Evidently.'

The door to the balcony was open, and through it I heard the wail of an old U2 song, studded with the sound of passing cars. The singer still had not found what he was looking for. I could see myself with Gabriel, at 5 a.m., kissing on that balcony for the first time, the city flung wide below us like the arms of a gregarious friend.

'What are you thinking?' he asked.

'Not much. Let's talk about something else. Are you writing anything new?'

'Sort of.'

'About the disappeared?'

'Yes. Of course.'

I didn't know how to ask my next question. I tried to sound casual. 'What would you do if I told you one of them came back?'

'One of who?'

'The disappeared.'

'From exile?'

'From the dead.'

'I'd kiss you.'

I hadn't expected this, even in a joking tone. It felt like something of an olive branch, or perhaps a guarded question. 'Be serious.'

'All right. I'd want to meet him.'

'Or her.'

'Right, yes, or her.'

'I thought you didn't believe in that. In coming back from the dead.'

'I don't. Of course not. But isn't this hypothetical?'

'What do you think?'

'Well then. Hypothetically, I'd want to meet him, or meet her.' He was closer and his arm brushed mine. The light touch made my whole body crave him; I wondered whether he felt it too. 'In any case, I might not believe in it, but does that really mean a thing can't happen? No one believed in disappearance, either. The world does things to people regardless of what we think is possible.'

I opened my mouth, but said nothing.

'Why do you ask?'

'No reason.'

'Oh, come on.'

'It just came into my mind, that's all.'

Gabriel looked worried. 'Something's going on with you.'

I looked away, out of the window, at the younger couple that was not yet a couple and was no longer there.

'Tell me what's really on your mind.'

'I can't.'

'Why not?'

'I don't have the words.'

'Start anywhere.'

'That's not the problem.' I imagined his face as he listened to a story of a drenched and dripping figure in my living room, a man who was not a man, who broke in without breaking anything, really just appeared, who smelled terrible and shed constant water and had memories that proved he had been alive and also when and in what circumstance, if there could be such a thing as proof in this mad story of a not-man who eats water, whom I could not stop thinking about, who had drowned my life and all the things of which I thought my life was made. 'I just can't.'

Very gently, he said, 'Try me.'

'I will, one day. I promise.' And I meant it. It occurred to me that if there were any person in this world who had a chance of taking in this story, of holding it close to the body with both hands, it would be he.

'As long as you're all right,' he said, and placed his hand over mine.

I stared at his hand. Hard as it was to believe, he seemed sincere. He was not thinking of himself, or at least not of the anger or the slights or even the uncertainty of days to come. I couldn't understand why he cared so much, when even I could stand myself only because I had no choice, because I was trapped inside my skin and could not peel it off and run away. Here was the hand that had reached inside me and found what I truly was, a feat my friends could not accomplish since my veneer was so convincing, a feat my mother seemed to avoid with a resistance that bordered on distaste, a feat my father had perhaps attempted but failed in why? – perhaps for fear of things that lurked inside our bond. That Gabriel should have reached and felt – and that his hand should still return to me, still arrive on mine, like this, warm, supple, with no trace of disgust. That such a thing could be.

'Gabriel.'

'Yes.'

'I wish we could begin again.'

I leaned in to his body. The air seemed to rush and form a shroud around us, dense and humming. His body told me with its bright electric language that desire was still there, that the gap between us could be easily dissolved, was already dissolving, and I turned my mouth in to his neck and closed the circle. He allowed me in, enveloped me, his hands were in my hair, under my shirt, my shirt was gone, his mouth returned to mine, my breasts returned to him, all the flesh that wanted to come home, he tried to talk but I said *Shhh, shhhhh querido, don't say anything,* and even here he acquiesced, even this he gave me, sounds free of the cage of language, bodies free of words, he let me strip him, let me take him as a canvas for my deepest colours. I wanted to exalt him with the shout of my bare hands. His tongue spoke to my neck, his hands spoke to my skin, his sex spoke inside me with a force that could surely defy gravity, keep a human from falling, shoot a body to the stars and spill its secrets into black and endless space.

Afterward, I lay curled on him, wrapped in afternoon light and carnal smells and the noise of traffic through an open window, through which our sounds had surely reached the street.

'Perlita.'

'Mmmm …'

'What are we doing?'

'Basking.'

'Yes. But where do we go from here?'

'Wherever you want.'

'Are you coming back to me?'

'Would you let me?'

'Conceivably.'

'Conceivably? That doesn't sound so good.'

'I'd have to hear your plea.'

'I don't have one planned.'

'No matter. Spontaneous is best.' He took my hand and raised it to his lips. 'Stay for a while. I'll cook something, we'll eat without putting on our clothes.'

I wanted to stay. I almost said yes, almost let myself sing into the notion, but then I thought of the guest, thirsty for his water, swimming in his memories, needing me, waiting, wondering when I would arrive.

'I can't.' I pulled myself up. 'I have to go.'

He stared at me, wounded.

'I'm sorry.'

'I can't take much more of this, Perla.'

'Don't give up on me,' I said, for the second time this week.

'You're the one who's leaving.' He searched my face. 'Again.'

'It's different this time. I just need to take care of something.'

'But you won't tell me what.'

'Not yet. I'll call you soon and I'll explain.' I stroked his chest, slowly, lingering among the wiry curls. 'I promise. I'll call you very soon.'

When I left, he was still on the floor, watching me with bewildered eyes.

10

Open

I don't have much time left to tell this story, judging from the
pain that just rushed through me – the most incredible sensation, like being gripped in the fervent fist of God.

As I said before and cannot say enough times, this is my
way of speaking to the heart of things, curving around it, in
the thrall of its gravitational pull. And now we're almost there,
almost at the core.

Let me tell you about the night that cut me open. I had
gone to Uruguay with Gabriel. It was ten days before the wet
man arrived. First, we went to Gabriel's family cottage on the
beach, after which we planned to spend some days in Montevideo with his parents. For a long time I had attempted to
put off meeting his parents, as I knew that they had not been
pleased to learn their son was dating a girl with a family like
mine. But Gabriel had been talking for years about the little
house in Piriápolis, on the very beach where his parents had
first met, where we could relax together in a place of calm and
beauty. And your parents won't mind that you're staying over-
night with someone you're not married to? He smiled at that.
Oh Perla, he said, they're not that kind of parents. You'll like
them, really, and they'll like you, they've had plenty of time to

get used to the idea of, well, of you, and once they meet you they'll see who you are instead of just where you come from.

I finally relented. The idea appealed to my hunger for adventure, and in any case, the summer was ripe, the millennium fresh and young and spreading itself before us like a dare. Even the lie to my parents wasn't hard; my friend Marisol was more than glad to provide an alibi, and even Mamá, who thought I had a new romantic interest in the form of Bruno, a physics student whose father was a doctor – when my imagination faltered all my invented dates were sons of doctors – accepted the story without question.

During the whole ferry ride across the wide Río de la Plata, as I watched the water rush below us, smooth and thick and silty, I thought of my parents, back at home, believing the lie. I had never crossed a border without them. I was drunk on the liquor of transgression, its hot thrill of guilt and power, the promise of standing at the helm of my own life. We landed in Montevideo and immediately boarded a bus to Piriápolis. The bus ride took us out of the city to the countryside, with its gentle hillocks and copious green. I leaned in to Gabriel as if to sleep, but could not relinquish wakefulness. The road was too open, my lust too large, the pop songs on the driver's radio too buoyant. Mine, I thought, this road is mine, I am a grown woman on the road with my lover and all of this – these moments, this body, the rattle of the bus – all of it is mine. I could almost sink into the delicious illusion of being free, able to become any woman I wanted. I lay in Gabriel's arms and watched Uruguayan fields ebb past, tranquil, lush, beckoning.

We arrived at the cottage and immediately began having sex on the living room floor, the kitchen counter, and finally the bed. The freedom of an entire night together, with no subway ride home, made me delirious with lust, I couldn't stop. Dusk fell and wrapped us in hot summer darkness. I growled and screamed without concern for neighbours. At one point, Gabriel laughed at my ferocity, which made me laugh, and then neither of us could stop.

'What are you laughing at?'

'I don't know anymore.'

'Me neither.'

'Ay, Perla,' he said, still laughing. I took that opportunity to kiss his chest, stomach, the bliss of his hip bone, my hand already on his sex.

'Wait a minute,' he said. 'Wait. Maybe we should go to the beach.'

'Why?'

'It's beautiful at night. You'll love it.'

'Not yet. I'm not done with you.'

'We can come right back.'

'I don't want to wash you off me.'

'Who says you have to?'

'I'm not going to the beach smelling like this.'

'You smell delicious.'

'You're crazy.'

'Want me to prove it?'

Before I could answer he sprang up, wrestled me onto my back, and pinned my arms above my head in a single gesture.

'I surrender,' I called out.

And I did.

We lost track of time. The night held us in its velvet folds.

'Now I can't let you outside.'

'Why not?'

'You smell so good that all the men will want you.'

'Gabriel.'

'They won't even know what hit them but what hit them is the sex and come and musky sweat all over you.'

'Don't be silly.'

'I'll have to beat them off with driftwood.'

'Oh come on.'

'Is that an order?'

I laughed.

'Well, in that case – '

'Gabo – '

It was two in the morning when we finally went outside. The Río de la Plata glimmered under a broken moon. The waves announced themselves over and over, *shhh, shhh, shh-hhhhh.* Lovers and families strolled the shore in little clusters, murmuring, laughing, drinking *mate.* I saw several clusters of young Uruguayan hippies, with their uncombed hair and marijuana smiles and baskets of fresh-baked goods and trinkets they sold on the beach to fund their continued wanderings. They were my age, or younger; they seemed full of ease, too relaxed to care about their hair or future. I had never been like them, never had a friend like them, could not imagine their inner worlds. While in the past I might have mocked their clothes or lazy stances, tonight I felt a stab of envy. They seemed free. All the denizens of this little beach town seemed free. It could have been the lovemaking, still making me feel as though my bones were made of nectar, or perhaps the long day of travel, but I had the strange sensation of having entered an alternative plane, an enchanted realm of sex and calm and pos-sibility. My family had often vacationed in Uruguay over the years, but only in Punta del Este, with its crowds of expensive bikinis and high-rises crushed up against each other. In Punta del Este, even the ocean seemed carefully groomed. Here the waves were just themselves, loose-maned, unabashed, mixing easily with the sand.

We walked. I walked arm in arm with Gabriel, cradling my weight against his body. We took off our shoes and walked toward the waves and when the water swallowed our feet like dark wet silk, I laughed.

'It's wonderful here,' I said.

'I thought you'd like it.'

'We should come back.'

'We'll bring our children.'

I laughed again.

'What's so funny?'

'What children?'

'You can't imagine it?'

'I didn't say that.'

He splashed me with his foot. 'Then what are you saying?'

He said it lightly, but I heard the edge in his voice. We had never talked about children before, not directly, though I had often wondered – late at night, naked, drifting in and out of sleep beside Gabriel – how a little boy or girl sprung from the two of us might look, how he or she might run or shout or laugh in a home we all shared, somewhere in the city, always in the city, an apartment where the child would fall asleep each night to lullabies shot through with the constant murmur of Buenos Aires. Surely that was what I wanted for my future, even if it meant long-avoided meetings, a double life exposed, a war with my parents that could end in my being cut from them like an amputated limb. I could have a life that contained Gabriel or a life that contained my parents, but I could not imagine having both. And so the thoughts of children, like all thoughts of the further future, stayed caught in the dim borderland between sleep and consciousness, never spoken. 'Nothing.'

'You don't want to have kids with me.' He sounded genuinely hurt.

'That's not true.'

'It's because of your parents, isn't it?'

I was quiet for a few steps. A low wave stroked our feet and then retreated.

'When are you going to live your own life?'

'I am living it.'

'But in their shadow.'

'Are you calling me a coward?'

'Do you feel like a coward?'

The waves, the waves, they were at my ankles, foaming and awake. 'Sometimes.'

'Let me meet them.'

'No.'

'You're about to meet my parents, but I can't meet yours.'

'If you met them you couldn't stand them.'

'Can you?'

I almost let it roll past me, it was such a beautiful night, but he had stopped walking and examined me with a gravity that bordered on a challenge. 'Please. Try to understand. They're my parents.'

His gaze softened and turned tender. 'Maybe they're not.'

'What?'

'Maybe they stole you.'

I said nothing. I couldn't move.

'It's been on my mind,' he said. 'I've been turning it over. Haven't you ever wondered?'

'No,' I said, and it was true. I hadn't. Or, more accurately, I had, but the wondering barely left an imprint on my conscious memory, it had been as rapid as a blink, shut-open-shut, fading into oblivion every time.

'Why not?'

'Why would I?'

'Well,' he said, and I could have slaughtered him for the pedantic tone, 'most of the abducted children were taken in by members of the regime. And from what you've told me about your father – '

'Shut up. I haven't told you anything about him.'

Very gently, he said, 'That's exactly my point.'

I didn't answer.

'You could find out, you know, at Las Abuelas' office.'

I didn't know what to say. I listened to the hostile whisper of the waves. Las Abuelas – the Grandmothers of the Plaza de Mayo – were a group within the Madres who wore the same white headscarves but who searched not only for their disappeared children but for their grandchildren as well. Fighting, they claimed, for the return of stolen babies. Who now, in 2001, were not babies anymore, but young adults with their own lives and destinies.

Old women with grim faces that had nothing, nothing to do with me.

'How long have you been thinking this?'

He shrugged. 'A while.'

'Have you talked to anyone about it?'

'No,' he said, then slowly added, 'not really.'

'Who?'

'My mother. Just my mother, honestly.'

I walked away from him, into the water, cold around my

calves. The night bellowed with stars. I wanted to climb into the sky and hurl myself into the black void between the constellations, where there was no air, no life, no mother in Montevideo preparing a dinner for a girl she thought was stolen, unbearable offerings heaped on the plates.

Gabriel was behind me now, hands on my shoulders. 'Listen, Las Abuelas, they do blood tests. They can see whether your DNA matches any of the disappeared. You don't have to think it's true. It's for anyone who's unsure of their identity.'

'I'm not unsure,' I said, too loudly.

'There's nothing to lose.'

'Stop it.'

'I could go with you.'

I whipped around to face him. 'Are you listening?'

He stared at me. A wave wrapped its supple body around our calves, then ebbed away. I walked out of the water, picked up my shoes, and started back toward the cottage. He caught up with me.

'I'm sorry,' he said. 'I'm really sorry. Let's just forget this.' He put his arm around me, and I stiffened, but stopped walking. I could have hit and scratched and clawed him, but my body burned to lean against him so I did, against his subtle swells and hollows that still smelled of sex and in whose supple warmth I longed to lose myself.

'Let's walk some more,' he said.

We traversed the boundary between dry and wet sand. The night sky vaulted above us, stung with stars, lulling me to forget my new dread of meeting Gabriel's mother, the fantasies of escaping the dinner she was preparing at which I now felt I would be less of an honoured guest and more of a hunted animal, *that one, she's a fake,* the conversation a field of pleasantries riddled with hidden traps. And other images rose into my mind, that I fought to push away, like the memory of my first brush with Las Abuelas, walking with my mother past an exhibit in a shop window. She sped our pace, but still I glimpsed children's drawings of shattered hearts and wailing mouths, and a banner reading IDENTITY IS A RIGHT, WE WANT THEM BACK WITH LIFE. *Those old bags,* my mother said, *have nothing better to do than try to destroy other people's families.* Of course at that time her scorn and hurried gait did not make me suspect anything, why would it, when everything to do with the disappeared was subject to such treatment, this was no different and it meant nothing, did it, that look in my mother's eyes as she looked back at the shop window. The look that Lot's wife might have had just before salt replaced her flesh. Nothing, it meant nothing, damn Gabriel and his ideas, twisting everything, tangling the skeins of my mind when all I wanted was to enjoy a summer night on the beach. He held me gently as we walked; I wanted to tear his clothes off and shut him up with my mouth everywhere and then we could forget this, everything was fine, we were walking on a smooth shore, two lovers on a night walk, an ordinary idyll after all. Our feet moved in time. The ocean carried the moon in a thousand splinters. The rhythmic water soothed me, and I began to feel the first specks of calm.

Then he said, 'I should tell you one more thing.'

A wave rushed up around our toes and ebbed away.

'I called them for you.'

'What? Who?'

'Las Abuelas. Perla, I worry about you.'

'Did you tell them my name?'

'Look, Perla, if your parents are really your parents, then there's no ha – '

'Did you tell them my name?'

He hesitated, and I pulled away. He looked stunned, dazed. His voice was so quiet that it almost got lost in the waves.

'I did.'

Down the shore, a pile of black seaweed glistened just beyond the reach of the waves. It probably turned green in the daylight, but now it was impenetrably dark, slick, something that the sea had coughed up from bowels where humans can't survive and shouldn't ever go, the inner organs of a monster, exposed on the sand. I felt far from my legs, they were not mine, they could buckle and betray me. I saw my family broken, police at our door, our house suddenly crowded with old women in white headscarves reaching for me and railing aloud and tearing apart the furniture but why would I think this if I did not have doubts Perla I thought Perla I shouted with my silent aching mind could it be that you have doubts?

I walked away.

'Perla – '

I kept walking. He followed, chased me, threw his arms out to stop me.

'Leave me alone.'

'Please don't shout.'

'Fuck you, Gabo.'

'Look, if you don't want – '

'I don't want you! What I don't want is you, you fucking prick, not your babies or phone calls or arrogant fucking speeches!'

We stared at each other, both breathing hard. An older couple slowed to stare at us.

'We can fix this,' he said.

I broke into a run.

I didn't know that I was running until I heard him call my name, once, and then a second time, already farther away. I ran to the cottage and picked up my purse and suitcase with whatever was still in it, left the rest behind and ran to the street, past homes where Uruguayans drank beer or *mate* on their patios, looking comfortable and happy and incapable of understanding why on earth a young woman would rush down the street on a lovely night like this with her suitcase buckles only half-secured, back out to the main road where the bus from the capital had let us off. I stood at the drop off spot, next to a family that was waiting for the bus, and I was grateful that they didn't try to talk to me. I stared down the bare two-lane highway, surrounded by low fields. Such calm, temperate land. Nothing to worry about, nothing to hide, the Uruguayan fields seemed to say. In that instant, I hated them for their serenity. I imagined Gabriel running up to find me here, grabbing my shoulders with both hands, *don't go, we can fix this,* redolent of sex, my sex, trying to draw me to the cottage. And part of me even then longed for him to make it to my side before the bus arrived so he could persuade me back to the little beach house, back in time, to the sumptuous innocence of who we were when we arrived here just eight hours ago, and after we'd made the sun rise again with the sheer force of our pleasure he'd say *I'm sorry, you're right, it was all a big mistake,* and we'd laugh at the absurd theories he and his mother had concocted, *she's a good woman, my mother, but she's watched* The Official Story *one too many times.* Theories that the morning sun would dispel like phantom shadows. But the bus came and Gabriel did not and some returns are impossible. Through a scratched and dirty window pane I watched the dark hills pass and gradually turn into the outskirts of the city, of Montevideo, with its flat-roofed houses that told nothing of the dreams being dreamed inside their walls. A city I had seen only through moving windows. Three hours from Buenos Aires, right across the river, and yet a mystery. Somewhere in the city was the house where Gabriel had grown up, where he would arrive alone in a few days with who knew what excuse for my absence, *Sorry, Mamá, she ran away in the middle of the night,* embarrassed and abandoned, his mother serving him more bread in quiet triumph, *Just as well, forget about her, you'll find a better girl.* I stared out at Montevideo and marvelled at how little I knew of the world beyond my home, for all my dutiful studies of classroom history. Even as close as here, in Uruguay, in this capital across the water, songs surely lurked at every corner – ballads, arias, dirges, tangos, chants, laments – and rippled through the unknown streets. Uruguay also had its secret wounds and stains. I wondered how they haunted the city. I wondered how my skin might feel if I remained here, pretending I could trade one set of wounds for another. I would disembark from the bus and simply wander without stopping until I lost my sense of direction, my foothold, my memories, my name. A blank slate of a woman, roaming the Montevideo streets, she lost her shoes, she lost herself, have you seen her, the wild hair, the look on her face? Will she ever stumble on her lost self again? And if she does, will she wear it or deem it torn beyond repair? But I did not disembark. Instead, I caught the 6:56 a.m. ferry home across the Río de la Plata. Wan light stroked the water the whole way.

He is still with Gloria, has been with her for an eternity, a swath of liquid moments that spill over any boundaries of time, she has been labouring and labouring and now the guards have come with a bed on wheels and a blindfold and chains, *no please not chains* but no one hears him, they tie her down and mask her eyes and roll her down a hall of gloomy doors that look the same and have no names or numbers to identify them or what lurks behind them, he follows them into an elevator that sinks down to the basement floor and down a hall into a bare room where two female nurses wait, the guards deposit their cargo and depart. Gloria is transfigured by the journey, she is naked and restrained and cannot see, the strong tongues of her hands cannot run across her body, and he cannot touch her either in the sour light of this room, he is pushed against the wall and cannot reach her, he is helpless to do anything but watch, Gloria is pinned and open, her belly huge as a pale whale, she is heaving like a beached whale, she sweats, her mouth is wrenched into a moan but he can't hear it and perhaps the moan is its own whale song, a sound that could travel for miles under the sea and be understood, recognised, an under-water music that speaks everything that never can be spoken and yet must be, must be, hurls out of her wideflung throat just as something else hurls out elsewhere, hurls slowly slowly through the tunnel of her flesh, her legs are spread wide open to the air and to the nurses who won't speak to her, they've been instructed not to do so, they know nothing about this woman exposed on the table except what they can guess, and they try not to guess, they are in a basement with no windows and it's dark and the first nurse would like some fresh air and a cigarette, the second nurse would like to bury her face in her man's and feel his hands rip off her dress and make her forget this place, this woman, stripped of name and clothes and sight but isn't she lucky she's allowed to scream although they cannot understand the sound as they aren't underwater, never have been, their touch is cool and professional, they don't remind her to push, they don't say *you can do this,* push, Gloria, push, Gloria, you can do this look you're doing it, he forms the words he never had the chance to say but Gloria cannot hear them and she also does not need them, she is not just pushing, she is bursting, breaking, growling, swelling, crashing, he has never seen her face like this, she looks like she could tear the world to pieces, her sex is large and throbbing and it splits open like a fruit that cannot bear its own ripeness, it widens until he glimpses flesh inside that is not hers, smooth, hairy, glistening, just a tiny teardrop patch of flesh at first and then more as Gloria's sex opens even further, becoming larger, the second nurse wraps gloved fingers around the head as it slips out, there is a face, there are cries, he cannot hear them but he sees the tiny fishmouth pop open and the eyes crunch (and there she is, the girl, you won't recall this place or this moment or your very first cries but they are yours and perhaps this moment will stay with you as you grow up, forming a silent nest inside your body, in your chest or nape or hips or spine), and Gloria's face changes again, falls open in wonder, she arches back as far as the chains will let her and the little body abandons her like a moth flying from its broken chrysalis. The nurses examine the baby, hold her upside down and smack her buttocks as if to ensure that she is made of materials solid enough to withstand the pressures of this world. Gloria breathes with her whole body, and when the afterbirth has come and gone and the nurses sponge her down and dry her off and the baby's cries seem to have settled into whimpers, she tells them *thank you,* the water is warm and the hands gentle but when she says *boy or girl? boy or girl?* the nurses, well-trained and afraid, wheel her from the room without an answer.

On my way back from Gabriel's apartment, before returning to the house with its wet guest, I stopped at a neighbourhood grocery store, where all the cans and cuts of meat stood in a fog. I could barely see the aisles because of what had happened to the air inside my mind, how unspeakably clear it had become. On the outside I was placing items in my basket like an ordinary woman in an ordinary world, but inside the world had cracked wide open and out swirled its stories in an unrelenting mesh of obvious truths, from genesis to denouement.

Once there was a boy whose name was Héctor. He was little and his father hit him and broke the jaw of the turtle that he loved, but he was a good boy who grew up to work hard and be proud of his pressed uniform and the strength he swore to use to serve his country. He would be the kind of man whose chest would glint with medals and whose presence stirred the perfect mix of awe and fear. He would hide his tender places and reserve them for his future child – only for her – to see. He married a girl called Luisa who had found her heart in the galleries of Madrid and then dashed it against a black and maroon canvas, leaving a sour cavity in its place, but who still mustered enough emotion to make vows to him in the most expensive wedding dress her family could find, a dress that should only portend great fruitfulness and multiplying of their goodness as the holy word had deemed for them at the very start of time.

They longed for a child, but no child came in the first years, a fact that brought surprise and a slim thread of gossip to their circles – and then the country changed and their dream came true, thanks to the intercession of God and to the natural order of things. They had a girl, or rather, they could not have her so they stole her from people whose existence was being erased as though they'd only lived in pencil. Surely, in their minds, it was not so much a stealing as a saving, an act of grace that followed an inevitable erasure and that, wrapped in silence, would itself disappear in the forgotten folds of time. The stolen girl or saved girl grew up without knowledge of the bitter glue that made her family, and she loved with her whole heart the man with the pressed uniform and wounded turtle, a man who sat beside her singing lullabies in the dark, smelling of scotch, and when he asked her in the dark *Do you love your dad?* she said *Yes,* and when he said *And will you always? no matter what?* She said, again, *Yes, yes,* and meant it with every cell of her body, even when, much later, she learned about the bodies he had treated like pencil strokes intruding on the canvas of the world, even then she said the *Yes* that surely made her monstrous a monster-girl, deformed by love – but that could not be helped, because this too, this loving of one's father, is the natural order of things.

And now the girl, in fact a woman but inside her skin the girl, still and always that same girl, walked down the street from the grocery store to the house that was not only haunted by a wet ghost of the past but had been haunted all her life by so many lies and shadows. And her feet carried her home or to the place she had been primed to always think of as her home, her feet braver than the rest of her, braver than the hands that gripped the grocery bags too tightly, the eyes that stung, the throat pulled shut by unseen string, the knees that melted as she fumbled with her key inside the lock and pushed open the door to find the smell of rotting apples and bright fish still present to surround her, and inside the house, the red pool that had held her as a small girl who bathed in lies, and there, inside the pool, the man or not-man whom she had longed to see all day and dreaded also and who, she now saw with her fresh and terrible lucidity, was beautiful. Beautiful. The drops along his skin resembled tears.

♣

She arrives home at last, and stands in the centre of the room without putting down her bags. She stares at him with an animal intensity. She stares at the water that surrounds him, high and deep and warm.

He thinks, It's over. She's tired of me. I'll apologise, I'll leave if I must, even though there's nowhere to go.

But then she comes to his side. Her eyes are wet.

Very quietly, she says, I know who you are.

THREE

11

Cradle

And the room becomes a cradle of light, holding them close. The walls and furniture disappear into shadows beyond the small sphere that holds everything and anything that matters, just him and the girl.

A thousand questions swarm in him. He cannot form them all at once. How do you know?

For many reasons, she says. The fact that you came here, to this house of all the houses in the country. And things about my family. And your eyes.

He longs to see his eyes in a mirror, if only to search them for hints of her, the annunciation of her coming in the slope and hue.

Now I want to ask you everything.

Ask me.

I don't know where to start.

Anywhere.

What was her name?

Your mother?

She is silent.

Her name was Gloria.

What was she like?

His mind explodes with light, and he says, She was beautiful. Stubborn. Sometimes she laughed in her sleep. She talked too loud in restaurants, everybody looked.

The girl says nothing.

He tries to gather more memories for her, tries to gather words to translate memory into sound. The gathering is laborious. He says, She came from Azul. She moved to the city when she was thirteen. We met in a bookstore, in the middle of the night. She liked to take long walks and get lost on purpose, just to see what she would find around the next corner and the next.

How old was she?

About your age.

And she disappeared?

They took her. When they took me, they took her.

He stops telling. At the brink of his lips is the image of her tied to a chair, bruised, blindfolded, pregnant, before a dozen black boots pushed him down. But he doesn't want to tell the image. He leaves the vague words *took her* in its place. It is an act of protection, a paltry replacement for the many years in which he could not fold his wings around the girl, but it is all he has. Instead, he says, You look like her.

I do?

You have her mouth, her hair.

Her hand rises to her lips, instinctively. And when she – when they took her. She was carrying me?

Yes. She was carrying you.

She stops, seems to gather herself to go on. When you arrived here. Did you already know?

No.

How long have you known?

Some days.

You got here anyway, though, without knowing.

Yes.

How can that be?

How can any of this be?

She moves to the sofa and lights a cigarette. They are quiet together. The air is unbearably full; it shimmers with a translucent weight that strains to spill out. He feels the physical distance between them as an ache throughout his skin, the little nest of their world stretched out too far, holding too much; but then, as if she too felt the pull, she comes back to the pool and sits close beside him. He is relieved. Smoke curls toward the ceiling, and she watches it with the focus of a hunter.

What are you thinking now? he asks.

I can't say it.

Why not?

Some things should not be said aloud.

No?

No.

All things can be spoken.

Bullshit.

It's true.

I'm afraid.

Say it anyway.

I was thinking about you. If you hadn't died. How it would have been for me. Who I would have been.

You would have been yourself.

But not the same self I am now.

What makes the self?

Experiences. Acculturation.

What else?

I don't know.

What's within you.

She says, I don't know what was within me and what got put there by my life as it was lived.

You can never know that.

No.

But there is a you that was there before you were born and that nobody shaped or changed or could have changed, not Gloria, not me, not the others.

How do you know that?

From the water.

What water?

The water I was in after I died.

She is silent.

Who would you like to have been?

I don't know, she says. Right now I can't even tell who I'll be in the morning. I feel completely naked, completely stripped of my own life. Like I've taken off the lies and there's nothing left. I don't know how else to explain it.

Her cigarette goes out; she lights another, and as she does, the small flame briefly illuminates her face. And he thinks, I would give anything, anything, ten years with my soft parts tied to their machines, to have stayed with you and watched you grow in place of the man you call your father.

Tell me about him.

Who?

Your other father.

She turns away.

He loves you?

Yes. I don't know. I don't know what that word means anymore.

He was good to you?

Yes. Overall. He has been a good father.

He moves his toes underwater, curls them shut.

He sang me to sleep. I was always clothed and fed. He wanted what was best for me, or what he thought was best.

It is not the whole story – he can feel in his bones that the portrait is incomplete, like a face cast half in light and half in shadow, and because of this, or perhaps because of something else, he longs to curse the man who could rightly be called a beast, an imposter, a prison warden disguised in father's clothing. He rallies all his strength into the task of reining himself in. He must not burst, he must not rage, and in any case he should be glad to hear that, in her early years, she experienced some doses of paternal tenderness, whatever their source. He must be gentle with the girl; he must control himself, be understanding. He must accept – must strain to accept – that she is not only discovering her parents on this night, but also losing them, or rather, losing the other parents who for years and years were the only ones she had. And no matter who they are or what they've done, they are her parents also. They raised her. Their fingerprints are indelible in her mind. He rails against this fact, in full knowledge that the fact will not be moved.

And you still love him.

Would you hate me for it?

Never.

How can you be sure?

I am sure.

Her voice turns to a whisper. Did you see him there?

Where?

In the place you were when you disappeared.

He glances at the wedding photo on the bookshelf, at the groom with the searching, restless gaze. No. I don't think so.

She looks relieved.

But most of the time my eyes were covered, I couldn't see.

Oh.

He was there?

I don't know. It might not have been the same place. She lowers her head, and hair curtains her face. You will. You'll hate me.

How could I ever?

Because of him.

But you're not him.

I'm his daughter – or I was. I thought I was.

His hands are not your hands.

But I was here.

You were a child.

I've defended him. I still defend him, she says, and pain throbs in her voice. I found out about his work and still said nothing.

It doesn't matter.

How could it not?

Because of who you really are.

And who is that? Who is that?

A memory juts into his mind, of the first time that he sensed her presence on this earth when she was still a scrap of flesh that had slipped into Gloria's body like the most carnal and tenacious miracle. He says, You are the glow.

What? What glow?

I'll try to tell you. Let me give you a memory, I will enter it and take you with me and tell it to you as it happens. It might take time. Will you listen?

She has been crying. She nods.

He shuts his eyes and dives into his mind.

He was terrified, not ready, but Gloria had room for nothing but delight. Six weeks, she said, the heart has formed two chambers, it is beating. A head has formed.

With eyes and ears?

No ears. Not yet. Just hollows where the aural passages will be.

Ah.

Stop looking so scared.

Who says I'm scared?

She laughed. I do. Come here.

He approached her and she put his hand to her belly, which felt the same as always, smooth and taut and warm, coaxing him down into the waist of her skirt.

Shhp, not now.

Why not?

I want you to feel my belly.

I feel it, it's sexy, you're sexy.

Not that. The baby.

Embryo.

She rolled her eyes. Just listen for it with your hand.

It's too early for that.

It's not. Just listen.

She was beautiful, he was distracted by the late afternoon light stroking her neck. This memory is vivid, rife with light, he can see the way it slants in through the tiny kitchen window, she sat at the kitchen table looking up at him with parted lips, he could never understand how a shy man like him had landed in the arms of such a woman. In a home with her, married, contemplating this phenomenon, *six weeks.*

He obliged her, placed his hand on her belly, waited. He felt nothing, no motion, no change. He tried to listen with his hand: six weeks are you in there? can you feel me? will you know me when you finally come out? He imagined a tiny being with eyes and no ears, you can't hear, you can't see, or if you can there's only the dark inside of Gloria, your nose your mouth your hands are coming and Gloria and I will be your template, and we will wipe your caca, wake to your cries, will you ever let us sleep? And then he felt it. A delicate glow beneath his palm, as if the nerves inside his hands had suddenly gained a seventh sense. As if his nerves themselves had found a spark in which they recognised themselves, a light in Gloria's body that was not the normal lust or warmth he had felt in her before; and it could have been his own imagination, but he could swear that near the centre of his palm, a few centimetres away, buried in his wife's flesh, there lay an essence that was linked to him and yet was not him, that was linked to Gloria but was not her, and that that essence glowed in a manner that had never in the history of the universe occurred anywhere else, but that belonged here, would be utterly itself, unique as a face or fingerprint but far more distilled, now, in its primeval state, unformed yet complete, beaming toward his hand, a pure unadulterated essence caught in a long slow gesture of growth.

Gloria was watching him closely.

Are we ready for this? he asked.

We will be.

How do you know?

I know.

The light had turned a deeper gold: in moments it would fall away to dusk. It fell across her shoulders like a shawl. He slid his hand down the waist of her skirt. Now can we?

She laughed. A brass bell in her laugh. We can, we can.

Her skin tasted of salt and summer heat. Her body on the kitchen table, legs wrapping around him, legs that could have crushed him as he slid into her body, which now evidenced new power, and this is a vivid memory, her body is damp and passionate, exuding fierce ecstatic joy at being entered, at breeding life, at being lit up from within by another being, at being whole and alive in a world that has not yet disappeared her from it, not yet revealed what is done to people in the unseen basements of the world. The sex ties them and unties them, binds the three of them into a burning knot and dissolves the boundaries between them, all at once. It is Gloria he is making love to but he can't help speaking also to the new one, the glow, the embryo, he pushes and pushes toward its nesting place and he is scared of disturbing it or revealing something children and babies should never see, he is scared that it is wrong to be together like this, the three of them rocking and whirling in a single bowl of heat, and yet an unknown instinct makes him do it anyway, makes him greet the new one, feel its presence, reach for its glow with the same part of his body that sent the seeds out hungry to create it, he reaches over and over, Gloria's thighs are warm and wide as gates but he will never arrive into her centre so he greets it from a distance, forms the word *hello* and sends it searing through his sex into the dark mysterious mazes inside Gloria.

That was just the beginning. Six weeks became seven and eight and ten and twenty, twenty-eight, each week a new revelation. Gloria's shape became a living testament to the miracle (and was it not, he thought, a miracle, for all that it had happened a trillion times in this world, and for all the carnal truths that caused this maculate conception?). He caught

Gloria stroking her belly in the shower, and in the morning as she dressed, and at the stove as she stirred onions in the pan. She not only stroked, she also murmured, divulging secrets or promises to the one inside. Private trysts not even he could enter. Gloria abounded with names, what about this one, or, if not, perhaps this for a boy and that for a girl, how could a single word ever sing the full resonance of this baby's identity to the world? She was a changed woman, the sharp edges of her temperament rounded into a voluptuous, almost complacent capacity for pleasure. She basked in the attention of strangers, who approached her on the street or in the market and placed their hands on her belly, *oh how lovely*, they rubbed her body without asking permission or so much as saying hello, *it's a girl, I can feel it*, or *it must be a boy*, and it enraged him that so many people had the nerve to touch his wife in public without even knowing her name. At first he tried to stop them, but Gloria intervened, *let them, it doesn't matter*, and then he saw that she not only didn't mind: she beamed at their touch, shone like a lantern, did not experience the touch of strangers as an invasion but rather as a form of benediction, even worship, the world offering its awe and blessings with many hands. It was her turn to walk the road of the madonna, and she savored it, every bit of it, even the great miracles of swollen ankles and indigestion, which she complained about with all the thrall of revelation. It's just incredible, she would say, I can barely bend to put on my own shoes. She took unparalleled pleasure in being pregnant. See how she stood before the mirror, caressing her round belly when she thought no one was looking. She did this naked sometimes so her touch could reach closer to the child-to-come. See how she prowled the apartment at night, awakened by kicks, foraging for chocolate *alfajores*. See how she wept for no reason or for all the reasons of the world, gazing out the window at secret messages only she could read in the skies. And all that time, it was you in there, bulging her waist and slowing her steps and flushing her cheeks with euphoria. It was your glow that she borrowed on the exalted days, your flush on her face. You were perfect then as you are perfect now. And just as you were in her then she is now in you, in your eyes and ears and ankles, the soft beneath your fingernails, the blood racing through your veins toward the muscle of your heart. The shape of her, it held your shape and gave it a place to begin, and there, right there inside her, you became yourself, the Who of you that you still are and that will always have its roots in the pure Who of Gloria: while you live and while cells hold their twisting secrets in your body, you are never fully lost and she is not entirely gone.

He returns to the room, looks up at her. She has lit another cigarette, and faces the wall. He told too much at once. Her first night hearing about her mother, and he talks about sex. He is an idiot. He has lost touch with the etiquette of the living, the terrains that are not meant to be discussed and that fathers are certainly not supposed to share with their children; from where he sits he has forgotten to see lust as a hushed secret rather than a radiant life force. He thinks, I'm a fool, I've lost her now, she's going to close back up, but then she faces him again and there is naked emotion in her face.

Was it really like that?

All that and more.

She stares at him. What's your name?

I don't have one.

How can that be?

The waters took it.

What was your name before the water?

He strains his mind, but it is no use. I don't know. It's gone.

That's all right, she says gently. That's all right. She becomes quiet and they sit, together, in that room, in a long silence that is not like any other they have shared. It is an amniotic silence that holds them together more than it keeps them apart. He could hover in it with her forever. Time stretches. Time slows and speeds and does not *tic tac tic* with any artificial calibrations; it melts; it pours. She is on the floor beside him, so close he smells her cigarettes and the sweet exhalations of her hair, and she is awake to him, she has unfurled herself, there are no veils left in her eyes. And this is more than just a night: it is a home carved into wasteland, a candle in black sky, salt on the tongue of the dying, defying the demands of oblivion.

He starts to hum. The sound rises from him without thinking. He has not sung since long before he died, and his voice is coarse at first, thick and wet at the back of his throat, but then it loosens and falls across the melody like a stream along stones. What is the song? It is old; he did not make it. His mother sang it to him as a boy and all the nights were crisp and safe and tinged with God, yes, now he knows, it is a lullaby. He hummed it into Gloria's belly in the darkness, under bedsheets, when the belly was wide and full and beckoned the admiring hands of strangers. In bed, at night, no one could touch Gloria but him, and he would touch and touch and sometimes hum and wonder, *Can you hear me?* How he wanted to be heard. To be remembered more than all the others. To hum his way into the tiny heart of the almost-child.

He hums, and his daughter sits beside the red pool and listens. Her gaze is on the wall, on the painting of the ship, but her head cocks toward the sound. The melody meanders and does not break the good silence between them, but rather feeds it, strengthens it, pours fluid into fluid into fluid.

The sound of his voice surrounded me and I wanted to crawl into it, wrap myself in the lullaby, its great white cloth of sound. I wished I could live inside this night, not just now, but always, so that from this moment forward, no matter where I went or what I saw, this night would cover and surround me, be a filter for the rest of the world. I was enveloped. I was carried. I longed to be carried this way for the rest of my life. I longed to have been carried this way when I was small, by this man, his voice, his company. There was a woman I could have been if I had lived all my life within the reach of this man's voice, if this man had stayed in the world to hold me from the beginning. That woman would never exist. I could not be rewritten. And yet, in those moments, in the delicate warmth of that night, that woman seemed more real than me, more rightful than the Perla who inhabited my skin. I wanted to reach out to her, wherever she was, somewhere in the torn corners of the cosmos where our might-have-beens skulk through the twilight, and I wanted to touch her, understand her, at the very least look her in the eyes. This alternative self. This woman never broken at the root. This Perla from whose mouth I longed to hear the words LOVE and TRUTH and FAMILY, to know how she'd pronounce them, whether she'd cast them out in easy sparks or the long slow syllables of song. Because I, the false twin, the Perla who had been allowed to exist, no longer knew how to hold those words. I closed my eyes. My new father, my first father, sang on. The melody sank into me, gentle, phosphorescent. He longed for me, despite everything the world had done. I wanted to absorb his stories, make them mine. I wanted to believe that there were threads between us all – between me, him, and Gloria – that had shuddered but not broken, that could stretch under the surface of reality, part of a secret webbing that glistens in the realms beyond time. Those threads felt like the only things I had left in the world.

Dawn came. It came slowly, reluctantly, as if the sun itself hated to impinge on the sounds and silence of this night, but it still arrived, and found us sitting together in the living room, close and quiet and awake. In the pale light, I put out another cigarette and left it on the pile of crushed carcasses in the ashtray. Then I moved to empty water from the pool. Cup to bucket, cup to bucket. He hummed again as I poured water, this time an aimless, wandering tune. I stared at the bucket full of his water. I didn't want to pour it down the drains in the house anymore – not the bathtub, nor the shower, nor the sinks. I wanted to spill it in the sun. I took the bucket outside, to the yard, to the old oak that always spoke to me of childhood climbs, reading in the shade, dextrous ants I watched on long hot summer days, wondering, where are they all going? where are they from? what is happening in their minuscule ant minds? I poured the water at the base of the tree. It left black streaks in the dirt that would be gone by the middle of the morning. Some of the water might evaporate in the sun, but the rest of it would sink deep into the earth and offer itself to the tree's roots. And the roots, I thought, would surely consume every drop.

12

Empty Hands, Clear Water

How, the book asked, *can a disappeared child form a true identity?*

I held the pages open in the morning light. The guest had finally closed his eyes; he had gone to sleep, or to whatever place he went to when he rested. I hadn't slept at all. I knew that I should, the night had been long and wakeful and my eyes burned with fatigue, but I could not do it. My mind was too crowded, as was this room, which palpitated with a thousand memories, thronging from the corridors of the past, demanding to be shaken open and seen anew. I saw my child-self eating ice cream from a crystal dish and also eating candy that had spent the day in Scilingo's trouser pocket while my father (could I still call him that?) and his friend Scilingo drank martinis and talked close by. I saw my mother (could I still call her that?) gently stroking the blooms of geraniums in those first days when they still received water and nurturance and were not yet left to die. I saw myself curled up with library books on the sofa beside Mamá while she read a magazine, our bodies close enough so that her delicate scent was in my lungs. I saw myself playing a card game with my father, *Don't let me win, Papá,* and the way his eyebrows rose in exaggerated alarm, *Of course not, Perlita, that victory was all yours,* and I also saw myself alone, the night Papá found out about my story in the newspaper and said *Oh yeah and who are you* and left me standing still as a pillar beside the sofa, unable to sit, unable to make a sound.

Hordes of memories, too many of them. I could not stand to look at them, but I also could not sleep surrounded by their clamor, so instead I turned to the library book I had brought home the day before. A book for children of the disappeared, written by Las Abuelas of the Plaza de Mayo, decades into their search, addressing the grandchildren they still longed to find. I looked over at the wet man, resting in his pool. His mother could be one of them. She could still be searching. I tried to picture her, a time-worn woman living just a handful of miles away, separated from her son (and granddaughter) by immense gulfs of reality, carrying the son's photo through the streets at marches, raised high above her head.

I leafed back to a photograph in the book of an Abuela with a white kerchief around her face and eyes like mournful wells. She gazed at me so intently that I could almost have believed that I was the still image and she the breathing presence. I wondered whether she might be the one.

But she was one of many. There were five hundred stolen infants, so it was believed, and only sixty so far had had their identities restored. *Restored,* the book said; as if the identity I had before birth were simply waiting for me, a folded piece of clothing, ready to slip back into, a perfect fit. As though I could simply become the woman who would have blossomed with her true parents if the nation had not fallen prey to the Process. *Restored,* like an old painting, the cracks and faded regions returned to their original state, to make it seem as though the intervening years had never occurred. I recoiled from the notion. I did not want to erase the person that I'd been all these years when I did not know where I came from. However false my identity might be, it was the only one I had. Without it I was nothing.

I wondered whether Las Abuelas, if I went to them, would want me to do this, to disown the person I had been. The thought made something ache below my rib cage.

I read on. These disappeared children, some were taken as babies, others while in their mothers' wombs. I looked at pictures of infants, from before they were lost, and I searched their wide primordial eyes for tales they could not tell. I did not want to read about the mothers, but I did it anyway. The book told me about things that were done to those women, pregnant women, in the same straits as the rest of the disappeared, enduring the same nightmares, except for the shackled hours of birth after which they might or might not see the baby before it disappeared from them, one disappearance inside of another, layers and layers of vanishing.

I closed my eyes. I did not want to think of my birth but the images arose and there were chains, blood, a dim medieval dungeon of a room although I knew that part was just my imagination. So many holes in memory and knowledge for imagination to fill. I had never really heard the false story of my birth, growing up, nor even seen pictures of Mamá pregnant. Oh, she'd said, I didn't want pictures taken of me, everything swelled up, you know, my calves, my face, forget about the waist. About the birth itself, she said only, The pain, you can't imagine, with a vague wave of her hand. Another lie, of course. It seemed that I would have to scour every memory of my childhood, that every centimetre was tainted with lies, that the cleaning and sorting would take the rest of my life. Even then there would always be holes, things I could never know, unless I filled the empty space with my imaginings.

Like the imagined picture of a man in Navy uniform arriving home from work one day with a squirming bundle in his arms.

Héctor, what's this?

Our baby.

How can that be?

I got a call in the office.

From the adoption agency?

From above them, direct from the government.

And the waiting list?

Don't ask too many questions, Luisa. Don't worry, she's ours. She was an orphan, no one to come for her.

A girl?

A girl. Her name is Perla.

Perhaps it went that way, perhaps not. But this version seemed plausible. Above all, it seemed right that he would have been the one to choose my name. When I was a child, he always said *I'm the one who named you, Perla,* with such emphasis that it now seemed like the only detail I could believe. I was his treasure, after all, wasn't that still true? A girl like gold to him. Stolen gold, I couldn't help but think. Which made me feel a bit like a spoil of war, an object claimed from battle, as warriors have done since ancient times. Gold, spears, slaves. Girls traded back and forth since the days of Troy. Girls raised to be loyal to their owners, so loyal you could remove the glimmering shackles and they'd stay, of course they'd stay, because after all the love circling their ankles was heavier than iron and in any case where could they go?

Stop it, I thought, these are ridiculous thoughts, you're not a slave, you're a grown woman, free to leave this house.

So will you?

The question curled open. It flared its enormous petals. I looked around at the bookshelf with its childhood photo and its bride and groom facing the future with closed mouths, the blue painting and still curtains and the patio beyond it that had once held too many flowerpots to count, the wet man resting in the pool whose humming lullabies had accompanied me all night, and I let all of it tear me open to see that I already knew the answer. I could not live here another day. I could not stay here in this haunted house where I would never form what the book called *a true identity,* and though I might never be *restored* – though I did not want to be *restored* if it meant erasure – though I still didn't know exactly where I was going or who I wanted to become or what it would take to carve the road of becoming, I knew in that moment that I wanted nothing more than to rip apart the self I had worn like heavy clothing that suffocates you but that you cling to for fear of the cold. I needed to be cold. I needed to be stripped down, hungry, alive – and also close to what was not alive, this phantom, because that, too, I thought, is who I really am. I wanted to spend a thousand and one more nights with this wet man, because he was linked to me and I to him. I wanted to be close to him and close to Perla, the stripped version of myself, I wanted to look in the mirror in the morning and know whom I was greeting, be capable of stroking her glass face no matter what she'd done.

The sun was ripe and heavy in the room. I had spent most of the morning perched here with the book as my sole companion. The guest was still asleep but I had catapulted to a space beyond sleep. All I could think of was the phone, sitting still and ready in the study. What would happen if I called my parents in Punta del Este, what would come out of my mouth. Do it now, I thought, before sense returns and fear sets in. I went to the study, sat in the plush leather chair, and dialled.

He wakes to the sound of her steps, walking away, down the hall. Last night rushes back to him and he thinks, Let tonight be the same, and the next night and the next, a long chain of incandescent hours, what a glorious future, the girl and him, sharing a room, sharing a sphere, his humming and her hair, his water and her thoughts, together and together and together.

The room is bright with day. The sofa's aggression has been silenced forever. The melted clocks in their dry landscape do not tick. The swan still bends its head, but there is no sense of burden to the posture, only a bowing to the mysteries inside or around it. Now he loves them, clock and swan and sofa, the way a fish loves the coral reef and stone and current that make his water possible, without thought, without the slightest flicker of a fin, *yes, here we all are, intrinsic to the ocean*. He will stay in this communion as long as the fates allow, this room is everything and every thing is contained within this room, or will be when she comes and stays and he can drink the molten air of their shared presence, and this, he thinks, is the true curve of the world – now I glimpse it: all things are blended under the surface like the mass of us were blended in the water, it's the separateness of skin and rock and mind that is the great illusion. We are not discrete; we are not solid. People and things and even cities are meant to flow together, they are meant to connect, and this is why we're always full of longing, the way I long for the girl, and the girl longs for truth, and the truth longs for volume, and volume longs for people to hear it, and people long for – what? – for everything, air, home, violence, chaos, beauty, hope, flight, sight, each other. Always, whether to stroke or maim, each other, above all.

He glows with his new knowledge, wants to share it with her, waits for her return. But then he hears her voice from a room down the hall. She has left the door open. Is she talking to herself? No, she is on the phone. Her voice sounds tight; he has never heard her sound this way. He strains to listen. He strains to understand.

My father answered the phone on the third ring. 'Hello?'

'Hi, it's me.'

'Ah, Perla. Hello.' His mood was amiable, relaxed. 'We were about to leave for the beach.'

'I was just calling to see how you were doing.'

'We're doing great, terrific. The only problem is that we have to pack up so soon.'

'Yes.'

'And you? How are you?'

'Fine.'

'Are you sure? You sound strange.'

'Do I?'

'I said it, didn't I? What have you been up to?'

He sounded as though he was really asking, and before I could stop myself, before I could pull the veil back over my own voice, I said, 'Thinking.'

'Hm! About what?'

'A lot of things.' I paused. My hands were shaking. 'For example, what exactly you did. And whether you would do it again.'

'Do what again?'

'The war. What happened at ESMA.'

We were both shocked by my words and timbre. Silence.

'Why are you bringing that up now?'

'It's been on my mind.'

He made no sound, and I thought the pause would never end; I was convinced that he had withdrawn from the topic, shut the window, drawn the drapes. But then he said, very softly, 'Perla. For God's sake.'

'For God's sake what?'

'Don't do this.'

But even if I'd wanted to I couldn't have stopped the woman who had taken possession of my body and tongue. 'Did you know their names?'

'Whose names?'

'The people under your charge. The' – disappeared, destroyed, disfigured – 'subversives.'

'Do you have to bring this up on my vacation?'

'Yes. I do.'

'Why?'

'I've been wondering about my parents.'

'Well, look, we never – '

'What did you do to my parents?'

He was silent again; it was a cavernous silence in which the question echoed, echoed, echoed. 'What the hell are you talking about?'

'I think you know, Papá.'

'Look,' he said, and now his voice was calm, carefully calibrated, a closely gauged voltage, 'you've been talking to the wrong people.'

'I want you to answer me.'

'Somebody has confused you.'

'I'm not confused.'

'You are. It's better to talk about this in person. We'll be home tomorrow night, we can talk then and clear the whole thing up. All right?'

He would not answer. He would never answer. It was no use continuing, and also no use pretending that the bomb had not been launched. I imagined the woman who was playing the part of my mother, across the room from him, sitting stiffly in her bathing suit as she followed one side of the conversation. *Perla,* I thought, *what have you done?* 'Fine.'

'None of this is what you think it is.'

My turn to go silent.

'Don't let anyone put ideas in your head. You can't be too careful these days, there are a lot of people out there spreading lies.'

I laughed, then – I couldn't help it, the sound escaped before I had a chance to bite it down.

'What the hell is so funny?'

'Nothing.'

'Perla.' He sounded nervous now. 'We'll chat when I get home, I promise. And then you can ask me anything you like.'

Anything? Anything at all? *Papá, this is our houseguest, don't mind his dripping skin – have you met before?*

'Okay?'

I was silent.

'Perla?'

I almost hung up or shouted at him, my hand burned to slam the receiver and my throat burned with unsaid words, but I did not do either because I suddenly saw my future clearly, one in which there would be no chat when he got home, a future in which I held this phone call in a locked drawer of my heart labelled THE LAST TIME I HEARD HIS VOICE. And this made me feel both free and numb, an arm on the brink of amputation, saying a dazed good-bye to the body. For this reason, and this reason only, I stayed on the phone.

I said, 'Okay.'

'Be careful out there. Don't think too much.' He paused, and I heard some shuffling. 'Your mother sends a kiss.'

'Okay.'

'Well? Do you send one for us?'

He said it with a laugh, trying to ease the mood, but I could hear the strain in his tone, almost a begging. I thought of leaving him in that position, ending the call with his question suspended and unanswered – he had left my question in that same state, after all – and perhaps I should have, but I could not bring myself to do so. I was a coward. A coward, or just a daughter, after all. 'Of course, Papá.'

'*Hasta pronto*. I love you.'

'*Adiós.*' I thought of saying *I love you* back; the words hung silent in my mouth; but before my mouth could comply, I saw my hand reach for the telephone cradle and press down. I heard a click as the line went dead.

I put the receiver down. The wood-panelled walls seemed to respire around me. *Now you've done it,* they breathed, *you can't turn back, the cutting has begun.* Even though my father was across the water in Uruguay, I was convinced that he would burst through the door at any moment and rush up to me, his hands landing on mine with warm authority, *Perla, what's all this crap, you're not going anywhere.* And then he would find a way to make me stay. But of course he didn't break through the door, I remained alone, and I wish I could tell you that I was glad he didn't come, that I sat there victorious and elated with no trace of longing for his presence. That's the story I would like to tell, but it would be a lie. I stared at the door for a long time. The walls bristled and pulsed around me. I felt sick. I felt gutted. I wanted to put my head down on the man called Héctor's desk and sleep for days, weeks, the rest of my life. But they were coming home the following night; I couldn't sleep yet, I had to act.

I picked up the phone receiver and dialed another number.

'Hello?'

'Gabriel.'

'Perla.' He sounded relieved and wary at the same time.

'How are you?'

'Fine,' he said curtly.

'I miss you.'

He was silent.

'I mean it.'

'Fine. Whatever.'

'Look, I know I've been horrible to you, I don't even deserve to ask this and if I were you I don't think I'd say yes, but I need your help.'

He was quiet for a moment, in which I tried not to fidget.

'With what?'

'I need to leave this house.'

'You want to go out somewhere?'

'I mean leave for good.'

He was quiet again, and this time I sat utterly still. I felt a kind of preternatural ease now that the words were out.

'Are you okay?'

'I am. I think so. Maybe more than ever.' Perla, I thought to myself, make some sense. No, to hell with that, it's much too late for sense. 'You were right.'

'About what?'

'About my parents.'

'Oh.' His voice became infinitely gentle. 'Perla.'

'What you said on the beach. You were right.'

'How do you know?'

'It's hard to explain.'

'Try me.'

'I will. But I want to do it in person.' Better, I thought, to show him the ghost than to try to describe the last few days. How could any of it ever be put into words?

'You're brave, you know.'

'Me?'

'What you're going through. I can't even imagine.'

I closed my eyes. 'I'm not brave. I haven't gone through a thing, haven't lived a single instant that could be called authentic life.'

'If it wasn't life, then what was it?'

'I don't know. I feel like I'm disappearing.'

'Maybe it's the opposite.'

'What do you mean?'

'Maybe you're finally appearing.'

I looked past the bookshelves to the window, with its shred of visible sky. 'Out of nothing? And with nothing?'

'With your true self.'

'I don't have a true self.'

'Of course you do.'

'It's all been false.'

'What about us? Was that false?'

'No. No.'

Silence hung between us; I could almost hear him thinking. 'Have you talked to your parents? I mean the – '

' – I know which ones you mean. They're not here. They're on vacation, they come back tomorrow night.'

'So you want to leave before then.'

'Right.'

'Do you need a place to stay?'

'If I could. For a little while. Until I find my own place.'

'How will you manage that?'

'I'll find a job. I'll drop out of school.'

'You can't drop out.'

'Of course I can.'

'You don't have to, Perla. You can stay with me.'

Gratitude rushed through me, mixed with relief. But then I tried to imagine our lives together – him, me, and the guest – with that ridiculous pool installed forever in his living room. It was too much. 'Thank you, Gabo. Really. But you don't know what you'd be getting into. There's something I haven't told you yet.'

The line between us seemed to prickle.

'It's not what you think.'

'I don't know what to think. I don't know what you're saying.'

'And I don't know how to say it. It can't be said, I have to show you. Can you come over?'

'When?'

'Tonight, if you can.'

'How about nine o'clock?'

'Okay, nine o'clock. Could you drive? So I can take some things in your car.'

'Sure.'

'Thank you. I love you.'

'No kidding?'

'No kidding.'

'Say it again.'

I laughed. 'I love you.'

'Well then.' He sounded lighter. 'See you soon.'

We hung up. I sat back in my father's leather chair, the chair of the man I had always called my father. I tried to imagine Gabriel's face on meeting the guest, his shock or disgust or fascination. I hoped he would not run away, and would agree to help me move the man to the backseat of his car. We'll have to wrap him in a blanket, I thought, and perhaps a plastic tarp. I should take the red pool. I should take some of my clothes, books, childhood photos. Not everything, of course, just the things I can't live without. Which may be no things at all. It may be that there's nothing in this house that I can't live without, that I could walk out with empty hands and survive. And then the exhaustion I had evaded all these hours swept its plush black hood over me, and I gave myself to sleep. I dreamed of ants, millions of them, scaling the oak in the yard, climbing and climbing toward the sky.

The light is fading. The corners lose their sun. There is so much he could shout into the gathering darkness. The turtle enters on slow legs and stands in the centre of the room and it is good to see him. *Clack,* his hard jaws say to the shadows. *Clack.*

Hours have passed since the two phone calls, and she is still in the other room, completely silent. She must have fallen asleep. Let her rest, he thinks. And let her go. He cannot steal her life. He does not want to be a burden. How moving that she planned to take him. She is a kind girl – and courageous, too, the way she talked to the man who had been her father. But no, he cannot live with whoever she called next, whoever is coming tonight with a car and prying eyes. A certain Gabo. Whom she loves, she says, and he hopes this Gabo loves her back and will be good to her, treat her like the miracle she is. In any case, she has a place to go *and you have to let her go.* He looks around the room now and he loves it, loves the painting of the ship made with the same strokes as the sea, the curtains where he has seen shards of Gloria's body, the walls that have sung with blinding light, the sofa with whom he warred, the porcelain swan that longs to spread its hard white wings and tell its secrets in a slash of flight. Where else will he go? He has no idea. He will follow the pull. He closes his eyes and searches, dives, reels until he finds himself in the chamber with electric devices and trained men, he sees it clearly around him but it is different now, this is not his own memory, he is not the one tied to the mattress, it is an older hairy man who lies there writhing, he can see the man at the machine and the guard at the door and the doctor with his clipboard: the man at the machine is as calm as a captain at the helm of his ship, upright, broad-shouldered, prepared to steer through any waves that come; the guard is young and clean-shaven and earnest, he is doing his part to save his nation, he does not watch; the doctor makes notes on his clipboard as the man at the machine turns a dial and the small hairy naked man thrashes against his restraints, the doctor watching keenly, a man of science, he rubs his nose and nods to himself. He watches the four men from the ceiling. A dance, a strained choreography, four men in a bare room. He is lighter than air, floating, he can float out into the hallway and he must, something pulls him out into the hall and down it and he goes because *she is not far and I must find her,* past the shut doors of cells with covered peepholes, one after the other, he is not so much searching for something as moving toward it the way a shard of iron moves toward a magnet. The pull grows stronger as he travels up a flight of stairs and down a hall past a room where guards play *truco,* a card game, and watch television (and they seem bored, their eyes are glazed, they laugh but do not look at each other), down another hall to another room where he finds her. She lies shaking. She is curled up like a foetus, her belly is smaller now but not yet down to normal size. She is blindfolded and unrestrained, bleeding down her legs, the guards have just had a round with her, they have used her like a dog but you are not a dog, my Gloria, *tesoro, mi vida,* I am here with you and I will stretch the nothingness I'm made of and cover you like a blanket, can you feel me across the boundaries of space and death and time? Do you feel warmer, Gloria? I would like to swaddle you, enfold you with myself, the soft of my conscious-ness a layer to blunt the edge of any fall. He unfurls the swath of his naked mind and strokes her with it. It is her skin, the same skin he has touched on many sweaty nights and languid mornings, supple and a joy to touch, like the joy of coming home after a long journey. *You. Come home.* Her breathing softens, her thin fingers move in the air as if playing a very quiet song on a piano, sensing for wayward keys. She tilts her head back, and her lips part. Yes, Gloria, I'm here, I'm here. She feels him, she must feel him, he believes it with his whole translucent being, he feels her body relax beneath his intangible caress. They lie together for an infinite instant or a brief eter-nity. When the guards come in to cuff and take her, he drapes himself around her shoulders like an unseen weightless shawl and stays wrapped around her in the Army truck that rumbles through the night, toward the outskirts of the city, carrying its cargo of dazed blindfolded people pressed close together in the dark, naked people merging with each other and straining to breathe air thick with the smell of unwashed bodies. They cannot see where they are going but some of them must know, they hang their heads as if in sleep or prayer. Gloria sways with the motion of the truck. He sways with her, the human shawl, he knows this journey, recalls the truck that led to the airplane and he tries to stroke her body with the limp invisible cloth of his mind. Once, Gloria, we drove through the pampas and your profile was so beautiful against the wheat fields passing by, such long flat land, how I loved you then, how I love you now, remember the wheat fields, Gloria. The truck stops and the guards unload their cargo on a dirt field beside a barracks, command the people to line up in the beam of the headlights, though the people cannot see and so the guards arrange them with their own hands, the air is cool and fresh and he can feel Gloria take deep breaths of it, her first night air in months, dark and sweet with the breath of leaves and rocks and the lingering taste of the sun, and she has just inhaled deeply when the shots begin and the air stays coiled inside her, she never lets it go. The guards roll the crumpled bodies into the ditch nearby, already prepared, large enough to take the whole pile at once, a mouth in the earth that swallows them all. She is gone now, lost under one female body and one male and the spray of falling dirt, and he unwraps from the shell that does not hold her anymore and rises, rises, out of the mass grave and high over the land so that the guards and truck and disturbed slash of earth become small below him, now he knows, he has seen, he knows that it was earth that took her (not sea, not fire) and with this knowledge slashing through him he can surely find her, Gloria, the glint of you must be somewhere, burrowing through mountains, trapped in the bedrock, curled into tree roots, riding a river, roaming the blue vaults of the sky, I will rove and rove for you, and when I find you I will have so much to show and give and pour, we will be together soon, none of this is finished, we are not finished, it's a girl, it's a girl, her name is Perla, her hair is rich like yours and her mouth is yours God help her, I have spent moments with her that are safely folded in my memory, the moments live and live and cannot be undone, they are more powerful than bullets or planes and see, see, I carry them toward you, wherever you are. He is higher now, beyond the trees, so high he sees the city to the east, Buenos Aires, glimmering with the lights of the living on an ordinary night, these things all happened on an ordinary night, the river glimmers black and long beyond it and even though he doesn't know what he's becoming he is not afraid, he is ready to change, ready to search, ready to rise.

The room was almost dark when I woke up, surprised to find my face against a desk. I felt groggy, disoriented. I had meant to pack some things before Gabriel arrived, but now he'd be coming any moment. And something wasn't right in the house, though I didn't know what. It was a feeling, a buzzing sound, or perhaps an absence of sound. I wondered how my guest was doing. I had to see him.

But when I entered the living room he was not there. The pool overflowed with water that had spilled over the edges to the hardwood floor, but there was no one in it.

No, I thought, *No* and *No.*

I tore back the curtains, ran to the kitchen, searched the hall closet, opened the sliding doors to the backyard and looked and looked around the rosebushes, the silent oak, the dark and unrevealing sky. He was gone. I had no name to call for him, no syllables to send into the heavens. But I knew him, I thought, he was mine and I was his. Every cell of my body screamed for his return, but he did not come. The loss of him crashed over me, surging in a tidal wave of losses. Too many losses to measure. Too many to contain. The yard stood utterly silent, the house loomed at my back, even the skies were empty, unresponsive, thick and dark where are the stars? where is my father? where am I? And at that point I seemed to watch myself, as if I were not the woman standing in the yard but a pure field of sight, watching the woman as she turned and went inside, where she stared at the pool for a minute, then took her clothes off and stepped in. The water rose and spilled around her, onto the floor, snaking out toward the walls. She crouched there, naked, for a long time. She thought of everything and nothing. She wept. She looked at her empty hands through the clear water. And then, in a sudden act of alchemy, she became herself, nothing less and nothing more. I felt the warm water embrace my limbs, murmuring of times long gone and times that still awaited. I looked around the room. I could not let it stay like this, false and immaculate. I rose out of the pool and let my hands take over, they knew just what they wanted to do, they took charge and grasped the bucket, filled it at the pool, aimed, and cast water against the wall. I plunged the bucket again and a great wave collided against the leather sofa and ruined it for good. I kept going, soaking another wall, where the Dalí print dripped and puckered, its dry landscape deluged with sudden rain to twist the clocks into new shapes; the wall wept streams of tears; I threw more water and the painting of the ship glistened with fresh moisture and I heard a sound now, a woman groaning with her own voice, not caring anymore about the proper use of voices or the proper place for wetness, let the waters rise and drown the house and draw its entire structure out to sea. Now the bucket heaved again and waters – memory-water, almost unbearably clear – splashed along the bookcase, soaked into the books, toppled the wedding photograph of one man and one woman who smiled with their mouths closed, and I wanted their mouths to open and swallow the sea that enveloped their house, I wanted the whole house to pour and swim and sway under these waters, and the hands flew the bucket to the kitchen, to the study, flooded the leather chair and desk and rug and books whose pages would forever curl from the force of this deluge, and from the front hall came a ringing bell and then a thudding sound, over and over, what the hell could it be, back in the living room the floor was wet and all was wet and I was wet and naked and still throwing water when the thudding sound came back coupled by a muffled voice from outside, calling, *Perla? Perla?*

I went to open the door. Gabriel made a strange sound when he saw me.

'Come in.'

'What – '

'Quickly.'

He came in, and I closed the door and returned to the living room. He followed me and stood, uncertain, gaping at the drenched room. I felt as though I'd just risen from a trance. I tried to imagine how the place looked through his eyes, and searched for words to account for the state of things, the source of the pungent water, my days with a guest who had appeared and just as suddenly disappeared. But nothing came. In the meantime, Gabriel seemed to recover himself.

'So this is your house.'

'It's not my house.'

'Oh. Right.'

'It's their house. Héctor and Luisa's house.'

'I understand.'

He was studying me now. I felt my nakedness. I thought of inviting him to sit but there was no dry surface to offer, so I just stood and let him look at me. In that moment, I realised that no matter what words I chose and no matter how much time I spent in telling, I would never be able to express my full experience. If I tried, he might choose to believe me – or pretend to believe me, for my sake, kind as he was – or he might discount the stranger parts of my story and try to rationalise them away. But it didn't matter. No matter what he really thought, no matter what I did or did not say, what had happened in this room – everything I'd seen and felt and come to understand – was impossible to convey to him, or to anyone. There are some experiences that only you can enter, that only you can truly hold. They are too vast to be imparted. You cannot even hold them wholly in your arms: they spill over into the dark beyond you, brimming, shooting out in ropes of light that make you ache with loneliness and yet yoke you to the world at the same time, because the vast things that have happened to you, however terrible, were always born out of the world, and so perhaps they offer you a place even as they push you out of another, even as they weigh you down with a self that can never fully be conveyed. Though most of us will try. We make bonds, we grow trust, we tell stories; we strive to articulate what it took to become who we are. Sometimes, if we're very fortunate, our listeners catch authentic glimpses of what we mean to say, like sparks in a dark room, but never the whole of it at once, not even with the best of friends or closest lover, because the whole of it at once is beyond speaking. It lives nowhere, absolutely nowhere, except inside your skin. That's where it flares, enormous, hazardous, utterly yours.

Finally, Gabriel stepped toward me. I owed him some kind, any kind, of explanation, and I opened my mouth to try.

But then he said, 'So this is what you wanted to show me.'

The room, I realised. He meant the state of the room. 'It wasn't this.'

'No?'

'It was more than this. What came before it.'

He stepped closer, and took my wet hand in his. 'Perla,' he said. 'It's all right. You thought this would scare me away, but it doesn't. I can see why you did it.'

'You can?'

'Of course. With everything you've been through.'

'But there's more, Gabriel. A lot happened these last few days.'

'I can imagine.' He stepped closer and embraced me. His hands on my back, they could surely hold up anything, a crumbling tower, a wounded tree. 'We'll go home and you can tell me all about it.'

'But I can't show you anymore.'

'Why not?'

'Because he's gone.'

'Who's gone?'

'My father's gone.'

Softly, he asked, 'Which one do you mean?'

'Both of them. They're both gone.' I was weeping now. 'Everybody's gone.'

'I'm not gone,' he murmured into my hair. 'And neither are you.'

I didn't fight the tears.

He was right. I wasn't.

13

Homecoming

The man and his wife arrived home late at night after a ferry ride from Uruguay, during which he stared out the window at the water spreading long and black in all directions, the water of the sea and then, gradually, though no one could say precisely where the shift occurred, the water of the river, still black and long and spread out like the mantle of a king in mourning.

His wife did not speak to him on the ferry or in the taxi ride that followed. Hours before, he had begged her to let him speak to their daughter first alone, *Give me a chance first,* but she had only said, *She already knows, there's no undoing that,* to which he had responded by slamming the suitcase shut on their vacation bed. On the ferry and also in the silent taxi he formed the words he would say to his daughter, carefully sculpted sentences he would not have the chance to speak because, when he arrived home and opened the door, he was met with a bizarre smell that made him afraid for his daughter, for what had happened in the house while he was gone. Though perhaps, he thought, she herself had caused the smell by leaving something (what on earth?) to decay and spread its stink inside their house, she should know better, he called her name in a stern voice as he turned on the light.

The devastated room reared up at him. Sofa, walls, books, all things soaked and destroyed. He looked and looked around him, called his daughter's name and looked in his study, the kitchen, the hall, came back into the living room where his wife stood still as a pillar. Then he saw the painting, the one created by his lost sister, of a ship at sea, the wall around it stained with streaks of water. The painting alone had withstood harm, its blue oils still miraculously in place. The ship rose from the waves with an unconquerable strength that struck him as almost violent.

I could kill her, he said.

His wife answered, You won't have the chance.

What is that supposed to mean?

She's gone.

I'll find her.

She'd still be gone.

No, I'll hold her down and –

Héctor, she's lost to us. It's over.

He was shocked by the cold edge in her voice, and the way she did not turn to look at him while speaking. No, he said. No. He ran up the stairs in search of his daughter, calling her name in sharp barks at first, and then in long protracted cries, her name, her name, the one he gave her when she was a little precious thing he salvaged from the depths of hell, that's how I chose your name, because of the way I dove for you, *hija,* that's how we started, how you became mine, you were not in the world until I brought you here because that nether place where you were born cannot be called part of the world and I was the one who fished you out of there, it was me, and no one else. As he reaches the upstairs landing, he recalls the very first time he saw her, the way she stared at him, and how he thought *a fish, she has the eyes of a fish.* She was four days old and, though in the coming days and nights there would be countless tears, at that moment she was not crying. She had just woken from a nap in a wooden drawer in a dim room. He had approached her quietly, thinking she was still asleep, but when he reached her side she turned and fixed her gaze on him, a black-eyed gaze that did not blink and seemed to have no bottom. Her gaze made the room – made the whole accursed building – disappear. Were all newborns like this? He did not know. He had no experience with babies. He had never heard of such a thing, of a person falling into a newborn's eyes the way a stone falls to the depths of the sea. With eyes like that no one would ever say she looked like Luisa, he thought, but no matter, she is still right for us, she is the one. He wondered, that first day, whether her eyes would lose that strange power over the years but they did not. You don't know that story, do you, *hija*? Of course you don't, there are so many things you don't know, so many things you can't begin to understand, now where are you, where are you, not in the bathroom, not in the hall, your room is in turmoil but you are not in it, the master bedroom is empty and the walls in here are screaming with the lack of you, and his joints loosened as if the glue of him had suddenly dissolved, bringing him slowly to his knees. His wife came up behind him and placed her smooth hands on his two shoulders, whispering, Let her go.

We'll get her back.

It's too late.

No.

She's not our daughter anymore.

How can you say that? he asked, although he knew this woman well enough that he felt no surprise. His wife's heart was a maze, things could fall into it and get lost without a trace, never to be seen or spoken of again. It was not a closed heart, exactly, but a complex one, full of darkened convolutions that were better left unprobed. And in any case, there was plenty to incriminate the girl; the water in the fine Italian sofa could never be expunged. He, for one, did not care about the sofa or the walls or the books, although he could not stand the thought that anyone would try to damage the painting, Mónica's painting, the last vestige of his sister, *hija,* how could you, if only you'd known Mónica who was a goodgirl once for all her delusions and mistakes, the one who brought me soup during my fevers, who taught me how to skate and catch beetles and steal the cookies in a manner where no one would find out. She was a lot like you, her face was similar to yours, if you'd stood side by side the whole world would have believed, without the shadow of a doubt, that you were related.

He said, No. I can't let her go.

She said, You have no choice. If you saw her now, what would you say?

He tried to form the conversation in his mind, the one he'd have with his girl, his daughter. He would rage at her, he would try to explain, she would melt and come back to him. Or she would resist until he became stern and his words broke her. Or he would be stern and try to break her but she would not let him, the girl capable of that downstairs room might keep on looking at him steadily with eyes that did not bend and then – and then – he could not complete the thought because dark water flooded his imaginings the way it had come to flood his house, and he was suddenly awash with memories, the ones of which he never spoke, they rose against his will and drenched his mind with sights and smells and sounds he had to push back and push back with all the force of a drowning man and then he realised, to his horror, that to keep those memories pushed back he had to let his daughter go. Only then did he see what he had lost, and it was radiant, like the sun. Like the sun, it blinded.

14

You

The day after my escape, I went to Las Abuelas' office, a warm, cluttered space in downtown Buenos Aires. I was welcomed by Marta, a kind woman with a yellow cardigan and sad eyes. She listened to me for longer than I expected to talk. She asked questions, but did not press for answers when I could not bear to give them. She filled out a form for me and arranged for the drawing of my blood. It would take a few months, she said, to decode the DNA. Did I want to look at the book of disappeared parents? I shook my head. I did not want to look. I had done as much as I could do on one evening. I left the office and took the elevator and once outside in the warm March air I thought, *Now what?*

I didn't know.

The city was so full, I was so empty.

For the next nine hours I walked and walked the streets, searching without knowing what I was looking for, staring at doors and faces and gutters with the slow intensity of an exile, though whether I was returning to my homeland or newly cast adrift in an unknown place, I could not say. Night fell and the streetlights came on. I lost my way. After five hours, my feet throbbed with pain. I thought of a fairy tale I'd read long ago, about a mermaid who longed to live on land. A witch transformed her tail into human legs, but condemned her feet to agony – every step would feel as though she were traversing shattered glass – so she would never forget her foreignness, never forget her liquid home. But I'm not a mermaid, I thought, I have no home. I walked on, block after block, on boulevards and through alleys, and my legs propelled me forward with surprising force despite the throbbing feet, and who knows, perhaps my legs were in fact bewitched. After all the madness I had seen, why not believe in this strange story? New legs for a new life. Fresh limbs for a broken girl. No, I thought, a broken *woman* – and this made me laugh aloud, not caring about the people glancing at me from a sidewalk café with eyes that said *that one's gone mad.* I walked right past them and continued on, across the street, around the corner, lost in the unceasing maze of Buenos Aires.

In the weeks that followed, I did very little. I spent long hours on Gabriel's balcony (it's *our* balcony, he would say), where I studied or pretended to study while the sun fell copiously on textbook pages. I sat alone in the apartment with Lolo, who had accompanied me as a stowaway in my purse, and stared at him as he stared at the wall. I cooked dinner with Gabriel, grateful for his chatter as well as for jazz albums that filled the silences so I did not have to. On some nights, we made love; on others he held me in his arms and demanded nothing from me, not even an explanation for my tears. I could not have explained them, not even to myself.

At school, I was able to catch up and retain my academic standing, largely thanks to Marisol, who provided me with class notes, study sessions, and, above all, the listening ear of true friendship. When you change, some friends don't follow you where you're going, and they fall away, whether abruptly or over time. This happened with most of my friends, but not with Marisol. In fact, we became closer than ever.

'I like this new Perla,' she said to me one day.

'She's more fragile than the old one,' I said.

'No, she's not. She just knows what she's made of.'

In the mornings, I often lay in bed for a long time before opening my eyes. It was strange to awaken in the heart of the city rather than at its margins, the throaty songs of car engines already in my ears, along with passing radios, raised voices, the inconsequential dramas of everyday urban life. At first it bothered me to have my mind infused with the city like that, with no respite, but soon I grew addicted and could not imagine waking any other way.

I thought often of the man who had been my guest. The time I'd spent with him seemed like the most real time of my life, more vivid than the years before it. I felt his absence keenly, but there were also times when I could have sworn I sensed his presence. I smelled him in the thick weight of a hot day, a sudden whiff of fish and copper that could not be traced to the open window or the kitchen. Or I'd hear a splash when no water lurked nearby. Or a wisp of lullaby hummed toward me in the depths of the night. And then I'd want to reach for him, to run for him, but it was impossible to know which way to run – whether I could find him to the left or right, forward or back – so instead I'd light a cigarette and send the smoke into the sky like a furled message. I wished that I could follow him wherever he'd gone.

In those first days, even dying seemed a fine price to pay. After all, we'd had only one night on which all barriers were removed. There were so many conversations left for us to have, blank lifetimes to fill, spaces we had never shared that begged for us to come to them, to hurl ourselves into them, as if the stolen past were a great blank canvas still waiting for us to give it colour.

But I could not die; there was no guarantee that death would help me find him, and in any case, when I imagined it, our nebulous reunion in a floating sphere of light, I could not see him welcoming me with open arms. Instead I saw him pushing me away, *You can't come in,* and I'd say But I came all this way to find you, and he'd close the sphere, *You're the one who's supposed to live,* and I could hear myself ask, Why, and could even hear his only possible answer, *Because you can.*

All this I saw in the perfect blackness of the ceiling as I lay awake beside Gabriel. On those long nights I felt the world sprawl out around me in all directions, huge, uncharted, and I was a tiny boat whose anchor had ripped away. How I faltered. How I spun with pain. How I feared that I might capsize at any moment. I have nothing, I told the blackness around me, but no, I thought, that's not true, make a list and hold it close: I have my body, my mind, my truth, my words. I have this bed with a warm man inside it, a turtle with a broken jaw, a stack of textbooks waiting on the balcony. And I have time. I have many years of time, if fate allows, and I have to find a way to live those years. I have to live. Not only that – I want to live. I found that wanting in myself and gripped it with both hands.

On good nights, in the blackness, I thought I saw the dance of tiny spirals, the twists of DNA, keepers of the most hallowed secrets. They magnified and whipped their tails and meandered through the dark.

Of course, I thought constantly about my other parents. The ones who raised me, who didn't have Gabriel's address but surely had other means to track me down. As far as I knew, they did not do so. I kept half-expecting my father to appear in the middle of the night, knocking and demanding I come home. I'd lie in bed and see him and Luisa burst through the door and run toward me through the dark, arms waving and outstretched to either slap me or pull me back to their house, or maybe both. Before arriving at my bed, they always dissolved into the blackness. I tried not to think about them. I failed. I often wondered how their homecoming had gone. I imagined the scene many times, watched their faces undergo endless variations as they discovered the deluge in their home. If the midnight raid was slightly far-fetched, it did seem plausible that they might hunt me down at the university if they wanted to find me, since it was a public building, perfectly easy to find, and nothing could stop them from invading its halls if they chose to.

But they didn't do it. This fact both filled me with victory and gutted me with grief. I wondered whether they ever would – specifically, whether Héctor might ever appear in the corridor outside one of my classes and accost me in front of all my peers. I could not tell whether this was my worst nightmare or my secret, feared desire. I held my breath every time I exited a lecture, and did not exhale until I'd made it outside without incident. He haunted those halls, a dim translucent figure, stalking me with his absence. At times I saw a person from afar on the street and thought it was Héctor or Luisa, and my body would go tight with heat until the stranger came closer and broke the spell. It was not them. It was never them. I was glad about this, and said so very clearly, in my own mind and to Gabriel.

'I never want to speak to them again.'

I thought that he would smile with reassurance and approval, but instead he studied me. 'Really?'

'Really.'

'Not even once?'

'Why would I?'

He shrugged. 'To answer your questions. They owe you that.'

It was hard to imagine this, at first. They were gone from my life and I wanted them gone. I did not want to hear their insufficient explanations, their voices, even the sound of their steps coming my way. But as I lay in blackness, in the deep recesses of night, unable to quiet the clamor of my mind, I glimpsed a distant future in which I might have the brazen strength to open contact. It would be many years later, if it ever happened, and even when it did the reunion could not take place at their house (which I always imagined perpetually soaked and destroyed, like a shipwreck). It would have to occur in the city. I imagined myself, older, a woman who had gathered confidence over the years in some mysterious harvest I could not yet fathom, walking into a café to find the man called Héctor waiting for her at a small round table. The confident woman would insist on paying for the coffee and croissants, and would look the man directly in the face even when he looked away. All her questions would be gathered carefully in her hands like a fan of playing cards that could easily rattle into chaos as soon as they began to talk, as soon as she said *If I ask you questions, will you answer?* and he nodded and obliged and exposed the stark terrain between them. Then the confident woman would have to find a way to take the urgent holes of understanding she was carrying and find a way to wrestle them into words, into pedestrian phrases such as *why did you* or *why didn't you* or *what have you been dreaming in your bed all these years,* questions that would flatten the enormity of what she was trying to bring to him cradled with both hands, but it's the best that we can do, isn't it? Words are incomplete and yet we need them. They are the cups that give our memories shape, and keep them from trickling away. And so she'd listen to the things he'd say. And she would take them in and drink her coffee and stash his answers somewhere in her sturdy mind where they could not hurt her, and where they would never be lost.

With luck, he would also listen to her, and then she would voice her own story, which, if she could be sufficiently brave and lucid, would contain him, contain the bustling café, perhaps contain the whole of Argentina.

Five weeks after my escape, I went to Montevideo with Gabriel, to visit his family. Their house was cluttered and warm, with photographs in every corner.

A sepia picture hung in the centre of the living room, of an older man with thick hair and a startling number of gold chains, who, Gabriel's mother told me, was her grandfather. He had come to Uruguay from Spain, and had once owned a traveling carnival that he named Calaquita, Little Skull, in honour of his own birthday, which was the Day of the Dead. *Calaca,* of course, was a Mexican word, strange to both Spaniards and Uruguayans – almost as strange as the Mexican custom of celebrating the Day of the Dead with music, cheerful flowers, and skeletons dancing in the street. He had grown up forced to spend his birthday in the village cemetery every year with his mother and aunts, who wept morosely, all dressed in black. And so, while he liked to tell of his carnival's name as a great joke, Talia saw it as equal parts humour and exorcism. She had grown up listening to his stories of roaming the countryside with his collection of brightly painted wagons, and of the motley cluster of performers who were his closest friends.

'I keep his picture up,' she said, looking at it with some bemusement, 'because he was the most eccentric person in my family.'

This comment, more than anything else, made me feel at ease. I had been bracing myself, not sure what to expect, anxious above all about Gabriel's mother. On the drive home from the ferry station, she had struck me as overly kind, too quick to laugh at my jokes, and I thought that she was doing so out of pity. But now, in her house, I saw her awkwardness as a sign of how fervently she hoped to make me comfortable. As she walked me through the photographs in the living room, her arm slinked through mine, an effortless, almost thoughtless touch.

'Call me Talia,' she insisted. 'And please drop that *usted*, and address me with *tú*. You'll make me feel like an old lady, or even worse, like you're not at home.'

The family set to preparing the *asado*, a collective process so familiar that the roles seemed automatic: Gabriel's father stoked embers at the grill with scientific precision, Gabriel and his sister Carla disappeared into the kitchen to prepare the meat, and I was hustled outside with the younger sister, Penélope, to talk over a glass of wine. She was clearly the quietest member of the family, but I drew her out by asking her about her studies. She was so passionate about chemistry that I could have listened to her for hours. I didn't understand much of what she said, but it sounded fascinating, this talk of molecules and ions and electron clouds, which made me think of the charts we had to draw in high school that connected one atom to another with little lines and headless arrows, which, when you thought about it, was an ingenious way to order the universe, even though the aspect of the universe being mapped was too small to be seen with the naked eye. The world has been written in a microscopic script that the naked eye can't begin to imagine, I thought to myself, as Penélope refilled my glass of red wine and kept on talking.

Carla's boyfriend joined us for the meal, and we crammed around the table on the patio, with its checkered tablecloth embroidered by hand. Everybody talked at once. They bickered, laughed. They seemed to agree on nothing, or, at least, to pick at their differences with relish. No one pressured me to speak, or brought up my parents, or uttered the word *disappeared*. My wine glass was always full, no matter how much I drank from it. Gabriel looked like a boy unwrapping a long-awaited gift.

That evening, at dusk, the whole family took a stroll to La Rambla, the walkway by the shore of the river. Many people had emerged to walk along the water with their *mate* gourds, the way they do in Uruguay, pouring hot water from their thermos into the gourds right out there in the open, on a bench, on the steps leading down to the sand, or even in mid-stride, instead of keeping to the kitchen as is the custom in Argentina. We walked in a gently amoebic cluster, Gabriel's arm around me, and I thought about the last time we'd walked together on a Uruguayan shore, before, before. Of course, that had been in Piriápolis, not Montevideo; but still, and this long dark sweep before us was the Río de la Plata, the same river I had known throughout my childhood, now seen from the other side. How wide it was. How strange, to walk on one side and imagine the existence of the other.

Talia made her way toward me with the gourd. In this family, she was the unquestioned *cebadora*, server of *mate*, and it was my turn. I took the gourd from her and drank.

'Perla,' she said in a low voice. 'If you ever want, I don't know, you know. To talk.'

The brew was perfect, bitter and fresh. The gourd gurgled as I drained it.

'She's fine, Mamá,' Gabriel said.

'I just want her to know – '

'Don't crowd her.'

'I'm not,' she said. 'Am I, Perla?'

I passed the gourd back to her, and shook my head.

'Look, I know we just met. But I want you to know I'm here. After all, a girl can't have enough mothers.'

An axe to the chest. The night, swiftly shattered, lay in pieces all around me.

'Mamá.'

'Oh, God. I said the wrong thing.' Talia sighed. 'I'm sorry. Sometimes I say the wrong thing.'

I meant to respond, but too much raged inside, I didn't dare open my mouth. I wished I hadn't drunk so much wine.

'I'm sorry,' she said again, and ebbed away.

After a few more minutes, the family stopped together at a jetty of rocks overlooking the water, all of a mind, all of a goddamn mind, this family with its lifetime of goddamn rituals. Gabriel moved us toward a rock where we could sit in private.

'Are you all right?'

I leaned in to him and listened to the roar inside myself, through which there threaded a slim whisper, It's not her fault, it's not her fault, the axe was there already and you keep falling on it when you least expect it but one day you'll have new skin and be a woman who can walk beside a river without mere words cutting you apart. I didn't quite believe the whisper, but I grasped it like rope.

'She can be clumsy, my mother. But she means well. She wants to be your friend.'

'Gabo.'

'Hmm.'

'Don't talk.'

'All right.'

'I'll be fine.'

'All right.'

'I just want to look at the water. Will you look at the water with me?'

He nodded. We looked out in silence, and when his family got up to move on we stayed, for hours, the two of us together before the vast river, gliding across it with our gaze, tracing infinite trajectories in the darkness.

♣

What I could not have guessed, at that time, was that Gabriel's mother would in time become one of my best friends. Tonight, six years later, as I sit here at this window, I can assure you that Talia is one of the most generous people you will meet in this world. When I graduated from the university, she arrived with a bouquet so large I could barely see her as she carried it toward me, and she wept as if she'd been waiting for that moment for years. And when, a year later, I married her son, it was her wedding dress I wore, tucked in here and let out there, adjusted for a new bride but the same white dress with its blend of classic lace and 1960s flair. And by that time, when she said, 'You are just like a daughter, my third daughter,' I could take the words in the way she meant them, with joy and love and almost without pain.

Six years. Of course I am still becoming myself; becoming is an infinite road. But I am a different person now from that scared and broken girl who ran from a house in the suburbs in an effort to save her own life. As a psychologist, each time a new client walks into my office I am floored by their trust and by the way our conversations slowly push open their inner maze of light and darkness. My work rivets me and makes me larger. So does my marriage. Because a marriage, it turns out, is not merely the empty space between two people, the passive sum of two parts, but a beast all its own, with its own breath and muscle, its own insistent rhythms, its own inimitable sounds. It vexes us. It makes demands. It startles with its beauty. It carries us when we are lost or tired. That is what Gabriel and I have formed: a connection so intense it has its own life and motion.

This is truer than ever since I started carrying you.

How perfect you are. How you sussurate of almost unbearable perfection. A toe, a spine, an eyelid, each part of you a revelation; where did my body store the knowledge to create you? How many bodies have passed such knowledge down through eons so that you could curl inside me now, small and complete, ready to be born? Soon after I became pregnant, I learned that baby girls have all their eggs already formed in miniature while they are in the womb. So that the egg of you was in me before I was born. So that when I was in my mother, whose face I never saw, a fleck of you was there, a fleck inside a girl inside a woman. Which means that when she disappeared we both disappeared with her, and every reappearance – yours, mine, into the future – belongs to all of us as well. That is why I've spent the night here at this window, telling you this story, preparing you for the world or perhaps preparing the world for you. It is your story as much as it is anyone's, and your existence has already brought new understanding: having carried you, I see the depth of what was lost. Carrying you has brought new floods of grief. But it has also helped me see the depth of what cannot be lost, the unbreakable threads, invisible to the mind, indelible to the body.

The body is the first gift you receive; the second is your name. And you already have yours, Gloria. You have everything you need to face this world, and you are ready now to enter it, I know this from these early contractions that press and shiver through me. They both hurt and thrill. I am not large enough to hold you inside anymore, you want more space now, don't you? It's time for me to give you, as they say, to the light.

I was afraid of birth, at first, but I'm not anymore. I don't know that I'm ready to be a mother but I do know that there is nothing, nothing I want more than to meet you face-to-face, to hold you against me, to look into your eyes. The world is going to begin again with you inside it. I know, that sounds extreme. Yet every new mother believes this, and – who knows? – perhaps all of us are right, perhaps it happens every time, millions of times a day around the globe. A child born, a world renewed. And that is what will happen later today, when you burst out of me, and I know it will happen before midnight because I always suspected that you would arrive on March 2, which was why I was not at all surprised when the contractions began last night, after your father had gone to sleep and left me alone to sit here on the balcony, gazing out at the streets of the city that is about to become your city, Gloria, and sifting through the past, for your sake and for mine. The waves are coming closer together now; you are roaring to be born. I will be reborn with you as mothers always are and Gloria there is still so much to tell you about these recent years, about the long past and even longer future, but it will not be told tonight because it is time for us to leave. Gabriel is still sleeping in the other room, with the suitcase in arm's reach for our sojourn at the hospital. He packed it with the utmost care, as if your safe passage depended on his perfectly folding miniature pajamas. He unpacked and repacked the suitcase several times, rearranging its contents, until finally I said, Gabo, don't worry, everything is in its place, the suitcase is perfect, you're going to be a wonderful father. And then for a moment he looked more terrified than I've ever seen him, even with everything we've been through, so I took his head in both my hands and bent it toward my belly so he could feel your kicks against his cheek. He never gets tired of your kicks. Just wait until you meet him – though there's no need to wait, of course, as it will happen very soon. There's more I want to tell you, but the surges are too great now and in any case there will always be more, the story has no end, it will circle and circle the whole of your life while I am here with you to tell it, so let me just give you this last piece and then we'll go and wake your father:

Two months after I left Héctor and Luisa's house, the call came in. I was in the kitchen, boiling squash for Lolo.

'Perla?'

'Yes, hello.'

'It's me, Marta, at Las Abuelas' office.'

'How are you?'

'Wonderful,' she said, her voice buoyant, a rising balloon. 'We've found a match.'

I stared at the pot, which was boiling now, bubbles roaring quietly to the surface.

'Your mother's name is Gloria.'

The steam writhed upward and I could not move.

'Gloria Rossella Ramos. Her parents have been looking for you, and so have your father's. Your father is Adelmo Rossella.'

Adelmo, I thought, and wished he would come back right then so I could tell him what I'd found, restore it to him. *Here it is, your name, take it back. Adelmo.* The woman was still talking, but I could barely hear her through the shimmering steam that seemed to fill the room and fill my skin and climb up to the ceiling and beyond it, through apartments through the roof into the blue vault of the sky.

'Perla? Are you there?'

'I'm here. I'm here.'

'I know this can be overwhelming, but – your grandparents can't wait to meet you. And aunts, and uncles. Cousins. Do you still want to meet them?'

'Yes.'

'When?'

'When can they?'

'Anytime. They're ready. It's up to you.'

'Today?'

'If you want.'

'At seven o'clock?'

'If you want.'

The water seethed over the sides of the pot, spilling onto the stove. I turned the fire down. 'Yes. I want.'

We said good-bye and hung up. Gabriel appeared in the doorway, naked hope on his face. 'You found them?'

I nodded. 'They found me. We found each other.'

'Perla,' he said, then stopped, as though no other words could hold this moment.

'I'm going to meet them tonight.'

'Do you want me to come with you?'

I shook my head. I knew that, on that night at least, I had to go alone. Nobody could walk through that door with me, not even Gabriel.

Five hours later I was on the subway, staring at the people around me – the solemn ones, the harried ones, the closed and proud and groomed and lonely ones – as if I had just arrived on their planet, in their city, *good sir can you tell me what to make of this place?* The train sped through its dark tunnels to my station and released me from the underground into the light. The sun hovered above the tops of downtown buildings and I could have shouted at sky and roofs *my mother's name is Gloria,* but I held the shouts inside and let them roil there as I reached the building where the office of Las Abuelas waited for me on the third floor. I opened the baroque wooden door that had swung open and closed for hundreds of years of this nation's history, pushed the button for the elevator and held my breath when it arrived for me and did not exhale as the doors closed and I rose to the second floor, the third, until the doors slid open on both sides and there, in the wood-panelled lobby, stood a crowd of people I had never seen before who stared at me with palms open and expressions on their faces like the ones that Lazarus' loved ones must have had when he returned from the grave. The faces hovered at the brink of cheers or sobs or exclamations, waiting for me to step out of the elevator into their midst, and when I did the sounds poured out in all their joy and unclasped sorrow. Two women rushed toward me first. The relatives around them made room as if their forward motion were the only possible step in an ancient choreographed dance. They were whitehaired, two grandmothers, in gold earrings and their best blouses, arms outstretched in unison, both smiling, both weeping, and they enfolded me together from both sides, saying *It's you, it's really you.* Though soon there would be food and names and bellow-laughs and infinite conversation, for now these women's arms became the world. I let myself lean into their embrace, a long and fierce embrace that spoke and spoke to me of things long gone and things to come and what had never been let go. We did not let each other go. We held each other tightly, and our bodies kept on speaking as the late sun gathered in a mantle all around us.

Acknowledgments

In his story 'The Library of Babel,' Jorge Luis Borges describes a universe in which infinite bookshelves contain all the written expressions of which human beings are capable. Only there could I ever hope to find a full record of my gratitude. It is that large and intricate. For now, until that library appears, I will make do with this humble sketch of my thanks.

With regard to research: my aunt Guadalupe López Ocón for accompanying me up and down the streets of Buenos Aires in search of traces of this story, and for the words with which she inscribed my personal copy of *Nunca más*; my aunt Cuti (Ester María López Ocón) for her wide-armed hospitality, and for walking beside me among the Madres de la Plaza de Mayo; my aunt Mónica López Ocón for her literary knowledge; Daniel Batlla, Claudio Batlla, Diego Batlla, and all my other relatives on the Argentinean side, for hosting, teaching, and embracing me during the hunting-and-gathering stage of writing this novel.

Vanesa González-Rizzo and Natalia Bruschstein for sharing their intimate stories over the course of one long Mexico City night. Evelyn Rinderknecht Alaga for the books. Las Madres y las Abuelas, for every drop of what they have done, and continue to do. Horacio Verbitsky, Ernesto Sábato, Marguerite Feitlowitz, Jacobo Timerman, and all the other writers whose courageous and unyielding pens have provided me, and the world, with indispensable sources. The filmmakers Estela Bravo and Peter Sanders, for sharing copies of their powerful documentaries *¿Quién soy yo?* and *The Disappeared,* respectively.

With regard to writing, I am indebted to Micheline Aharonian Marcom, under whose brilliant mentorship this book was born. I am also indebted to Daniel Alarcón, for his luminous insights and guidance. I thank the Mills College M.F.A. Program, the Hedgebrook Residency, and the Macondo Workshop for the space and support to work on this book, as well as Fernando Sasco and Enrique Loedel of the Uruguayan consolate in California for their steadfast generosity. I also thank the following friends for reading drafts or offering help along the way: Erika Abrahamian, Leila Abu-Saba (we miss you, *querida*), Eduardo Cabrera, Sara Campos, Héctor Mario Cavallari, Aya de León, Marcelo de León, Jenesha de Rivera, Frances Hwang, Shanna Lo Presti, Marc Anthony Richardson, Julia Azar Rubin, Cleavon Smith, Joyce Thompson, and Allison Towata. You are all fantastic.

In the publishing world, unending thanks to Victoria Sanders, stellar agent and human being, whose powers are so formidable we should all be grateful that, like a Jedi, she uses them only for good. Thanks also to her wonderful associates, Chris Kepner, Bernadette Baker-Baughman, and Benee Knauer, who make so much happen every day. Chandler Crawford, foreign agent extraordinaire, for working ceaseless miracles. And Sara Nelson, who humbles me with her great support of, and belief in, my books.

As for my editor at Knopf, Carole Baron: her passion, genius, and dedication are without equal. What a difference – what a joyous difference – she has made for this book. My deepest thanks to Sonny Mehta, as well, for his leadership and peerless vision. Emily Milder, another member of the editorial team, provided incisive comments, for which I am most grateful. And really, the whole team at Knopf and Vintage, not to mention at my fifteen-plus international publishers: you are superheroes. You should wear red capes to work.

Finally, vast thanks to my family, beginning with Pamela Harris, wife, soul sister, without whom none of this would be – and stretching out all over the world to the whole sprawling De Robertis–Marazzi–Canil–Martínez–Grimaldi–Batlla–López–Ocón–Pascal–Aldama–Edwards–Friarson tribe. A map of my heart would be full of roads to you.

A Note About the Author

Carolina De Robertis grew up in a Uruguayan-Argentinean family that immigrated to England, Switzerland, and California. Her first novel, *The Invisible Mountain,* was an international best seller translated into fifteen languages; an *O, The Oprah Magazine* 2009 Terrific Read, a *San Francisco Chronicle* Best Book of the Year, and the recipient of Italy's Rhegium Julii Prize. Her translations of Latin American fiction have appeared in *Granta, Zoetrope: Allstory, The Virginia Quarterly Review,* and elsewhere. She lives in Oakland, California.